"[This is] a terrific series of French noir novels, a Marseilles trilogy of sun-baked bad guys and beautiful women, smart cops and mean situations. Mr. Izzo was a marvelous food writer in addition to being a poet of violence and regret. His books are filled with winning descriptions of Provençal meals run through with the flavors of north Africa, Italy, Greece."
—Sam Sifton, *The New York Times*

"Caught between pride and crime, racism and fraternity, tragedy and light, messy urbanization and generous beauty, the city is for Jean-Claude Izzo a Utopia, an ultimate port of call for exiles. There Montale, like Mr. Izzo himself perhaps, is torn between fatalism and revolt, despair and sensualism."—*The Economist*

"What makes Izzo's work haunting is his extraordinary ability to convey the tastes and smells of Marseilles, and the way memory and obligation dog every step his hero takes."—*The New Yorker*

"In Izzo's books . . . Marseilles is a '*ville selon nos coeurs*,' a city in tune with our hearts, as we can read in the penultimate sentence of *Total Chaos*. A cosmopolitan, maritime city, greedy, sensual and warm, but undermined by racism, hatred, money, mafia, and religious fundamentalism—and passive complicity in the face of these scourges."—Michel Samson, *Slow Food*

"Jean-Claude Izzo's Marseille trilogy . . . delve deep into the guts of multiracial Marseilles, a city that is at once a hopeful symbol of the Mediterranean's rich cultural past and an urban dystopia burdened by unemployment, racism and violence . . . Noir at its finest: compelling, sophisticated literature with a biting social edge."—Hirsh Sawhney, *The Times Literary Supplement*

"Like all tragic noir heroes, Montale treads a dangerously narrow line between triumphant . . . ger."—*The Village Voice*

"*Total Chaos* is undeniably literature . . . Part of this is due to Izzo's amazing characterization . . . Izzo takes a convention of noir—the lost soul who finds himself in vengeance—and packs it with enough realism to make it utterly lifelike . . . *Total Chaos* is a noir through and through, but it feels so real that it reminds us that the clichés of noir were originally drawn from real life."—*The Quarterly Conversation*

"A few years ago I was planning a trip to Madrid and Paris from Los Angeles. I was also deep into Jean-Claude Izzo's *Total Chaos* . . . By the time I finished the book, I had replaced the Paris leg of my trip with Marseilles. I'd found Lagavulin, the main character's scotch of choice. (Mine was always Laphroaig.) And a whole lot of interesting jazz . . . The story had leapt out from the book and into my life."—Valla Vakili, CEO, Small Demons

"Like the best American practitioners in the genre, Izzo refrains from any sugarcoating of the city he depicts or the broken and imperfect men and women who people it."—*Publishers Weekly*

"Jean-Claude Izzo's *Total Chaos* is a marvelous noir novel in which passions and feelings are thrown into the narrative mix without reserve and without gratuitousness."—*La Repubblica*

"*Total Chaos* . . . draws from the deep, dark well of noir . . . Izzo's plot is labyrinthine, but his novel is rich, ambitious and passionate, and his sad, loving portrait of his native city is amazing."—*The Washington Post*

# CHOURMO

ALSO BY

JEAN-CLAUDE IZZO

*Total Chaos*
*Solea*
*The Lost Sailors*
*A Sun for the Dying*
*Garlic, Mint, & Sweet Basil*
*Living Tires*

Jean-Claude Izzo

# CHOURMO

*Translated from the French
by Howard Curtis*

Europa
*editions*

Europa Editions
214 West 29th Street
New York, N.Y. 10001
www.europaeditions.com
info@europaeditions.com

Copyright © 1996 by Éditions Gallimard
First Publication 2006 by Europa Editions
This edition, 2018

Translation by Howard Curtis
Original Title: *Chourmo*
Translation copyright © 2006 by Europa Editions
*Eulogy for Jean-Claude Izzo* © 2006 by Massimo Carlotto,
translation from the Italian by Michael Reynolds

This work has been published thanks to support from
the French Ministry of Culture – Centre National du Livre
Ouvrage publié avec le concours du Ministère
Français chargé de la Culture – Centre National du Livre

Library of Congress Cataloging in Publication Data is available
ISBN 978-1-60945-450-0

Izzo, Jean-Claude
Chourmo

Book design and cover illustration by Emanuele Ragnisco
www.mekkanografici.com

Prepress by Grafica Punto Print – Rome

Printed in the USA

# CONTENTS

# EULOGY FOR JEAN-CLAUDE IZZO
## *by Massimo Carlotto*

Recalling the work and the person of Jean-Claude Izzo will forever remain painful for those who knew him. Izzo was first and foremost a good person. It was impossible not to feel warmth for that slight man who always had an attentive, curious look in his eyes and a cigarette in his mouth. I met him in 1995, in Chambery, during the Festival du Premier Roman. Izzo was there to present *Total Chaos* (*Total Khéops*). I bought the book because its author stirred my interest: he seemed a little detached in many of those cultural gatherings, as if faintly annoyed by them, as he was most certainly annoyed by the quality of food and wine offered by the organizers. I read his book traveling between Chambery and Turin, where the Salone del Libro was underway. I found it a superb, innovative book, an exemplar in a genre that was finally starting to establish itself here in Italy. I recommended it to my publishers. And not long after Izzo arrived in Italy. A few sporadic meetings later, I went to Marseilles for a conference. Izzo was not there. He was in hospital. Everyone knew how serious his illness was. Marseilles was rooting for its noirist. Every bookshop in town filled its display windows with Izzo's books. Then, on January 26, Jean-Claude left us. He wasn't even fifty-five. He left us with many fond memories and several extraordinary novels that convincingly delineated the current now known as "Mediterranean Noir."

Autodidact, son of immigrant parents, his father a barman from Naples, his mother a Spanish seamstress. After lengthy battles as a left-wing journalist, having already written for film and television, and author of numerous essays, Izzo decided to take a stab at noir, penning his Marseilles Trilogy, *Total Chaos*, *Chourmo* and *Solea*. The protagonist: Fabio Montale; a cop.

Montale, son of immigrant parents, like Izzo, and child of the interethnic mix that is Marseilles, defiantly stakes out his ground in the city that gave birth to the *Front National*.[1] In *Solea*, Izzo writes:

> It was good to be in Hassan's bar. There were no barriers of age, sex, skin color, or class among the regulars. We were all friends. Whoever came there to drink a *pastis* sure as hell didn't vote for the *Front National*. And they never had, not once, not like some others I knew. Here, in this bar, every single one of us knew why we were from Marseilles and not some other place, why we lived in Marseilles and not some other place. Friendship mixed with the smell of anise and filled the place. We communicated our feelings for one another with a single look. A look that took in our fathers' exile. It was reassuring. We had nothing to lose. We had already lost everything.

Izzo's writing is political, in the tradition of the French neo-polar novels[2], and the writing of Jean-Patrick Manchette. But compared with Manchette, who does not believe in direct political action inasmuch as he believes it is ineffective and doomed to failure, and who limits himself to using noir as an instrument with which to read reality, Izzo goes further. His use of the noir genre is not limited simply to description but penetrates deep into the heart of the incongruities, leaving room for sociological

---

[1] The party was founded in 1972 by Jean-Marie Le Pen and is currently led by Marine Le Pen. It is generally considered to be of the far right, although its leaders deny this qualification.

[2] Neo-polar: the 1970s-80s version of the French mystery novel, after the rebirth of the genre following May '68. Often a politically-oriented novel with a social message.

reflection and for a return to his generation's collective memory, and above all, gives sense to the present day. Via Montale's inner journey, Izzo declares his inexorable faith in the possibility of transformation, both individual and collective. The point that matters most to Izzo, politically speaking, that is, the point that cannot be abandoned, is the existence of a united culture. From the defeats of yesterday come the losers of today. From this perspective, Montale is an extraordinary figure. Son of marginalization, he joins the police so as to avoid the criminal margins. He abandons his group of childhood friends, a group that embodies multiple ethnic differences, but he will never forget his roots. This becomes a source for his feelings of guilt when faced with his role as cop in a society that is becoming increasingly intolerant. An internal gestation and growth obligates him to leave the police force and to become a loner in search of the justice that is not furnished by the courts. What gets him into trouble is the ethic of solidarity and the desire, common to culturally and ethnically mixed milieus, to find a place and a moment in which he can live peacefully.

*On Mediterranean Noir*
*Solea*, the concluding installment in Izzo's Marseilles Trilogy, is flamenco music's backbone, but also a song by Miles Davis. Indeed, music is one of the author's passions. Particularly jazz and the mix of Mediterranean rhythms that characterize contemporary southern European and North African music. In Izzo's writing, however, music does not simply represent rhythm and a source of nostalgia, but also a key to understanding generational differences. Montale contemplates the merits of rap music. He doesn't like it much, but his reflections represent a kind of understanding as to its intrinsic worth:

I was floored by what it said. The rightness of the intentions behind it. The quality of the lyrics. They sang incessantly about the their friends' lives, whether at home or at the reform school.

With *Solea*, Jean-Claude Izzo gives substance to the political intuition that is the cornerstone of Mediterranean Noir. He understands that the sticking point the movement must face consists in the epochal revolutions that have transformed criminality. Babette Bellini's investigation[1] does not result in the typical affirmation of the Mafia's superiority and organized crime's collusion with higher powers. Izzo defines the outlines of Mediterranean Noir when he introduces into his novel the principal contradiction present in the crime-society dyad: the annual income of transnational criminal organizations worldwide is US$10,000 billion, a sum equal to the GDP of many single developing countries. The need to launder this mountain of dirty money is at the root of the dizzying increase in the corruption of institutions, of police forces. It is also the catalyst for strategic alliances between entrepreneurs, financial policing bodies, politics, and organized crime. The society in which we live is criminal inasmuch as it produces crime and "anti-crime," resulting in an endless spiral in which legal and illegal economies merge in a single model. Call it, if you will, a socio-economic "locomotive," as in the case of northeast Italy.

Mediterranean Noir, in this sense, departs from the existing conception of French Noir, and likewise from the modern police novel. The novel no longer recounts a single "noir" story in a given place at a given moment but begins with a precise analysis of organized crime.

Another of Izzo's intuitions was his having individuated the Mediterranean as the geographical centre of the universal criminal revolution. There is a rich fabric of alliances in this region between new illegal cultures emerging from the east and from Africa. These alliances are influenced by local realities,

---

[1] Babette Bellini: a character in the Marseilles Trilogy. Journalist and activist, friend of Fabio Montale.

which they in turn absorb into themselves. As a result, they possess the means to pursue direct negotiations with established power structures.

This is what Mediterranean Noir means: to tell stories with a wide swath; to recount great transformations; to denounce but at the same time to propose the culture of solidarity as an alternative.

For Isabelle and Gennaro,
quite simply, my mother and father

## AUTHOR'S NOTE

Nothing of what you are about to read actually happened. Apart, of course, from what's true. And what you may have read in the newspapers, or seen on TV. Not so much, when you come down to it. And I sincerely hope that the story told here will stay where it should: in the pages of a book. Having said that, Marseilles itself is real. So real that I really wouldn't like you to look for any resemblances to people who actually lived. Even with the main character. What I have to say about Marseilles, my city, is once again nothing but a series of echoes and reminiscences. In other words, whatever you can read between the lines.

These are bad times, that's all.
RUDOLPH WURLITZER

To the memory of Ibrahim Ali,
killed in North Marseilles,
February 24, 1995,
by billposters from the National Front.

# MARSEILLES TERMINUS, SAINT-CHARLES STATION

From the top of the steps in front of the Saint-Charles station, Guitou—as his mother still called him—looked down at Marseilles. "The big city." His mother's birthplace. She'd often promised to bring him here, but she never had. Now, here he was. Alone. As an adult.

And in two hours, he'd be seeing Naïma again.

She was the reason he was here.

His hands deep in the pockets of his jeans, a Camel between his lips, he slowly descended the steps. With the city in front of him.

"At the bottom of the steps," Naïma had said, "is Boulevard d'Athènes. Go along it until you get to the Canebière. Then turn right. Toward the Vieux-Port. Two hundred yards along, on your right, you'll see a big bar on the corner, called the Samaritaine. Let's meet there. At six o'clock. You can't miss it."

He was glad he had two hours to spare. He'd find the bar. He'd be on time. He didn't want to keep Naïma waiting. He was eager to see her again. To take her hand, to clasp her in his arms, to kiss her. Tonight, they'd sleep together. For the first time. His first time, and hers. Mathias, a classmate of Naïma's, was leaving them his studio apartment. It'd be just the two of them. At last.

The thought of it made him smile. A shy smile, like when he'd first met Naïma.

Then he thought of his mother, and grimaced. He was sure she'd give him a hard time when he got back. Not only had he taken off without permission, three days before the start of school, but before he left he'd taken a thousand francs from the cash register in her store. A very upmarket ready-to-wear boutique in the Gap shopping mall.

He shrugged. A thousand francs certainly wasn't going to jeopardize the family's lifestyle. He'd smooth things over with his mother. He always did. It wasn't his mother who worried him. It was the fat bastard who called himself his father. He'd already beaten him once because of Naïma.

Crossing the Allées de Meilhan, he spotted a phone booth. He ought at least to phone his mother, he told himself. To stop her worrying.

He put down his little rucksack and put his hand in the back pocket of his jeans. Shit! His wallet was gone! In a panic, he felt the other pocket, then, even though he wasn't in the habit of putting it there, the pocket of his denim jacket. Nothing. How could he have lost it? He'd had it when he left the station. He'd put his train ticket away in it.

He remembered now. As he'd come down the station steps, an Arab had asked him for a light. He'd taken out his Zippo lighter, and at that moment, he'd been jostled, almost pushed, from behind, by another Arab who was running down the steps. Like a thief, he'd thought. He'd almost lost his balance on the steps and the first Arab had caught him. They'd really screwed him, and they'd done it in style.

He felt quite dizzy with anger and worry. Everything was gone: his papers, his phone card, his train ticket, above all almost all his money. All he had left was the change from the train ticket and the pack of Camels. Three hundred and ten francs. "Shit!" he said out loud.

"Are you all right?" an old lady asked him.

"My wallet's been stolen."

"Oh, you poor boy. Nothing you can do about it! It happens all the time." She looked at him sympathetically. "Just don't go to the police. Whatever you do! It'll only cause more trouble!"

And she went on her way, holding her little purse tight to her chest. Guitou watched her as she walked away. She melted into the motley crowd of passers-by, most of them blacks and Arabs.

Things hadn't gotten off to a good start in Marseilles!

To chase away his rotten luck, he kissed the gold medallion of the Virgin hanging on his chest, which was still tanned from his summer in the mountains. His mother had given it to him on the morning of his first communion, taking it from around her neck and putting it around his. "It's come a long way," she'd said. "It'll protect you."

He didn't believe in God, but like all children of Italians he was superstitious. And besides, kissing the Virgin Mary was like kissing his mother. When he was still just a kid and she put him to bed, she'd plant a kiss on his forehead, and as she did so the medallion would come closer to his lips, borne along on his mother's opulent breasts.

He dismissed this image, which always excited him. And thought about Naïma. Her breasts weren't as large as his mother's, but they were just as beautiful. Just as dark. One evening, kissing Naïma behind the Rebouls' barn, he'd slipped his hand inside her sweater. She'd let him stroke them. Slowly, he'd lifted the sweater to see them, his hands shaking. "Do you like them?" she'd asked in a low voice. He hadn't answered, only opened his lips to take first one, then the other, in his mouth. He started to get a hard-on. He was going to see Naïma again, and that was all that mattered.

He'd get by.

Naïma woke with a start. A noise upstairs. A strange, muffled noise. Her heart was pounding. She listened hard, holding her breath. Nothing. Silence. A weak light filtered through the blinds. What time was it? She wasn't wearing a watch. Guitou was sleeping peacefully, lying on his stomach, his face turned toward her. His breathing was almost inaudible but regular. It reassured her. She lay down again and snuggled up close to him, with her eyes open. She'd have liked to smoke, to calm down. To get back to sleep.

Gently, she moved her hand over Guitou's shoulders, then

down his back in one long caress. He had silky skin. Soft. Like his eyes, his smiles, his voice, the words he spoke. Like his hands on her body. It was that softness that had attracted her to him. An almost feminine softness. The boys she had known, even Mathias, with whom she'd flirted, were rougher in their ways. From the first time she'd seen Guitou smile, she'd wanted to be in his arms and rest her head against his chest.

She wanted to wake him, she wanted to have him caress her as he had before. She'd liked that: his fingers on her body, his eyes filled with wonder, making her feel beautiful. And in love. Making love with him had seemed the most natural thing in the world. She'd liked that too. Would it be just as good the second time around? Was it always like that? Her whole body quivered at the memory of it. She smiled, planted a kiss on Guitou's shoulder, and snuggled even closer to him. He was warm.

He moved. She slid her leg between his legs. He opened his eyes.

"Are you awake?" he murmured, stroking her hair.

"A noise. I heard a noise."

"Are you afraid?"

There was no reason to be afraid.

Hocine was sleeping upstairs. They'd talked to him a little, earlier in the evening. When they'd come to get the keys, before they went out for a pizza. He was an Algerian historian, specializing in the ancient world. He was interested in the archeological excavations being carried out in Marseilles. "Incredibly rich finds," he'd started to explain. It had sounded fascinating. But they hadn't paid too much attention. They'd been in a hurry to be alone together. To declare their love for each other. And then to make love.

Hocine had been staying in Mathias' parents' house for more than a month. They'd left to spend the weekend in their villa at Sanary in the Var. And Mathias had left Naïma and Guitou his studio apartment on the first floor.

It was one of those beautiful renovated houses in the Panier, on the corner of Rue des Belles-Écuelles and Rue du Puits Saint-Antoine, near Place Lorette. Mathias' father, an architect, had redesigned the interior. A three-storied house, with an Italian-style terrace on the roof, giving a magnificent view of the whole harbor, from L'Estaque to La Madrague-de-Montredon.

"Tomorrow morning," Naïma had said to Guitou, "I'll go out and buy bread. We'll have breakfast up there. It'll be beautiful, you'll see." She wanted him to love Marseilles. Her city. She'd told him so much about it. Guitou had been a bit jealous of Mathias. "Have you been out with him?" She'd laughed, but she hadn't answered. Later, when she'd confessed, "It's true, you know, this is my first time," he'd forgotten all about Mathias. The promised breakfast. The terrace. And Marseilles.

"Afraid of what?"

She slid her leg over him, moving it up toward his stomach. Her knee brushed against his cock, and she felt it get hard. She placed her cheek on his pubescent chest. Guitou held her tight. He stroked her back. Naïma quivered.

He wanted her again, really wanted her, but he didn't know if it was the right thing to do. If it was what she wanted. He didn't know anything about girls, or about love. But he was getting a massive hard-on. She looked up at him. Their lips met. He drew her to him and she moved until she was on top of him. Then they heard a cry: Hocine.

They froze.

"My God," she said, almost voicelessly.

Guitou pushed Naïma away and leaped out of the bed. He pulled on his shorts.

"Where are you going?" she asked, not daring to move.

He didn't know. He was afraid. But he couldn't stay that way. He couldn't show he was afraid. He was a man now. And Naïma was watching him.

She'd sat up in bed.

"Get dressed," he said.

"Why?"

"I don't know."

"What's happening?"

"I don't know."

They heard footsteps on the stairs.

Naïma picked up her scattered clothes and ran to the bathroom. Guitou put his ear against the door and listened. More steps on the stairs. Whispering. He opened the door, not really aware of what he was doing. As if his fear was stopping him from thinking rationally. The first thing he saw was the gun. The second was the man's eyes. They looked so cruel. His whole body started shaking. He didn't hear the shot. But he felt a burning pain in his stomach, and he thought of his mother. He fell. His head hit the stone stairs so violently that the arch of his eyebrows was torn off. He felt the taste of blood in his mouth. It was disgusting.

"Let's get out of here." That was the last thing he heard. He was aware of them stepping over him. Like a corpse.

# 1.

## In which happiness is a simple idea when you've got the sea in front of you

There's nothing more pleasant, when you have nothing to do, than to have a snack in the morning and sit looking at the sea.

As a snack, Fonfon had made an anchovy purée, which he'd just taken out of the oven. I'd come back from fishing, and was feeling happy. I'd caught a fine bass, four bream and a dozen mullet. The anchovy purée added to my happiness. I've always been happy with simple things.

I opened a bottle of Saint-Cannat rosé. The quality of Provençal rosés was getting better every year. We drank, to whet our appetite. The wine, from the Commanderie de la Bargemone, was delicious. Beneath your tongue you could feel the warm sun on the low slopes of the Trevarese. Fonfon winked at me, and we started dipping slices of bread in the anchovy purée, seasoned with pepper and chopped garlic. My stomach was aroused at the first mouthful.

"God, that's good!"

"You said it."

It was all you could say. One more word would have been one word too many. We ate without talking. Gazing out over the surface of the sea. A beautiful autumn sea, dark blue, almost velvety. I never tired of it. I was constantly surprised by the attraction it had over me, the way it called to me. I'd never been a sailor or a traveler. I'd had dreams, adolescent dreams, of sailing out there, beyond the horizon. But I'd never gone very far. Except once. To the Red Sea. A long time ago.

I was nearly forty-five, and like many people in Marseilles I liked stories of travel more than travel itself. I couldn't see myself taking a plane to Mexico City, Saigon or Buenos Aires.

I belonged to a generation to which travel meant something very particular. Liners, freighters. Navigation. The rhythm of the sea. Ports. A gangway thrown onto the quay, the intoxication of new smells, unknown faces.

I was content to take my boat, the *Tremolino*, with its pointed stern, out beyond Ile Maire and the Riou archipelago, and fish for a few hours, wrapped in the silence of the sea. I didn't have anything else to do. Go fishing, when the mood took me. Or play *belote* between three and four. Or a game of *pétanque* with aperitifs as the stake.

A well-ordered life.

Sometimes, I'd set off along the *calanques*, the rocky inlets that line the coast: Sormiou, Morgiou, Sugiton, En-Vau, and so on. I'd walk for hours, with my rucksack on my back, sweating, breathing hard. It kept me in shape. It allayed my doubts, my fears. My anxieties. The beauty of the *calanques* reconciled me to the world. Always. And they really are beautiful. Saying it is nothing, you have to see them. But you can only reach them on foot, or by boat. Tourists always thought twice about it, which was just as well.

Fonfon got up about a dozen times, to serve his customers. His regulars, guys like me. Old guys especially, who weren't put off by his bad temper. Or even by the fact that you couldn't read *Le Méridional* in his bar. Only *Le Provençal* and *La Marseillaise* were allowed. Fonfon was an old Socialist Party activist. He was broad-minded, but not so broad-minded that he could ever tolerate the National Front. Especially not here, in his own bar, where so many political meetings had been held. Gastounet, as the former mayor was familiarly known, had even come once, with Milou, to shake hands with the Socialist activists. That was in 1981. Then disillusionment had set in. And bitterness.

One morning, Fonfon had taken down the portrait of the President from over the coffee machine and had thrown it in the big red plastic trash can. We'd heard the glass breaking.

From behind his counter, Fonfon had looked at us, one after the other, but nobody had breathed a word.

Not that Fonfon kept his views hidden after that. Nor did he hold his tongue. Fifi-Big-Ears, one of our *belote* partners, had tried to explain to him the previous week how *Le Méridional* had changed. Sure, it was still a right-wing newspaper, but on the liberal side. And anyhow, outside Marseilles, the local pages were the same in *Le Provençal* and *Le Méridional*. So there was no point in making so much fuss . . .

They'd almost come to blows.

"Look, a paper that made its name inciting people to kill Arabs makes me sick. I feel dirty just looking at it."

"Damn! We can't even talk to you!"

"My friend, that's not talking. That's raving. Look, I didn't fight the Boches to hear your crap!"

"Oh, no, here we go again," Momo had said, trumping Fonfon's ace of clubs with the eight of diamonds.

"Nobody's talking to you! You were with the riffraff who fought for Mussolini! Count yourself lucky I even let you in here!"

"*Belote*," I said.

But it was too late. Momo had thrown his cards on the table.

"Well, I can go play someplace else."

"All right then. Go to Julien's. At his place, the cards are red, white and blue. And the king of spades wears a black shirt."

Momo had left and hadn't set foot in Fonfon's bar again. But he didn't go to Julien's. He just didn't play *belote* with us anymore. And that was sad, because we liked Momo. But Fonfon was right. Just because you were getting old was no reason to keep your mouth shut. My father had been just like him. Worse, maybe, because he'd been a Communist, and in the world today Communism was nothing but a cold heap of ashes.

Fonfon returned with a plate of bread rubbed with garlic

and fresh tomato. Just to soften up the palate. Another good reason to drink more of the rosé.

The harbor was slowly waking up with the first warm rays of the sun. There wasn't the same commotion here as there was on the Canebière. Here it was just a background hum. Voices, bursts of music. Cars setting off. Boat engines being started. And the first bus arriving, and filling up with school kids.

When summer was over, Les Goudes, only half an hour from the center of the city, reverted to being a village of six hundred people. Since I'd come back to live in Marseilles, a good ten years before, I hadn't been able to settle anywhere but here, Les Goudes. In a small cottage—two rooms and a kitchen—that I'd inherited from my parents. In my spare time, I'd fixed it up as best I could. It was a long way from being luxurious, but eight steps led down from my terrace to the sea, and my boat. And that was a whole lot better than waiting to find paradise.

Unless you'd walked all the way here, you'd find it impossible to believe that this little sun-baked harbor town is an urban district of Marseilles, the second largest city in France. It feels like the end of the world. Half a mile away, at Callelongue, the road turns into a white, stony path, and the vegetation becomes sparse. It was from there that I set out on my walks. Through the Vallon de la Mounine and the Plan de Cailles to the Cortiou and Sormiou passes.

The boat from the diving school emerged from the fairway, heading for the islands of the Frioul. Fonfon watched it go by, then turned to me and asked, solemnly, "So what do you think?"

"I think we're going to get screwed."

I didn't know what he was talking about. With him, it could be the Ministry of the Interior, the Islamic Salvation Front, or President Clinton. Olympique Marseilles's new coach. Or even the Pope. But my answer was almost certainly the right one. Because the one sure thing was that we were going to get screwed. The more they droned on about society, democracy, freedom, human rights and the rest of it, the more screwed we were. As sure as two and two make four.

"Yeah," he said. "That's what I think too. It's like roulette. You keep betting, but there's only one hole and you always lose. They always trick you."

"But as long as you're betting, you're still alive."

"These days, you have to play for big stakes. And I don't have enough chips anymore, my friend."

I finished my drink and looked at him. His eyes were trained on me. The big purplish rings below them accentuated the thinness of his face. I hadn't noticed Fonfon get old. I wasn't even sure how old he was. Seventy-five, seventy-six. Not as old as all that.

"You're going to make me cry," I said, as a joke.

But I knew *he* wasn't joking. It was a major effort for him to open the bar every morning. He couldn't stand the customers anymore. He couldn't stand being alone anymore. Maybe one day he wouldn't be able to stand me anymore either, and I was sure that worried him.

"I'm going to quit, Fabio."

He made a sweeping gesture to take in the whole of his bar, a vast room with twenty-odd tables, table soccer in one corner—a rare specimen from the sixties—and a zinc and wood bar counter, which Fonfon polished carefully every morning. And the customers. Two guys at the counter, the first engrossed in *L'Équipe* and the second peering at the sports results over his shoulder. Two old guys, almost facing each other, one reading *Le Provençal*, the other *La Marseillaise*. Three school kids waiting for the bus, telling each other about their vacations.

Fonfon's world.

"Come on, you're talking crap!"

"I've always been behind a bar. Ever since I arrived in Marseilles with my poor brother Luigi. You never knew him.

We were sixteen when we started. At the Bar de Lenche. Then he became a longshoreman, and I carried on. The Zanzi, the Jeannot bar at the Cinq-Avenues, the Wagram on the Vieux-Port. After the war, when I had a little money, I settled here. In Les Goudes. It felt good here. That makes forty years.

"We all used to know each other. One day you'd be helping Marius repaint his bar, the next day he'd be giving you a hand to fix up the terrace. You'd go fishing together. Honorine's husband, poor old Toinou, was still around. The things we caught! We'd put it all together and make huge *bouillabaisses*. One time at my house, another time at someone else's. With the women and children. Twenty or thirty of us there were, sometimes. We had a good laugh! I'm sure your parents, God rest their souls, wherever they are, still remember."

"I remember, Fonfon."

"Yeah. You always made a scene, because the only thing you'd eat was soup with croutons. No fish. Your poor mother was so embarrassed."

He stopped speaking, lost in memories of "the good old days." I was a worm in those days. I'd pretend to drown his daughter, Magali, in the harbor. We were the same age. Everyone thought we'd get married. Magali was my first love. The first girl I ever slept with. In the blockhouse above the Maronnaise. In the morning they bawled us out because we hadn't come home till after midnight.

We were sixteen.

"That was a long time ago."

"That's what I'm saying. You see, we each had our own ideas. We bawled each other out, worse than fishwives. And you know me, I was as bad as any of them. I've always been loud. But all the same, we had respect. Nowadays, if you don't dump on those who are poorer than you, they spit in your face."

"What are you going to do?"

"Close down."

"Have you talked to Magali and Fredo?"

"Don't make yourself out to be stupider than you are. When did you last see Magali here? Or the kids? For years now, they've been playing at being Parisians. With all the things that go with it, the car and everything. In the summer, they prefer to get their asses tanned in Benidorm or Turkey or on some island or other. This is just a place for deadbeats like us. As for Fredo, maybe he's dead. The last time he wrote me, he was going to open an Italian restaurant in Dakar. The blacks have probably eaten him alive! You want a coffee?"

"I'd love one."

He stood up. He placed his hand on my shoulder and leaned toward me, his cheek brushing against mine.

"Fabio, put one franc on the table, and the bar is yours. I've been giving it a lot of thought. You're not going to spend the rest of your life doing nothing, right? Money comes and goes, but it never lasts. I'll keep the cottage, and when I die you just make sure they put me next to my Louisette."

"You're not dead yet, dammit!"

"I know. So you still have time to think about it."

He left me and walked to the bar before I could say another word. Not that I knew what to say. His proposition had left me speechless. So had his generosity. But I couldn't see myself behind a bar. I couldn't see myself anywhere.

I was waiting to see what the future would bring.

What it was bringing, right now, was Honorine. My neighbor. She was walking briskly, her shopping bag under her arm. For an old woman of seventy-two, her energy never ceased to amaze me.

I was finishing my second cup of coffee and reading the newspaper. I could feel the gentle warmth of the sun on my back. It helped me not to despair completely about the state of the world. The war was still going on in the former Yugoslavia. Another had just broken out in Africa. Another was brewing in Asia, on the borders of Cambodia. And it seemed almost inevitable that all hell was about to break loose in Cuba. Or Central America, or somewhere in that neck of the woods.

Closer to home, things weren't exactly rosy either.

"Burglary in the Panier Leaves Two Dead," read a headline in the local pages of *Le Provençal*. It was a brief item, in the stop press. Two people had been found murdered in a house whose owners had spent the weekend in Sanary. It wasn't until last night that they'd discovered the bodies of two friends who'd been staying there. The house had been emptied of anything that was worth reselling: TV, VCR, stereo, CD player, and so on. According to the police, the victims had died during the night of Friday to Saturday, about three in the morning.

Honorine came straight up to me. "I thought I'd find you here," she said, putting her shopping bag down.

At the same moment, Fonfon appeared, smiling. The two of them liked each other.

"Hi, Honorine."

"I'll have a coffee, Fonfon. But not too strong, eh, I've already had too much." She sat down, and pulled her chair toward me. "Guess what? You have a visitor."

She looked at me, waiting for my reaction.

"Where? At my place?"

"Yes, of course at your place. Not at mine. Who do you think would come see me?" She was waiting for me to question her, but I could see she was burning to tell me anyway. "You'll never guess who it is!"

"No, I can't."

I couldn't imagine who'd be visiting me. Just like that, at nine-thirty on a Monday morning. The love of my life was with her family, somewhere between Seville, Córdoba and Cádiz, and I had no idea when she'd be back. I didn't even know if Lole would be back at all.

"You're going to be surprised." She looked at me again, a crafty gleam in her eyes. She couldn't hold back anymore. "It's your cousin. Your cousin Angèle."

Gélou. My beautiful cousin. That really was a surprise. I hadn't seen Gélou for ten years. Since her husband's funeral. Gino had been shot dead one night as he was closing his restaurant in Bandol. As he wasn't a crook, everyone thought he'd fallen foul of racketeers. The investigation ended up forgotten, like so many others, at the back of a drawer. Gélou sold the restaurant, took her three children and left to start a new life elsewhere. Since then I hadn't heard from her.

Honorine leaned toward me. "The poor woman doesn't seem like her old self," she said, in a confidential tone. "I'd swear she's in trouble."

"What makes you say that?"

"It's not that she wasn't nice. She gave me a kiss, and lots of smiles. We had coffee and chatted a little. But I could see that under all that, she's going through a hard time."

"Maybe she's just tired."

"In my opinion, she's in trouble. And that's why she's come to see you."

Fonfon returned with three coffees, and sat down facing us. "I thought you'd like another one, OK?" he asked, looking at us.

"It's Gélou," Honorine said. "Do you remember?" He nodded. "She's just arrived."

"What of it?"

"I think she's in trouble."

Honorine was never wrong about things like that. I looked at the sea, and told myself that my peaceful life looked as if it might be coming to an end. In a year, I'd put on four and a half pounds. I'd been so idle, I was starting to get fat. So, whether she was in trouble or not, Gélou was welcome. I emptied my cup and stood up.

"I'm going."

"How about I bring a *focaccia*, around noon?" Honorine said. "She'll want to stay for lunch, won't she?"

## 2.

## IN WHICH, WHEN YOU OPEN YOUR MOUTH, YOU ALWAYS SAY TOO MUCH

Gélou turned, and the whole of my youth caught me by the throat. She'd been the most beautiful girl in the neighborhood. She'd turned a lot of heads, none more than mine. She'd been there all through my childhood, and had haunted my adolescent dreams. She'd been my secret love. My inaccessible love. Because Gélou was a grown-up. Nearly three years older than me.

She smiled at me, and two dimples lit up her face. A smile like Claudia Cardinale's. Gélou had always known she looked like her. Almost the spitting image. She'd often played on it, even dressing and doing her hair like the Italian star. We never missed any of her movies. Luckily for me, Gélou's brothers didn't like going to the movies. They preferred soccer matches. Gélou would come and get me on Sunday afternoons and we'd go together. Where we lived, a girl of seventeen never went out alone. Even to meet up with her girlfriends. There always had to be a boy from the family with her. And Gélou liked me.

I loved being with her. On the street, when she gave me her arm, I was on top of the world! The time we went to see Visconti's *The Leopard*, I nearly went crazy. Gélou had leaned toward me and whispered in my ear, "Isn't she beautiful?"

Alain Delon was taking her in his arms. I'd placed my hand on Gélou's, and had replied, almost voicelessly, "Like you."

Her hand stayed in mine for the rest of the movie. I had such a hard-on, I didn't know what the movie was all about. I was fourteen. But I didn't look anything like Alain Delon, and Gélou was my cousin. When the lights came back on, life reasserted itself. I knew at that moment that it was going to be totally unfair.

Her smile was fleeting. Like a flash of memory. Gélou came toward me. I barely had time to see the tears misting her eyes before she was in my arms.

"I'm so glad to see you," I said, holding her tight.

"I need your help, Fabio."

The same cracked voice as the actress. But it wasn't a line from a movie. We weren't at the movies anymore. Claudia Cardinale had married, had children and led a happy life. Alain Delon had gotten fatter and made lots of money. The two of us had grown older. Life, as I'd foreseen, had been unfair to us. And it still was. Gélou was in trouble.

"Tell me all about it."

Guitou, the youngest of her three sons, had run away. On Friday morning. He hadn't left a note, or any clue about his whereabouts, but he'd taken a thousand francs from the cash register in the boutique. Since then, she'd heard nothing. She'd hoped he'd call her, like he did when he went to stay with her cousins in Naples. She'd thought he'd come back on Saturday. She'd waited all day. Then all of Sunday. Last night, she'd finally broken down.

"Where do you think he went?"

"Here. Marseilles."

She'd spoken without hesitation. Our eyes met. Hers were staring into the distance, at some place where it couldn't be easy being a mother.

"I have to explain."

"I think so, yes."

I made coffee again, for the second time. I'd put on a Bob Dylan album. *Nashville Skyline*. My favorite. The one with *Girl from the North Country*, a duet with Johnny Cash. A fantastic album.

"That's an old one. I haven't heard it in years. You still play it?"

She sounded almost disgusted.

"That and other things. My tastes haven't really changed.

But I can put on Antonio Machin if you prefer. *Dos gardenias para tí.*" I hummed, doing a few bolero steps.

It didn't make her smile. Maybe she preferred Julio Iglesias! I didn't ask her, and went into the kitchen.

We'd sat down on the terrace, facing the sea. Gélou was sitting cross-legged in a wicker armchair, my favorite. She was smoking, lost in thought. From the kitchen, I watched her out of the corner of my eye, as I waited for the coffee to boil. Stashed away in a cupboard somewhere, I have a superb electric coffee maker, but I prefer to use my old Italian coffee maker. A question of taste.

The years had been kind to Gélou. She was pushing fifty, but she was still a beautiful, desirable woman. The few lines on her face, fine crow's feet at the corners of her eyes, only made her more attractive. But there was something about her that bothered me. That had bothered me since she'd freed herself from my arms. She seemed to belong to a world where I'd never set foot. A respectable world. Where you can smell Chanel No. 5 even on the golf course. Where there's always something being celebrated: first communions, engagements, weddings, christenings. Where everything matches, right down to the sheets, the quilt covers, the nightdresses and the slippers. And the friends and acquaintances you invite to dinner once a month always return the compliment. I'd seen a black Saab parked in front of my door and I was willing to bet that the gray tailored suit Gélou was wearing hadn't come from a mail order catalog.

There must have been whole chunks of my cousin's life since Gino had died that I'd missed out on. I was dying to know more, but that wasn't the priority right now.

"This summer, Guitou met a girl. Just a flirtation, you know. She was camping with a bunch of friends at Lake Serre-Ponçon. He met her at a village fête. At Manse, I think. There are village fêtes all summer, dances, that kind of thing. Ever since, they've been inseparable."

"It's normal at his age."

"Yes. But he's only sixteen and a half. And she's eighteen."

"Well, your Guitou must be a handsome kid," I said, jokingly.

Still no smile. Nothing I could say would cheer her up or console her. She was too anxious. She picked up her bag, which was lying on the floor by her feet. A Louis Vuitton bag. She took out a purse, opened it, and handed me a photo.

"Skiing, last winter. At Serre-Chevalier."

Her and Guitou. He was a whole head taller than her, and as thin as a rake. Long, unkempt hair falling over his face. An almost effeminate face. Gélou's face. And the same smile. But standing next to her, he seemed out of sync. While she radiated self-confidence and determination, he appeared not frail but fragile. I told myself that he was the baby of the family, who'd come along when she and Gino hadn't planned on having another child, and she must have spoiled him rotten. What surprised me was that although Guitou's mouth was smiling, his eyes weren't. They stared sadly into the distance. And from the way he was holding his skis, I guessed that he was bored by the whole thing. I didn't say that to Gélou.

"I'm sure you wouldn't have been able to resist him when you were eighteen."

"Do you think he looks like Gino?"

"He has your smile. Irresistible, like . . ."

She didn't catch the allusion. Or didn't want to. She shrugged and put away the photo.

"Guitou has a vivid imagination. He's a dreamer. I don't know who he gets it from. He spends hours reading. He doesn't like sports. He hates making the least effort to do anything. Marc and Patrice aren't like that. They're more . . . down to earth. More practical."

I could imagine. Realists, they were called these days.

"Do Marc and Patrice live with you?"

"Patrice is married. He got married three years ago. He runs one of my shops, in Sisteron. With his wife. It's going really well for them. Marc has been in the States for a year. He's studying tourism. He went back ten days ago." She paused to think. "She's Guitou's first girlfriend. Well, the first I know about."

"Has he talked to you about her?"

"She left on August 15, and since then they haven't stopped phoning each other. Morning, noon and night. At night, they talked for hours. Imagine if things had continued like that! I had to talk to him about it."

"What were you hoping? That they'd break up, just like that? A last kiss, and so long, it's been great to know you?"

"No, but—"

"Do you think he came to Marseilles to see her? Is that it?"

"I don't think it, I know it. First he wanted me to invite her for a weekend at our house, and I refused. Then he asked permission to go see her in Marseilles, and I said no. He's too young. And besides, I didn't think it was a good idea, just before the start of the school year."

"You think this is better?" I said, and stood up.

This conversation was getting on my nerves. Of course I could understand how afraid a mother might be, seeing her son fly the nest to be with another woman. Especially the youngest. Italian mothers are great at that game. But it wasn't just that. I sensed that Gélou wasn't telling me the whole story.

"It isn't advice I want, Fabio, it's help."

"If you think you're talking to a cop, you've come to the wrong address," I said, coldly.

"I know. I called police headquarters. You haven't been with them for more than a year."

"I resigned. It's a long story. In any case, I was only an insignificant neighborhood cop. In North Marseilles."

"It's you I came to see, not the cop. I want you to find him. I have the girl's address."

This is where it got hard to follow.

"Wait, Gélou. Explain something to me. If you have the

address, why didn't you go straight there? Why didn't you at least call?"

"I did call. Yesterday. Twice. I got hold of the mother. She told me she didn't know Guitou. That she'd never seen him. And that her daughter wasn't there. That she was at her grandfather's, and he didn't have a phone. Nonsense like that."

"It may be true."

I was thinking, trying to see clearly in all this mess. But there was still something missing, I was sure of it.

"What are you thinking about?"

"What kind of impression did the girl make on you?"

"I only saw her once. The day she left. She came to see Guitou at the house. She wanted him to go with her to the station."

"What's she like?"

"So-so."

"What do you mean, so-so? Is she pretty?"

She shrugged. "Well . . . "

"Yes or no? For God's sake! Is there something wrong with her? Is she ugly? Disabled?"

"No. She's . . . She's pretty."

"Anybody would think you find that painful. Does she seem genuine?"

She shrugged again, which was really starting to irritate me. "I don't know, Fabio."

There was a touch of panic in her voice now, and an evasive look in her eyes. We were getting close to the truth.

"What do you mean you don't know? Didn't you talk to her?"

"Alex threw her out."

"Alex?"

"Alexandre. The guy I've been living with since . . . almost since Gino died."

"Oh! And why did he do that?"

"She's . . . She's an Arab. And . . . well, we're not crazy about Arabs."

So that was it. That was the sticking point. Suddenly, I couldn't look at Gélou anymore. I turned to the sea. As if it had the answer to everything. I felt ashamed. I'd have gladly thrown Gélou out, but she was my cousin. Her son had run away, he might miss the start of the school year, and she was worried. I could understand that, in spite of everything.

"What were you afraid of? That this Arab girl would stick out like a sore thumb where you live? For fuck's sake, Gélou! Don't you know where you're from? Don't you remember what your father was? What they called him? Your father, and mine, and all the *nabos*? Harbor dogs! That's right! And don't tell me it didn't hurt you, the fact that you were born there, in the Panier, among the harbor dogs! And now you talk to me about Arabs!

"Just because you drive a Saab and wear a tailored suit like some fucking high-class whore, it doesn't mean you've changed. If they did a blood test before they gave you your identity card, they'd put Arab on yours."

She stood up, beside herself with anger. "My blood's Italian. Italians aren't Arabs."

"The South isn't Italy. It's the land of the wops. You know what the people in Piedmont call us? The Mau Mau. That includes niggers, Gypsies, and all the wops south of Rome! Fuck, Gélou! Don't tell me you believe in all that bullshit."

"Alex fought in Algeria. They really gave him a rough time. He knows what they're like. Devious and—"

"So that's it. You're afraid she'll give your kid a blow job and he'll get AIDS!"

"You're really gross."

"Yeah. It's the way I react to bullshit. Take your bag and get out of here. Tell your Alex to go see the Arabs. Maybe he'll come back alive, with your son."

"Alex doesn't know anything about it. He isn't here. He's away on a trip. Until tomorrow night. We have to bring Guitou back by tomorrow, or else . . . "

"Or else what?"

She collapsed back in the armchair and burst into tears. I crouched in front of her.

"Or else what, Gélou?" I asked again, more gently.

"He'll beat him again."

Honorine finally appeared. She probably hadn't missed a word of my screaming match with Gélou, but she'd deliberately kept out of it. It wasn't her style to interfere in my business. Unless I asked her.

Gélou and I were both silent, lost in thought. When you open your mouth, you always say too much. And then you have to take responsibility for what you've said. The little that Gélou had told me about her and Alex didn't make it sound as if their life was always a bed of roses.

She put up with it. Because when she's fifty, she said, even an attractive woman doesn't have many choices. The most important thing is having a man. At least as important as financial security. And that was worth the occasional unhappiness, the occasional humiliation. The occasional sacrifice too. She was quite prepared to admit that she'd lost Guitou somewhere along the way. For the best of reasons. Fear. Fear of arguing with Alex. Fear of being dumped. Fear of being alone. The day would come when Guitou would leave home. As Patrice had done, then Marc.

Guitou, admittedly, hadn't been planned, by Gino and her. He'd come along years later. Six years. An accident. The two others were already big. She hadn't wanted to be a mother anymore, she wanted to be a woman. Then Gino had died, and she was left with this child. And her terrible grief. She became a mother again.

Alex had taken care of the kids. They got along fine. There were no problems. But as he grew, Guitou started to hate this father who wasn't his father. His real father, the one he hadn't had time to get to know, became a paragon of virtue. Guitou started to like everything that Alex hated and hate everything Alex liked. After his two brothers left home, the bad feeling between Guitou and Alex had gotten worse. Everything became an excuse for a confrontation. Even the choice of which movie to watch on TV would end in an argument, and Guitou would shut himself in his room and play music, loud. First rock, then reggae. Raï and rap in the past year.

Alex started hitting Guitou. Nothing bad, a couple of slaps. Gino would have done the same. Kids deserve it sometimes. Guitou more than most. He'd gotten a slap when the girl, the Arab girl, had showed up at the house, but then things had degenerated. Guitou had protested, and Alex had been forced to hit him. Hard. She'd come between them, but Alex had told her not to interfere. The kid did just what he liked, he said. They'd taken too much from him already. Listening to Arab music in the house was one thing. But inviting one of them home was a step too far. It was the same old story. First it would be her, then her brothers, and then all the tribe. Deep down, Gélou pretty much agreed with Alex.

Now she was panicking. Because she didn't know what to do anymore. She didn't want to lose Alex, but Guitou running away, and then not getting in touch with her, made her feel guilty. He was her son. She was his mother.

"I've fried a few *panisses*," Honorine said to Gélou. "Look, they're still warm." She handed me the plate, and the focaccia she was holding under her arm.

During the summer, I'd built a little passageway between her terrace and mine. With a little wooden door. That avoided her having to come out of her house to get to mine. I didn't have anything to hide from Honorine. Not my dirty linen, not my love affairs. I was like the son her Toinou hadn't been able to give her.

I smiled, and brought water and a bottle of *pastis*, and got ready to charcoal-grill the bream. When you're in trouble, you might as well take your time.

## 3

## IN WHICH WHERE THERE IS ANGER, THERE IS LIFE

The kids were playing really well. They weren't showing off. They were playing for the pleasure of the game. They wanted to learn, they wanted their team to be the best one day. The basketball court, which was fairly recent, had taken part of the space away from the parking lot in front of the two big blocks of the La Bigotte housing project, on the heights of Notre-Dame Limite, on the "border" between Marseilles and Septèmes-les-Vallons. A housing project that towered over North Marseilles.

It was no worse—and no better—here than anywhere else. A mass of concrete in the middle of a twisted landscape of rock and chalk. The city down below, on the left. A long way away. You're a long way from everything here. Except poverty. Even the washing drying in the windows bears witness to that. It always looks colorless, in spite of the sun and the wind. Poor people's washing. But one thing the people "down there" don't have is the view. A stunning view, the most beautiful view in Marseilles. You open the window and you have the sea all to yourself, for free. When you have nothing, owning the sea— the Mediterranean—means a lot. Like a crust of bread when you're starving.

The idea of the basketball court was down to one of the kids, who was called OubaOuba. Not because he was a wild man from the jungles of Senegal, but because he could jump higher to reach the basket than a kangaroo. He was a true artist.

"When I see all these cars taking up so much space, it bugs me," he'd said to Lucien, a friendly guy from the Social Committee. "The place where I live may not be very big, fair enough. But these parking lots, dammit!"

The idea had spread. A race had started between the mayor and the deputy, much to the amusement of the departmental councilor who, unlike them, wasn't running for re-election. I remembered it well. The kids didn't even wait for the end of the official speeches to take over "their" court. It wasn't even finished. It never was, in fact, and now there were cracks all over the thin layer of asphalt.

I smoked a cigarette and watched them playing. It felt strange being back here, in North Marseilles. This had been my patch. Since I'd resigned, I hadn't set foot here again. I had no reason to come here. Here, or La Bricarde, or La Solidarité, or La Savine, or La Paternelle . . . There's nothing in these projects. Nothing to see. Nothing to do. Not even anywhere to buy a Coke. At least in Le Plan d'Aou, one grocery store survived as best it could.

You had to live here, or be a cop, or a youth worker, to go anywhere near neighborhoods like this. For most people in Marseilles, the north of the city is nothing but an abstraction. They know the place exists, but they've never been there, and will never go there. Their vision of it comes exclusively from TV. Like the Bronx, I guess. They fantasize about it. And they fear it.

Of course, I'd let myself be persuaded by Gélou to look for Guitou. We'd avoided talking about it during the meal. We were both embarrassed. She because of what she'd told me, and me because of what I'd heard. Fortunately, Honorine had kept the conversation going.

"I don't know how you manage up there in those mountains of yours. I've only ever left Marseilles once, to go to Avignon. One of my sisters, Louise, needed me. I was so unhappy . . . But I only stayed two months. What I missed most was the sea. Here, I can spend hours looking at it. It's never the same. They have the Rhône over there, of course. But it's not the same thing at all. It never changes. It's always gray and doesn't smell of anything."

"You don't always get to choose in life," Gélou had replied, wearily.

"It's true, the sea isn't everything. Happiness, your kids, your health, come first."

Gélou was on the verge of tears. She'd lit a cigarette. She'd barely touched her bream.

"Please do it, please go," she'd murmured when Honorine had gone out to fetch the coffee cups.

Now here I was. Outside the block where the Hamoudi family lived. And Gélou was waiting for me. She was waiting for Guitou and me. Anxiously, even with Honorine there to reassure her.

"She's in trouble, isn't she?" Honorine had asked me in the kitchen.

"It's her youngest son. Guitou. He's run away. She thinks he's here, in Marseilles. Don't needle her too much while I'm gone."

"You're going to find him?"

"Someone has to go, right?"

"Yes, but why not . . . ? I don't know . . . Does she live alone?"

"We'll talk about it later, all right?"

"Ah, so it's like I said, your cousin's in trouble. Not just with her youngest."

I lit another cigarette. OubaOuba scored a basket that left his friends speechless. They were a damn good team, these kids. But as for me, I was still hesitating. I lacked the courage, or rather, the conviction. How would it look, showing up at these people's door? "Hello, my name's Fabio Montale. I've come to get the boy. This affair's gone on long enough. You cool it, your mother's worried enough as it is." No, I couldn't do that. What I was going to do was take the two kids to my place, and let them explain it all to Gélou.

I spotted a familiar figure. Serge. I recognized him from the clumsy, almost childish way he walked. He was coming out of section D4, right in front of me. He seemed to have gotten thinner. Half his face was covered by a thick beard. He crossed to the parking lot, his hands in the pockets of his denim jacket, his shoulders bent. He seemed quite sad.

I hadn't seen him for two years. I didn't even know he was still in Marseilles. He'd been a youth worker in North Marseilles for several years, and he'd been dismissed, partly because of me. Whenever I collared kids who'd committed some offense or other, he was the one I called to the station house, even before the parents. He'd give me information about the families, and advice. The kids were his life. That was why he'd chosen that line of work. Because he'd had enough of seeing teenagers end up in the can. He trusted them, that was the main thing. He had the kind of faith in people that some priests have. In fact, he was a bit too much like a priest, for my taste. We'd gotten on well, without ever becoming friends. Because of that side of him that was like a priest. I've never believed men are good. Just that they deserved to be treated equally.

My links with Serge set tongues wagging. And my bosses didn't like it at all. A cop and a youth worker! We were made to pay for it. Serge was the first to go. He was dealt with harshly. When my turn came, it was a little more subtle. After all, it wasn't so easy to get rid of a cop whose appointment to the neighborhood had deliberately been made into a media event a few years earlier. Gradually, my workforce was reduced, and more and more responsibilities were taken away from me. Although I didn't believe in it anymore, I'd carried on, because being a cop was the only thing I knew how to do. It had taken the deaths of too many people I loved before disgust finally prevailed and set me free.

What the hell was Serge doing here? I didn't have time to ask him. A black BMW with tinted windows suddenly appeared as if from nowhere. It was moving very slowly, and Serge didn't take any notice of it. When it came level with him, an arm emerged through the rear window. A hand carrying a revolver. Three shots, at point blank range. The BMW took off, disappearing as suddenly as it had come.

Serge was lying on the asphalt. Dead. There was no doubt about it.

The shots echoed between the blocks. Windows opened. The boys stopped playing, and the ball rolled across the roadway. Time froze, and for a moment there was silence. Then people came hurrying from all sides.

I ran to Serge.

"Move aside," I cried to the people who were gathering around the body. As if Serge might still need space and air.

I crouched beside him. A movement that had become familiar to me. Too familiar. As familiar as death. The years had gone by, and that seemed to be all I ever did: crouch to look at a corpse. Shit! It couldn't be starting all over again, could it? Why were there so many corpses in my life? And why were more and more of them people I knew or loved? Manu and Ugo, my friends from childhood and hard times. Leila, so beautiful, and so young I hadn't dared live with her. And now my pal Serge.

Death wouldn't let go of me. It was like a kind of glue I'd trodden in without realizing it. But why? Why, dammit?

Serge had taken the shots full in the stomach. High caliber. .38, I suspected. Professional weapons. What kind of mess had the idiot gotten himself mixed up in? I looked up at D4. Who had he been to see? And why? It was unlikely that whoever it was he'd just visited was going to put his head out of the window and show himself.

"Have you seen him before?" I asked OubaOuba, who'd come up beside me.

"Never seen the guy."

The police siren could be heard at the entrance to the project. They were quick, for a change! The kids vanished in less than two minutes. Only the women, the children and a few ageless old people were left. And me.

They arrived like cowboys. From the way they screeched to a halt alongside the group of onlookers, I guessed they'd been spending a lot of time watching *Starsky and Hutch* on TV. They must even have rehearsed that arrival, because it was so damn accurate. The four doors opened at the same time and they all ejected. Except Babar. He was the oldest cop in the neighborhood station house, and it was a long time since he'd enjoyed playing remakes of old cop shows. He wanted to reach retirement the way he'd started his career, without too much effort. And preferably alive.

Pertin, known as Four Eyes by all the kids in the project, because of the Ray-Bans he never took off, glanced at Serge's corpse, then stood looking me up and down.

"What are you doing here?"

Pertin and I weren't exactly best buddies. Although he was a chief inspector, for seven years I'd been the person in charge of North Marseilles. His neighborhood station house had been no more than an outpost of the Neighborhood Surveillance Squad, which I led. He was at our disposal.

From the beginning, it was war between Pertin and me. "In the Arab neighborhoods," he'd say, "there's only one thing that works, and that's force." That was his credo, and for years he'd applied it to the letter. "The thing with the Arabs, all you gotta do is grab one from time to time, take him out to a deserted quarry, and beat the crap out of him. They've always done some stupid thing that you don't know about. You hit the scum, they always know why. That's a damn sight better than a lot of ID checks. It avoids paperwork at the station house. And it does wonders for your nerves after the Arabs have been fucking you around."

According to Pertin, they were just "doing their job honestly." That's what he'd told the journalists the day after his team had "accidentally" shot down a seventeen-year-old Arab during a routine ID check. That was in 1988. Marseilles was up in arms about the blunder. That year, they thrust me into the position of head of the Neighborhood Surveillance Squad. I was the supercop who was going to restore order and calm to North Marseilles. I had to, because we were on the verge of a riot.

Everything I did showed him that his approach was a mistake. But I made mistakes too, more than my share, by trying too hard to play for time, to be conciliatory. Trying too hard to understand what couldn't be understood. Poverty and despair. I guess I didn't act enough like a cop. That was what my bosses told me. Later. I think they were right. From the police point of view, I mean.

Since my resignation, Pertin had re-established his power over the projects. His "law" prevailed. The beating sessions in the disused quarries had resumed. The high-speed chases through the streets too. Hate. The escalation of hate. Fantasies were becoming reality and any citizen, armed with a rifle, could shoot on sight at anything that wasn't completely white. Ibrahim Ali, a seventeen-year-old Comorian, had died like that, one night in February 1995, running after a night bus with his friends.

"I asked you a question. What are you doing here?"

"Sightseeing. I missed the neighborhood. The people, that kind of thing."

Of the four of them, only Babar smiled. Pertin bent over Serge's body. "Shit! It's your friend, the faggot! He's dead."

"I saw."

He looked at me, a wicked gleam in his eye. "What was he doing here?"

"No idea."

"And you?"

"I told you, Pertin. I was passing. I wanted to see the kids play, so I stopped."

The basketball court was empty.

"What kids? No one's playing."

"The game ended when the shooting started. You know how they are. It's not that they don't like you. But they'd rather not meet you."

"Save the comments, Montale. I don't give a shit. What's your story?"

I told him.

I told him a second time. At the station house. Pertin hadn't been able to resist the pleasure. The pleasure of having me sitting there opposite him, being interrogated. In this station house, where, for years, I'd ruled the roost. It was a meager revenge, but he was as happy about it as only a loser could be, and he wanted to savor it as much as he could. The opportunity might not come again.

And behind those fucking Ray-Bans, the wheels were turning in Pertin's brain. Serge and I had been buddies. Maybe we still were. Serge had just been whacked. Which meant he must have done something he shouldn't. I was there, on the scene. A witness. Yes, but why not an accomplice? That made me a lead. Not to collar the guys who'd gunned down Serge, but to collar me. I could just imagine the kick he'd get out of that.

I couldn't see his eyes, but I was sure that was what I'd have read in them if I could. Just because you're stupid doesn't mean you can't think logically.

"Profession?" he'd asked, contemptuously.

"Unemployed."

He burst out laughing. Carli stopped typing and laughed as well.

"No! So you're on welfare, are you? Like the niggers and the Arabs?"

I turned to Carli. "Are you getting this down?"

"Only the answers."

"Mustn't offend Superman here!" Pertin said. He leaned toward me. "And what do you live on?"

"Where do you think you are, Pertin? On TV? Or at the circus?"

I'd raised my voice a little. To set the record straight. To remind them I was just a witness. I didn't know anything about this business. I had nothing to hide, except the reason I'd gone to the project. I could tell my story a hundred times, it wouldn't change. Pertin had figured that immediately, and it made him really mad. He'd have liked to hit me. He'd have done it if he could. He'd stop at nothing. In the days when he was under my authority, he'd always make sure the dealers were tipped off when I was getting ready to make a raid. Or he'd tip off the narcs, if he felt the haul would be a good one. I still remembered the failure of a bust in Le Petit Séminaire, another project in North Marseilles. The dealers were a family. Brothers, sisters, relatives: they were all in on it. They operated where they lived, like good neighbors. And the kids paid them in stolen hi-fi equipment, which they then resold immediately, at three times the price. The profits were reinvested in drugs. The raid was a damp squib. The narcs succeeded three years later, with Pertin in charge.

He smiled. It wasn't a genuine smile. I was scoring points, and he knew it. To show me he was still in control, he picked up Serge's passport from the table in front of him and waved it under my nose.

"Tell me, Montale, you know where your buddy was crashing?"

"No idea."

"Are you sure?"

"Should I know?"

He opened the passport, and smiled again. "At Arno's place."

Shit! What was that all about? Pertin was watching for my reactions. I didn't have any. I waited. He hated me so much, he was making mistakes. He should never have revealed information to a witness.

"It isn't written in here," he said, waving the passport like a fan. "But we have our sources. In fact, we've been quite well informed, since you left. Seeing as how we're cops, not priests. You see the difference?"

"I see," I replied.

He leaned toward me. "He was one of your blue-eyed boys, wasn't he, that little Gypsy bastard?"

Arno. Arno Gimenez. I'd never been sure whether or not we'd made a mistake with him. Eighteen years old, crazy, cunning, stubborn sometimes to the point of stupidity. With a passion for motorbikes. The only guy capable of lifting a bike on the street with a chick still on it and carting her off, without her crying rape or theft. A mechanical genius. Every time he got involved in selling stolen goods, Serge would show up, then me.

One day, we'd cornered him in a bar called the Balto, in L'Estaque.

"Why don't you get a job?" Serge had said.

"Oh, yeah, great. I could buy a TV, a VCR, save for a pension, watch the Kawasakis passing on the street. Like cows watching the trains go by. That's it, huh? Yeah, great, guys. Real cool . . . "

He was making fun of us. Of course we weren't great at arguing for the benefits of society. Talking about morality, on the other hand, now that was something that came easily to us. Beyond that, it was a dead end.

"Guys want bikes," Arno had continued. "I find them bikes. I fix the bikes up for them and they're happy. It's cheaper than getting them from a dealership, and there's no sales tax to pay, so . . . "

I'd put my nose in my glass of beer, thinking how pointless conversations like this were. Serge tried to come out with a few more fine phrases, but Arno cut him off.

"For clothes, there's Carrefour. A big choice. Same with food. You just have to order." He looked at us, craftily. "Want to come with me one day?"

I often thought of Serge's credo: "Where there is revolt, there is anger. And where there is anger, there is life." It was beautiful. And maybe we'd trusted Arno too much. Or not enough. Maybe it really wasn't enough, because he didn't come to us the night he decided to hold up a drugstore on Boulevard de la Libération, at the top of the Canebière. All alone, like an idiot. And not with a crappy plastic gun. No, a real gun, big and black, shooting real bullets that could kill. All because Mira, his big sister, had the bailiffs on her back and needed five thousand in cash, otherwise she'd be out on the street with her two kids.

Arno had been given five years. Mira had been thrown out of where she lived. She'd taken the kids and left for Perpignan, where her folks were. The social worker hadn't been able to do anything for her, nor had the neighborhood committee. Serge and I were equally unsuccessful on behalf of Arno. Our testimonies were dismissed, like shit being flushed down the toilet. Society needs examples, sometimes, to show its citizens that it has the situation well in hand. And no more dreams for the Gimenez kids.

It put years on Serge and me. In his first letter, Arno had written: "I'm bored to death. I can't talk to the guys here. There's one who does nothing but talk about his exploits. The bozo thinks he's Mesrine. The other's an Arab, who's only interested in scrounging your smokes, your sugar, your coffee . . . The nights are long. But I can't get to sleep, even though I'm exhausted. I'm too worked up. I can't stop thinking . . . "

Pertin hadn't taken his eyes off me, pleased that he'd made an impression.

"How do you explain that, huh? That he was crashing at that son of a bitch's place?"

I slowly lifted my ass off the chair, and moved my face closer to his. I grabbed his Ray-bans and slid them down his nose. He had little eyes. Dirty yellow eyes, like a hyena's. It gave me the creeps looking into those eyes. He didn't blink. We stayed like that for a suspended moment. With my finger, I thrust the Ray-Bans back onto the bridge of his nose.

"I think we're done here. I've got other things to do. Forget about me."

Carli's fingers hung in midair above the keyboard. He was looking at me, open-mouthed.

"When you've finished the report," I said, "sign it for me and wipe your ass with it. OK?" I turned back to Pertin. "Bye, Four Eyes."

I went out. Nobody stopped me.

# 4.

## IN WHICH THE MAIN POINT
## IS FOR PEOPLE TO MEET

Night had fallen by the time I got back to La Bigotte. Back to square one. Outside D4. On the roadway, the chalk outline of Serge's body was already fading. Inside the buildings, they must have talked about the guy who'd been shot until the eight o'clock news. Then life had regained the upper hand. Tomorrow, it would again be gray in the North and sunny in the South. And even if you were unemployed, you thought that was great.

I looked up at the buildings, wondering which of the apartments Serge had been coming out of, who he'd been to see, and why. And what on earth he could have been doing to be killed like a dog.

My eyes came to rest on the windows of the Hamoudi family. On the tenth floor. Where their daughter Naïma lived. The girl Guitou loved. But I didn't think the two kids were here. They weren't in these blocks. They weren't in one of the bedrooms, listening to music. They weren't in the living room, calmly watching TV. These projects weren't a place for love. Any kid who'd been born here, grown up here, knew that. You didn't live in a place like this, you died slowly. Love needs dreams, and a future. The sea, instead of warming their hearts, as it had their parents', was an incentive to get away.

I knew that. Manu and Ugo and I, as soon as we could, would leave the Panier and go to watch the freighters sail away. Wherever they were going, it was better than living in poverty in the damp alleys of the neighborhood. We were fifteen years old, and that was what we thought. The same thing my father had thought sixty years earlier, in the port of Naples. Or my mother. And so, I supposed, had thousands of Spaniards and

Portuguese. Armenians, Vietnamese, Africans. Algerians, Comorians.

That's what I was thinking as I crossed the parking lot. I was also thinking that there was no way the Hamoudi family had taken in a young French boy. Any more than Gélou could have received a young Arab girl in her house. It was the weight of tradition. Sad as it might be, racism cut both ways. Today more than ever.

But here I was. With no illusions, but always ready to believe in miracles. I'd find Guitou, take him back to his mother and a bastard whose only language was his fists. If I found him, I'd decided I'd be gentle. I didn't want to make things worse. Not for these two kids. I believed in first love. In "The first girl you took in your arms," to quote the Brassens song.

All afternoon, I'd been thinking about Magali. That hadn't happened in years. Since that first night in the blockhouse, time had passed and we'd met again and made love. But that night was one I'd never taken out of my box of souvenirs. I was pretty much of the opinion that, however old you are when it happens—fifteen, sixteen, seventeen or even eighteen—the first time you sleep with someone, and break once and for all with your mother, or your father, is the decisive moment. It isn't a question of sex. It's the way you look at other people, women, men, after that. The way you look at life. And the feeling—right or wrong, good or bad—that you have for the rest of your life, about love.

I'd loved Magali. I should have married her. I was sure my life would have been different. Hers too. But there were too many people hoping that what she and I wanted so much would come true. My parents, hers, our uncles and aunts . . . We didn't want these old people, who knew it all, who laid down the rules, to be right. So Magali and I had played at hurting each other. Her letter reached me in Djibouti, where I was doing my military service, in the Colonial Army. "I'm three months pregnant. The father wants to marry me. In June.

Kisses." Magali was the first screw-up in my life. She wasn't the last.

I didn't know if Guitou and Naïma were in love the way we'd been in love. But I didn't want things to go bad for them. I wanted them to have the chance to spend a weekend, a month, a year together. Or forever. Without the adults sucking the air out of them. Without them being messed around too much. I could do that for them. I owed it to Magali, who, for twenty years, had been champing at the bit with a guy she'd never really loved, as she'd told me much later in a letter.

I took a deep breath, and climbed the stairs to the Hamoudis' apartment. Because, of course, the elevator was "temporarily out of order."

Behind the door, I could hear loud rap music. I recognized the voice of MC Solaar. *Prose Combat.* One of his hits. Since he'd taken part in a rap writing workshop with the kids in the projects, on 1 May one year, between two concerts, he'd been their idol. A woman shouted, and the sound dimmed. I took advantage of that to ring a second time. "There's someone at the door," the woman cried. Mourad opened.

Mourad was one of the boys I'd watched earlier on the basketball court. I'd noticed him. He had a good sense of teamwork.

"Oh," he said, recoiling. "Hi."

"Who is it?" the woman asked.

"A man," he replied, without turning around. "Are you a cop?"

"No. Why?"

"Well . . . " He looked me up and down. "Well, because of what happened earlier, you know. The French guy who was shot. I just thought. You were talking to the cops like you knew them."

"You're very observant."

"Well, we don't really talk to them, you know. We avoid them."

"Did you know the guy?"

"I didn't really get a look at him. But the others say they'd never seen him around here."

"So there's nothing to worry about."

"No."

"But you thought I was a cop. And you were scared. Any particular reason?"

The woman appeared in the corridor. She was dressed in European style, and on her feet she wore Turkish slippers with big red pompons.

"What is it, Mourad?"

"Good evening, Madame," I said.

Mourad retreated behind his mother, but didn't go away.

"What is it?" she repeated, to me this time.

She had magnificent black eyes. Her whole face was magnificent, framed by thick curly hennaed hair. She was barely into her forties. A beautiful woman, just starting to fill out a bit. Imagining how she must have been twenty years earlier gave me an idea of what Naïma looked like. Guitou had good taste, I said to myself, and it made me feel quite happy.

"I'd like to talk to Naïma."

Mourad came forward again, boldly. His face had grown somber. He looked at his mother.

"She isn't here," she said.

"May I come in for a moment?"

"She hasn't done anything stupid, has she?"

"That's what I'd like to find out."

She touched her heart with her fingertips.

"Let him come in," Mourad said. "He's not a cop."

I told my story, drinking a mint tea. Not my favorite drink after eight o'clock at night. I was dying for a glass of Clos-Cassivet, a white wine with a vanilla fragrance, which I'd recently discovered during my trips inland.

That was what I usually did at this time. I'd sit on my terrace, facing the sea, and drink, earnestly, savoring the taste. And I'd listen to jazz. Lately, Coltrane or Miles Davis. I was rediscovering them. I'd dug out the old Miles Davis album *Sketches of Spain* and, on evenings when I particularly missed Lole, I played *Solea* and *Saeta* over and over. The music made me think of Seville. That's where I'd have liked to be, right now, this minute. But I was too proud to do that. Lole had gone. She'd be back. She was a free agent, and I shouldn't go running after her. It was a lousy argument and I knew it.

In my desire to convince Naïma's mother, I mentioned Alex, saying that he "wasn't a very nice man." I told her how Guitou and Naïma had met, how Guitou had run away, how he'd taken money from the cash register, how his mother, my cousin, hadn't heard from him since, and how worried she was.

"You can understand that," I said.

Madame Hamoudi understood, but didn't reply. Her French vocabulary seemed to be limited to "Yes. No. Maybe. I know. I don't know." Mourad hadn't taken his eyes off me. Between him and me, I felt a kind of rapport. His face, though, remained inscrutable. I was starting to think that things weren't as simple as I'd imagined.

"Mourad, this is serious."

He looked at his mother, who sat with her hands clasped on her knees. "Talk to him, Ma. He doesn't mean us any harm."

She turned to her son, took him by the shoulders, and hugged him to her chest. As if she was afraid that someone would take her child away from her. It wasn't until afterwards that I realized it was the gesture of an Algerian woman assuming the right to speak under the authority of a man.

"She doesn't live here anymore," she began, her eyes lowered. "She hasn't been here for a week. She's living with her grandfather. Since Farid left for Algeria."

"My father," Mourad explained.

"About ten days ago," she went on, still without looking at me, "the Islamists attacked my husband's village, looking for hunting rifles. My father's brother still lives there. We're worried because of what's happening in our country. So Farid said, 'I'm going to find my brother.'"

She drank some of her tea.

"I didn't know what we were going to do. We don't have a lot of room here. That's why Naïma went to live with her grandfather. They love each other." Then she hastened to add, looking me in the eyes this time, "It's not that she doesn't get on with us, but . . . Well . . . There's the boys . . . And Redouane, Redouane's the eldest, he's . . . how shall I say? . . . more religious. So he's always after her. Because she wears pants, because she smokes, because she goes out with her girlfriends . . . "

"French boyfriends," I cut in.

"A *roumi* in our home, no, it's not possible, monsieur. Not for a girl. It isn't done. As Farid says, there's tradition. When we go back to our country, he doesn't want to hear people say, 'You wanted France, and now, you see, France has swallowed your children.'"

"Right now, it's the fundamentalists who are swallowing your children."

I immediately regretted being so direct. She stopped short, and looked around her, anxiously. Then she looked back at Mourad, who was listening without saying anything. He gently freed himself from his mother's embrace.

"It's not for me to talk about that," she said. "We're French. Their grandfather fought for France. He liberated Marseilles. With the Algerian artillery regiment. He got a medal for it . . . "

"He was badly wounded," Mourad said. "In the leg."

The liberation of Marseilles. My father had gotten a medal too. And a citation. But that was a long time ago. Fifty years. Ancient history. The only thing people still remembered was the American soldiers, on the Canebière. With their cans of Coke and packs of Lucky Strikes. And the girls who threw themselves at them for a pair of nylon stockings. The liberators. The heroes. People had forgotten about their indiscriminate bombardment of the city. Just as they'd forgotten about the Algerian infantry's desperate attempts to dislodge the Germans from Notre-Dame de la Garde. Cannon fodder for the French commanders.

Marseilles had never thanked the Algerians for that. Nor had France. And at the very same time, other French officers were violently suppressing the first pro-independence demonstrations in Algeria. People had also forgotten about the Sétif massacres, in which men, women and children were slaughtered. We all have short memories when it suits us . . .

"French, but also Muslims," she went on. "Farid used to go to cafés, drink beer, play dominoes. Now he's stopped. He prays. Maybe one day he'll go to Mecca, on the Hadj. That's how we are, there's a time for everything. But . . . We don't need people to tell us what to do and what not to do. The FIS are scary. That's what Farid says."

She was a good woman. And a clever one. She was expressing herself now in very correct French. Talking slowly, going into detail, but always skirting the true issue, like a true Eastern woman. She had her own opinions, but she concealed them beneath those of her husband. I had no wish to offend her, but I had to know.

"Redouane threw her out, is that it?"

"You should leave," she said, getting to her feet. "She isn't here. And I don't know the man you mentioned."

I also stood up. "I have to see your daughter," I said.

"It's not possible. Her grandfather doesn't have a phone."

"I could go there. It won't take long. I just have to talk to her. And I really have to talk to Guitou. His mother's worried. I have to reason with him. I don't wish them any harm. And . . . " I hesitated for a moment. "This is just between us. Redouane doesn't need to know. You can discuss it later, when your husband returns."

"He's not with her anymore," Mourad said.

His mother looked at him reproachfully.

"So you've seen your sister?"

"He's not with her anymore. He left, that's what she told me. They had an argument."

Shit! If that was true, Guitou was out there somewhere, brooding over a first love affair that had turned sour.

"I still have to see her," I said, turning back to the woman. "Guitou hasn't come home yet. I have to find him. You must understand that."

Her eyes were full of panic. Tenderness too. And a lot of questions. She stared at me, seeming to look right through me, searching for answers. Or for someone to trust. When you're an immigrant, trusting people is the hardest thing. She closed her eyes for a fraction of a second.

"I'll go to her grandfather's and talk to her. Tomorrow. Tomorrow morning. Call me around noon. If her grandfather agrees, then Mourad will go with you."

She walked to the door of the apartment. "You must leave. Redouane will be back, he's always home at this time."

"Thank you," I said. I turned to Mourad. "How old are you?"

"Almost sixteen."

"Carry on with the basketball. You're really good."

I lit a cigarette as I left the building, and walked toward my car. Hoping it would still be intact. OubaOuba must have been waiting for me. He came straight up to me before I reached the parking lot. Like a shadow. Black T-shirt, black pants. And a matching Rangers cap.

"Hi," he said, still walking. "I have some information for you."

"I'm listening," I said, following him.

"The French guy they shot, they say he's been nosing around lately. At La Savine, La Bricarde, everywhere. Especially at Le Plan d'Aou. This was the first time they saw him here."

We kept walking past the buildings, side by side, chatting away like old friends.

"What do you mean, nosing around?"

"Asking questions. About the young guys. Just the Arabs."

"What kind of questions?"

"About the fundamentalists."

"What do you know about that?"

"What I'm telling you."

"What else?"

"The guy who was driving the car. He's been seen around here a few times, with Redouane."

"Redouane Hamoudi?"

"Sure, you've just come from his place, haven't you?"

We'd walked around the project, and were coming back to the parking lot and my car. I wouldn't get any more information.

"Why are you telling me all this?"

"I know who you are. So do some of my friends. I know Serge was a buddy of yours. From before. From when you were sheriff." He smiled, his face lit by the crescent moon. "He was an OK guy. He did a lot of favors, they say. So did you. A lot of kids owe you. The mothers know that. So people trust you."

"I don't know your first name."

"Anselme. Haven't fucked up big time yet, so they don't know me down the station house."

"Carry on like that."

"I have good parents. Not everyone can say that. And the basketball . . . " He smiled. "And there's the *chourmo*. Know what that is?"

I knew. *Chourmo*, a Provençal word derived from *chiourme*, the rowers in a galley. In Marseilles, we knew all about galleys. No need to kill your mother and father to find yourself in the galleys, just like two centuries ago. No, these days, you just had to be young, whether you were an immigrant or not. The fan club of Massilia Sound System, the craziest bunch of kids around, had taken over the expression.

Since then, the *chourmo* had become not so much a fan club as a friendship club. There were two hundred and fifty, maybe three hundred of them, and they now "supported" several bands. Massilia, the Fabulous, Bouducon, the Black Lions, Hypnotik, Wadada . . . They'd just brought out a brilliant joint album called *Ragga baletti*. That certainly got things rocking on a Saturday night!

The *chourmo* organized sound systems, and used the revenue to publish a newsletter, distribute cassettes of live recordings, and arrange cheap travel so the kids could follow the bands on tour. It worked that way at the stadium too, around OM. With the Ultras, the Winners or the Fanatics. But that wasn't the main point of the *chourmo*. The main point was for people to meet. "To mingle," like they say in Marseilles. To get involved in someone else's business, and have them get involved in yours. There was a *chourmo* spirit. You weren't just from one neighborhood, one project. You were *chourmo*. In the same galley, rowing! Trying to get out. Together.

Crazy Rastas!

I hazarded another question as we reached the parking lot. "Is something going down in the projects?"

"Something's always going down, you should know that. Think about it."

When we got to my car, he continued walking, without saying goodbye.

I took a Bob Marley cassette from the glove compartment. I always had at least one with me, for moments like this. And *So Much Trouble in the World* seemed to fit, as I drove through the Marseilles night.

# 5.

## IN WHICH A LITTLE TRUTH
## DOESN'T HURT ANYONE

On Place des Baumes in Saint-Antoine, I made up my mind. Instead of turning onto the coastal highway and heading for home, I went around the giratory, and took the road from Saint-Antoine to Saint-Joseph. Heading for Le Merlan.

I was thinking about my conversation with Anselme. The fact that he'd thought it was worth coming to me and talking about Serge meant there must be something more to find out. I wanted to know what it was. To understand, as always. A real sickness. I must have the mind of a cop. To leap into things at a moment's notice. Unless I was *chourmo* too! It didn't matter. A little truth, I told myself, never hurt anyone. Not the dead anyway. And Serge wasn't just anyone. He was a good man, someone I'd respected.

I had a head start, a whole night to nose around in Serge's affairs. Pertin was arrogant, and driven by hatred. But he wasn't a good cop. I couldn't imagine him being prepared to waste a single hour turning over a dead man's apartment. He'd rather leave that to the "pencil pushers," as he called his colleagues at the station house. He had something more interesting to do. Like playing cowboys and Indians in North Marseilles. Especially at night. There was every chance I'd be left in peace.

The truth was, I wanted to gain time. How could I go home, with my hands in my pockets, and look Gélou in the eyes? What could I say to her? That Guitou and Naïma might be spending another night together. That it wasn't harming anyone. Something like that. Lies. It would hurt only her pride as a mother. But she'd been hurt worse than that in her life. And sometimes I chicken out. Especially with women. And especially the ones I love.

At Le Merlan-Village, I spotted an empty phone booth. There was no answer at my place. I tried Honorine.

"We didn't wait for you. We sat down to eat. I made some spaghetti with basil and garlic. Have you seen the boy?"

"Not yet, Honorine."

"She's getting worried. By the way, before I pass her to you, you remember the mullet you caught this morning? There's enough eggs to make a nice *poutargue*. What do you say?"

*Poutargue* was a specialty from the Martigues, similar to caviar. It was years since I'd last eaten it.

"Don't put yourself out, Honorine. That's a lot of work."

What you had to do was extract the two clusters of eggs, without tearing the membrane that protects them, salt them, crush them, then leave them to dry. Making it could take a week.

"It's nothing. Besides, it's a good opportunity. You'll be able to invite poor Fonfon to dinner. I have the feeling he isn't himself in the fall."

I smiled. It was true that I hadn't invited Fonfon in a long time. And if I didn't invite him, those two didn't invite each other either. As if there was something indecent about a man and a woman in their seventies, both widowed, wanting to see each other.

"OK, I'll pass you Gélou, she's dying to speak to you."

I was ready.

"Hello?"

Claudia Cardinale speaking. Gélou's voice sounded even more sensual on the phone. It went down as smoothly as a glass of Lagavulin. Soft and warm.

"Hello?" she repeated.

I had to chase away the memories. Gélou's memories too. I took a deep breath and gave her the speech I'd prepared.

"Listen, it's more complicated than we thought. They're not

at her parents'. Or her grandfather's. Are you sure he hasn't come home?"

"No, I left your phone number on his bed. And Patrice knows what's going on. He knows I'm here."

"What about . . . Alex?"

"He never calls when he's on a trip. There's still a chance. It's . . . It's always been like that, ever since we met. He has his business. I don't ask questions." There was a silence, then she went on, "Guitou, he's . . . They may be staying with a friend of hers. Mathias. He was one of the friends she went camping with. This Mathias was with her when she came to say good-bye to Guitou, and . . . "

"Do you know his surname?"

"Fabre. But I don't know where he lives."

"The Marseilles phone book is full of Fabres."

"I know. I looked it up last night. I even called several of them. I felt such a fool. After the twelfth one I gave up. I was exhausted, on edge. And even more foolish than before I'd started."

"In any case, I think we've missed the start of the school year. I'm going to see what else I can do tonight. Tomorrow, I'll try to find out a bit more about this Mathias. And I'll go see Naïma's grandfather."

A bit of truth in the middle of all the lies. And the hope that Naïma's mother hadn't taken me for a ride. That the grandfather really existed. That Mourad would go with me. That the grandfather would agree to see me. That Guitou and Naïma were there, or not too far from there . . .

"Why not right away?"

"Gélou, have you seen what time it is?"

"Yes, but . . . Fabio, do you think he's all right?"

"Sure, he's in bed with a nice girl. He's forgotten we exist. Don't you remember what it was like? It wasn't bad, was it?"

"I was twenty! And Gino and I were going to get married."

"It must have been good, though, all the same, eh? That's what I'm asking."

There was another silence. Then I heard her sniffing at the other end. There was nothing erotic about it. It wasn't Claudia Cardinale playing a role. It was simply my cousin crying, as a mother.

"I think I really screwed up with Guitou. Don't you think so?"

"Gélou, you must be tired. Finish eating and go to bed. Don't wait up for me. Take my bed and try to get some sleep."

"OK," she sighed.

She sniffled some more. I heard Honorine coughing behind her. Her way of saying I shouldn't worry, she'd take care of her. Honorine never coughed.

"Take care," I said to Gélou. "You'll see, tomorrow, we'll all be together."

I hung up. Rather abruptly, in fact, because for the last few minutes two young bozos on a moped had been circling my car. I had forty-five seconds to save my car radio. I ran out of the booth, yelling. More to let off steam than to scare them. I really did scare them, but that didn't clear my head of all the thoughts buzzing around in it. Zooming past me, the driver of the moped shouted, "Fucking dickhead!"—even less compensation for them than the price of my rotten car radio.

Arno had lived in a place called the Old Mill, a spot on the road to Le Merlan curiously neglected by the developers. Before and after it, there was nothing but low-cost Provençal housing developments. High-rises for bank clerks and middle managers. I'd only been here once before, with Serge. The place was rather sinister. Especially at night. After eight-thirty, the buses stopped running, and very few cars passed.

I parked near the old mill itself, which had been turned into a furniture warehouse. The area directly in front of it was an automobile scrap yard, owned by a distant cousin of Arno's, a Gypsy named Saadna. Arno's place was behind it, a parpen shack with a canvas roof. Saadna had built it with the intention of making it into a small body shop.

I went around the mill, and walked along the Marseilles water canal for about a hundred yards, until I came to a bend, just behind the scrap yard. I ran down an embankment of garbage to Arno's place. A few dogs barked, but I wasn't bothered. Most dogs were asleep in the houses. Dying of fear, like their masters. And Saadna didn't like dogs. He didn't like anyone.

Around, there were still a few carcasses of motorbikes. Stolen, I guessed. Arno fixed them at night, bare-chested, with slippers on his feet and a joint in his mouth.

"You could go down for that," I'd said to him one evening when I'd paid him a visit. Just to make sure he was at home, and not out selling stolen property in the Belleville project. In an hour, we were going to make a raid on the cellars of the project and pick up whatever we found. Drugs, dealers and other human filth.

"Don't jerk me around, Montale! Not you too. You and Serge, you crack me up, you know? It's work. OK? I don't have job security, but it's my life. Looking after number one. You know what I mean?" He'd dragged furiously on his joint, thrown it away angrily, then had looked at me, his wrench in his hand. "I'm not going to live here all my life, you know. So I work. Do you really think . . . "

I didn't think. That was what worried me about Arno. "Money stolen is money gained." The logic Manu, Ugo and I had used when we came on the scene, at the age of twenty. However often you tell yourself that fifty million is a good figure and when you reach it you'll stop, one of you always eventually does something you didn't expect. Manu had shot someone. Ugo had gloated, because it was our biggest haul. But I'd thrown up, and left to join the Colonial Army. A whole chapter of our lives had ended abruptly. Our adolescence, our dreams of travel and adventure. Of being free and happy, and not working. No bosses, no chiefs. No God or master.

At any other time, I could have sailed away on a liner.

Argentina. Buenos Aires. "Reduced prices on one-way tickets," as they said on the old Messageries Maritimes posters. But by 1970 there were no more liners. The world was like us now. No destination, no future. I'd left for free. Spent five years in Djibouti. I'd already done my military service there, a few years earlier. It was no worse than being in prison. Or working in a factory. In my pocket, to keep going, to stay sane, I always had *Exile* by Saint John Perse. The same copy that Lole used to read aloud to us, on the Digue du Large, facing the sea.

> *I had, I had this taste for living among men, and now the earth exhales her foreign soul . . .*

Enough to make you weep.

Then I'd become a cop, without really knowing why or how. And lost my friends. Now Manu and Ugo were dead. And Lole was away, in a place where it ought to be possible to live without memories. Without remorse. Without rancor. Coming to terms with life meant coming to terms with your memories. That was what Lole had said to me one night. The night before she left. I agreed with her about that. It was pointless to question the past. It was the future you had to question. Without a future, the present is nothing but chaos. Of course. But I couldn't get away from my past, that was my problem.

Now, I wasn't anything anymore. I didn't believe in cops and I didn't believe in robbers. Those who represented the law had lost all sense of moral values, and the real thieves weren't the ones who stole to put food on the table. They sent ministers to prison, of course, but that was just one of the ups and downs of political life. It wasn't justice. They all came back sooner or later. In the business world, politics washes everything white. The Mafia is the best example of that. But for thousands of kids in the projects, prison was the start of the downward slope. When they got out, the best was behind them and the worst lay ahead. Whatever dreams they'd had had turned to dust.

I pushed open the door. It had never had a lock. In winter, Arno put a chair against it to keep it closed. In summer, he slept outside, in a Cuban hammock. The interior was as I remembered it. A military surplus iron bedstead in a corner. A table, two chairs. A small wardrobe. A little gas stove. An electric heater. Next to the sink, the dishes from a meal, all washed. A plate, a glass, a fork, a knife. Serge had lived alone. I couldn't see him bringing a girl here. Living in a place like this, you'd really have to want it badly. In any case, I'd never known Serge to have a girlfriend. Maybe he really was gay.

I didn't really know what I was looking for. Something to give me an idea of what he was involved in, something to explain why he'd been shot down on the street. I didn't think I'd find anything, but it was worth a try. I started with the wardrobe, from top to bottom. Inside, a couple of jackets, two pairs of jeans. Nothing in the pockets. The table had no drawers. There was an envelope lying on it, already opened. I put it in my pocket. Nothing under the bed. Or beneath the mattress. I sat down to think. There was nowhere to hide anything.

Beside the bed, on top of a pile of newspapers, two paperback books. *Fragments of a Paradise* by Jean Giono and *The Astonished Man* by Blaise Cendrars. I'd read both books. I had them in my house. I leafed through them. No papers. No notes. I put them down. There was a third book, hardback this time. This one wasn't one of my bedside books. *The Lawful and the Prohibited in Islam* by Yusuf Al-Qaradawi. There was a press cutting with it, saying there'd been an order banning the sale and distribution of this book "because of its strong anti-Western stance and because the ideas it contains are contrary to the fundamental laws and values of the Republic." No notes in this one either.

I came across a chapter entitled "What to Do when Your Wife Is Proud and Rebellious." I smiled, telling myself maybe it'd teach me how to deal with Lole, if she ever came back. But could you regulate the relationship between a man and a woman with a law? Only religious fanatics—Islamists, Christians or Jews—thought you could. When it came to love, the only things I believed in were freedom and trust. Which didn't make relationships any easier. I'd always known that. Now I was living with the consequences.

The newspapers were from the day before. *Le Provençal*, *Le Méridional*, *Libération*, *Le Monde*. This week's *Le Canard Enchaîné*. Several recent issues of the Algerian dailies *Liberté* and *El Watam*. More surprisingly, a pile of issues of *Al Ansar*, the clandestine newsletter of the Armed Islamic Group, the GIA. Beneath the newspapers, in folders, several more press cuttings. "The Marrakesh Trial: A Trial with a French Suburban Background." "Biggest Raid Ever on Islamist Groups." "Terrorism: How the Islamists Recruit in France." "The Islamist Spider Spins Its Web in Europe." "Islam: Resistance to Fundamentalism."

This, along with the Al-Qaradawi book and the issues of *Liberté*, *El Watam* and *Al Ansar*, might be the beginnings of a lead. What on earth had Serge been up to since I'd seen him last? Was he writing an article? An investigation into Islamists in Marseilles? There were six folders full of press cuttings. I noticed a FNAC bag under the sink and put the book and all the papers in it.

"Don't move!" someone cried behind me.

"Don't be an idiot, Saadna, it's Montale!"

I'd recognized his voice. I had no desire to meet him. That was why I'd come via the canal.

The light came on. A single bulb hanging by a thread from the ceiling. A white, crude, harsh light that made the place look even more squalid. I turned slowly, blinking, my FNAC bag in my hand. Saadna was aiming a hunting rifle directly at me. He took a step forward, dragging his limp leg. He'd had polio and it had never mended.

"You came by the canal, eh?" he said with a ugly smile. "Like a thief. Have you taken up burglary, Fabio?"

"I wouldn't get rich here," I said sarcastically.

Saadna and I made no secret of our hatred for each other. He was the archetypal gypsy. Non-Gypsies were all jerks. Every time a young Gypsy got into trouble, it was of course the non-Gypsies' fault. For centuries, we'd persecuted them. We were only there to cause them problems. We'd been invented by the devil, to piss off God the Father who, in his infinite goodness, had created the Gypsy in his own image. The Roma. Man. Since then, the devil had made things even worse, by bringing thousands of Arabs to France, just to piss off the Gypsies even more.

With his beard and long salt-and-pepper hair, he liked to think of himself as a wise old man. The younger ones often asked him for advice. It was always the worst kind of advice. Inspired by hatred, scorn. Cynicism. Through them, he was avenging himself for the bad leg he'd had since the age of twelve. Without the affection he felt for him, Arno might never have done so many stupid things. He'd never have ended up in prison. And he'd still be alive.

When Arno's father, Chano, died, Serge and I had intervened on his behalf to get him granted leave. He was really upset, and was determined to be at the funeral. I'd even flirted with the social worker—"hotter than the youth organizer," Arno had said—to get her to intervene too, personally. The leave was granted, then withdrawn, on the express orders of the warden, apparently because Arno was stupid. He was only authorized to see his father, one last time, at the morgue. Between two gendarmes. When they got there, they wouldn't remove his handcuffs. So Arno refused to see his father. "I didn't want him to see me with those things on my wrists," he'd written to us soon afterwards.

On his return, he broke down, kicked up an almighty fuss, and found himself in solitary again. "Look, you guys, I'm fed up with this shit, people treating me without respect, all those things. The walls, the contempt, the insults . . . It stinks! I've looked at the ceiling two thousand times, and I've had enough."

When he came out of solitary, he slit his wrists.

Saadna lowered his eyes. And his rifle.

"Honest people come in through the main door. Would it have hurt you to come say hello to me?" He looked around the room and his eyes came to rest on the FNAC bag. "What have you got in there?"

"Papers that Serge doesn't need anymore. He was killed. This afternoon. Right in front of me. You'll be getting a visit from the cops tomorrow."

"Killed?"

"Any idea what Serge was up to?"

"I need a drink. Follow me."


Even if he'd known anything, Saadna wouldn't have told me. All the same, he didn't need much prodding to start talking, and he didn't launch into any convoluted explanations, like he did when he was lying. That should have surprised me. But I was too much in a hurry to leave his rat hole.

He'd filled two dusty glasses with a foul-smelling brew he called whisky. I hadn't touched it. Hadn't even clinked glasses. Saadna was one of those people I didn't even clink glasses with.

Serge had come to see him the previous fall, to ask if he could stay in Arno's shack. "I need it for a while," Serge had said. "I need a hiding place." He'd tried to get him to talk, but to no avail. "You're not in any danger, but the less you know, the better." They didn't see much of each other, rarely talked. About two weeks ago, Serge had given him a thousand francs and asked him to make sure nobody was following him when he came back at night.

Saadna hadn't much liked Serge either. Youth worker,

cop—we were all the same fucking bunch of jerks to him. But Serge had been good to Arno. He wrote to him, sent him packages, went to see him. Saadna mentioned that now, in his usual spiteful tone, to make it quite clear that he made a distinction between Serge and me. I didn't say anything. I didn't have any desire to suck up to Saadna. How I behaved was up to me, and my conscience.

It was true I hadn't written much to Arno. Letters have never been my thing. The only person I ever wrote to a lot was Magali. When she was at teachers' training college in Caen. I'd tell her about Marseilles, Les Goudes. She missed it a lot. But words aren't my forte. I'm not even very good at talking. I mean, about what I really feel. Idle chatter I'm fine with, like everyone in Marseilles.

But every two weeks, I went to see Arno. First, at the young people's institution in Luynes, near Aix en Provence. Then at Les Baumettes. A month later, they put him in the infirmary because he wasn't eating anything and was spending all his time on the toilet, having a crap. He was emptying himself. I'd brought him some Pepitos, he loved those.

"I'll tell you what it is about Pepitos," he said. "One day, when I was—what?—eight or nine, I was hanging out with my brothers, the older ones. They'd scrounged a smoke from a *payo* and were smoking and talking dirty. Obviously, I found it fascinating. Suddenly Le Pacho said, 'Marco, how many calories is a natural yoghurt?' Of course, Marco had no idea. At the age of fifteen, he didn't eat a whole lot of yoghurt. Next, Le Pacho asked, 'What about a hard-boiled egg?' 'Get to the point!' the others said, not sure where he was going with this.

"Le Pacho had heard that when you fuck, you burn up eighty calories. And that's the same as a hard-boiled egg, or a Danone. 'So eat an egg or a yoghurt,' he said, very seriously, 'and you'll come.' We all laughed our heads off. Marco didn't want to be left behind. 'I heard that if you can't get it up, you eat fifteen Pepitos and it works fine!' Since then, I've been eating Pepitos! You never know! I know what you're going to say, not much use for it in here. You saw what the nurse looked like!"

We'd both laughed.

I suddenly needed air. I had no desire to talk to Saadna about Arno. Or about Serge. Saadna soiled everything he talked about, everything he touched, everything around him. And the people he talked to as well. He'd agreed to Serge coming here not because of his friendship with Arno but because knowing he was in the shit made him feel as if he was a kindred spirit.

I stood up.

"You haven't touched your drink," he said.

"You know, Saadna. I never drink with guys like you."

"You'll live to regret it."

And he drained my glass in one go.

In the car, I lit the ceiling light and had a look at the letter I'd taken. It had been posted on Saturday, from the Colbert post office in the center of town. On the back, the sender, instead of putting his or her name and address, had written, in a clumsy hand, "Because the cards have been so badly dealt, we are reaching a level of chaos at which life becomes impossible." I shivered. Inside, there was a single sheet of paper torn from an exercise book, in the same handwriting. Two short sentences. I read them feverishly, driven by the urgency of their cry for help. "I can't stand it anymore. I need to see you. Pavie."

Pavie. My God! She was all we needed.

# 6.

## IN WHICH THE CHOICES WE MAKE IN LIFE DO NOT DETERMINE EVERYTHING

It wasn't until I indicated a right turn onto Rue de la Belle-de-Mai that I realized I was being followed. A black Safrane had been tailing me, keeping at a fair distance, but never losing sight of me. On Boulevard Fleming, it had even overtaken me after a red light. When it had stopped next to me, I'd felt eyes on me. I'd glanced toward the car. But it had smoked windows, protecting the driver from prying eyes. All I'd seen was the reflection of my own face.

The Safrane then drove on in front of me, scrupulously keeping to the speed limit in town. That should have alerted me. At night, no one keeps to the speed limit. Not even me in my old Renault 5. But I was too busy trying to put my thoughts in order to worry about being followed. Besides, it had simply never occurred to me that anyone might be tailing me.

I'd been thinking about the way circumstances come together, the way, for example, you wake up in the morning with not a care in the world, and by nighttime your cousin's son is missing, a buddy of yours has been shot down in front of your eyes, a kid you barely know befriends you, and you're forced to talk to a guy you have no desire to see. And your memories grab you by the throat. Magali. Manu, Ugo. Arno too. I was reminded of him by his ex-girlfriend, who was permanently high. Pavie, little Pavie, who'd had too many dreams. And had realized all too soon that life is a bad movie, in which the fact that it's in Technicolor doesn't improve the story. Pavie, who was calling for help, and Serge, who'd never be able to answer that call now.

That's how life is. Our paths crisscross. We make choices that lead us along roads different from the ones we'd hoped to take, depending on whether we turned right rather than left. Whether we said yes to one thing and not another. It wasn't the first time I'd found myself in a situation like this. I sometimes got the feeling I always chose the wrong direction. But would the other road have been better? Or even different?

I doubted it. But I wasn't sure. I'd read somewhere, in a cheap novel, that "men are led by the blind man inside them." That was it, that was the way we moved forward. Blindly. Choice was just an illusion. A trick that life used to get us to swallow its bitter pill. It wasn't choice that determined everything, but how open we were to other people.

When Gélou had arrived that morning, my life had been empty. She'd set off a chain reaction. The world around me had begun moving again, like an engine being started. And backfiring, as usual.

Damn!

A glance in the rearview mirror showed me that I was still being followed. Who by? And why? The questions were pointless, because I had no way of answering them. I assumed I'd been followed since I left Saadna's. But it could just as easily have been since I said goodbye to Anselme. Or since I'd come out of the station house. Or since I'd left home. No, it couldn't have been since I left home, that made no sense at all. But at some point since Serge was killed, yes, that was plausible.

I started the Bob Marley cassette again, with *Slave Driver*, to put me in the right mood, and on Rue Honorat, alongside the railroad track, I accelerated to 43 mph. The Safrane hardly reacted. I went back to my normal speed.

Pavie. She'd been there at Arno's trial. She hadn't protested, hadn't cried, hadn't said a word. Proud, like Arno. But after that, she'd plunged back into the drug scene, with all the little hustles you were forced into to get a fix. Her life with Arno had been just a brief happy episode. Arno had been her last hope. But her last hope hadn't been enough to cope with all the shit. He'd slipped, and she'd plunged headlong.

On Place d'Aix, the Safrane went through a yellow light. Good, I told myself, it's nearly eleven, and I'm feeling hungry. And thirsty. I turned onto Rue Sainte-Barbe, without signaling, but without accelerating either. Then Rue Colbert, Rue Méry and Rue Caisserie, toward the old neighborhood, my childhood territory. Where my parents had lived when they left Italy. Where Gélou was born. Where I'd known Manu and Ugo. And Lole, who still seemed to haunt the streets with her presence.

On Place de Lenche, I parked the way everyone did here, somewhere I shouldn't, my right wheel up against the front step of a small building. There was a parking space available on the other side, but I wanted the guy following me to think I wouldn't be gone for long, which was why I hadn't parked properly. That's the way we are here. Sometimes, even if it's just for fifteen minutes, people prefer to double park, with the hazard lights on.

The Safrane appeared as I was locking my door. I ignored it. I lit a cigarette, and strode back up Place de Lenche, turned right onto Rue des Accoules, then right again onto Rue Fonderie-Vieille. Down a flight of steps, and I was back on Rue Caisserie. All I had to do now was get back to Place de Lenche, to see what had become of the guy following me.

He'd shamelessly taken the space I'd left free, parking impeccably between two other cars. The driver's window was open, and smoke wafted out. He didn't seem to be in any hurry. I wasn't worried about him. Cars like that even had stereos. The Safrane had a Var license number. I made a note of it. It didn't tell me anything right now. But tomorrow was another day.

Time to eat, I told myself.

When I reached Chez Félix, two couples were just finishing dinner. Félix himself was sitting at a table toward the rear of the restaurant, his Gitanes filters on one side, his *pastis* on the other, reading *The Pieds Nickelés in Deauville*. His favorite reading matter. In fact, his only reading matter. He didn't even bother with the newspapers. He had a collection of Pieds Nickelés and Bibi Fricotin comics, and enjoyed them whenever he had five minutes to spare.

"Céleste!" he called, when he saw me come in. "We have a guest!"

His wife came out of the kitchen, wiping her hands on her black apron, which she never took off until the restaurant closed. She'd put on another six pounds at least. Where it was most conspicuous. On the chest and the buttocks. Just seeing her, you felt like eating.

Her *bouillabaisse* was one of the best in Marseilles. Scorpion fish, gurnard, conger, dory, angler fish, weever, pandora, rainbow wrasse . . . A few crabs, too, and sometimes a lobster. Only rock fish. That's what made it different. And for the sauce, she had a particular genius for combining garlic and peppers with potatoes and sea urchin. But her *bouillabaisse* was never on the menu. You had to phone regularly to know when she was making it. Because you needed at least seven or eight people for a good *bouillabaisse*. So that you could make a copious amount of it and put in as many kinds of fish as possible. The only people there when she served it were friends and connoisseurs. Even Honorine had to admit Céleste was good. "Well, you know, it's not my profession . . . "

"You're just in time," she said, kissing me. "I was cooking a few leftovers. Clams in sauce, like a fricassee. And I was planning to grill some *fegatelli*. How about a few pickled sardines to start?"

"Whatever you're having."

"No need to ask him, dammit!" Félix said. "Just bring it!"

He knocked back his *pastis*, then went behind the bar and poured a round without being asked. Félix's average intake of *pastis* was ten or twelve at noon and ten or twelve in the evening. Today, he was drinking it in a normal glass, with a drop of water. In the old days he used to serve it, almost entirely neat, in very small glasses. Everyone lost count of the rounds. Depending on the number of friends drinking, a round could be eight to ten *pastis*. Never less. Whenever Félix said, "It's my round," they'd start all over again. It was just the same at the Péano or the Unic, before the first was taken up by a hip crowd and the second became a rock venue. *Pastis* and *kenia*—black and green olives, pickles and all kinds of vegetables cooked in vinegar—were part of the art of living, Marseilles style. Those were the days when people still knew how to talk to each other, when they still had things to say to each other. Of course, it made you thirsty. And it took time. But time didn't matter. Nobody was in a hurry. Everything could wait a few more minutes. Those days were no better and no worse than now. But it was a time when you could share your joys and your sorrows. You didn't hold back. You could even tell people you were poor. You were never alone. You just had to come to Chez Félix. Or Chez Marius. Or Chez Lucien. And whatever problems kept you awake at night vanished in a haze of *pastis*.

Celeste would often shout to a customer, "Hey! You want me to lay a place for you?"

"No, I'm going home to eat."

"And does your wife know you're going home to eat?"

"What the hell? I told her this morning."

"She can't still be waiting for you, you know. Have you seen what time it is?"

"Oh, shit!"

And he'd sit down to a plate of spaghetti with clams and eat it quickly, so that he could get to work on time.

Félix placed the *pastis* in front of me, and we clinked glasses. He looked at me with his bloodshot eyes. He seemed happy. We'd known each other for twenty-five years. But in the last four he'd transferred his fatherly affections to me.

Dominique, their only son, who'd had a passion for wrecks

on the sea bed between the Riou islands and the Maire islands, had dived one day and hadn't come up again. He'd heard that fishermen from Sanary were constantly snagging their nets on the bottom of the Blauquières plateau, twelve miles off the coast, between Toulon and Marseilles. It might have been a protuberant rock. It might have been something else. Dominique had never returned with the answer.

But his hunch had been right. A few months ago, at that very spot, quite by chance, two divers from the maritime survey team, Henri Delauze and Popof, had brought up, from a depth of sixty-five feet, the intact wreck of the *Protée*, the French submarine that went missing between Algiers and Marseilles in 1943. The discovery had been widely reported in the local press, and Dominique's name had been mentioned. At noon that day, I'd gone to Chez Félix. The discovery of the *Protée* hadn't brought his son back to life. But it had given his name a new luster. It had made him a pioneer. He was part of legend now. We'd drunk to that. Crying with happiness.

"Your health!"

"Damn that's good."

I hadn't been back since that day. Four months. When you don't go anywhere, time rushes by at a tremendous speed. I suddenly realized that. Since Lole had gone, I hadn't left my cottage. And I'd neglected the few friends I still had.

"Could you do me a favor?"

He nodded. "Yeah, sure."

He'd have done anything for me, except drink water.

"Phone Jo, at the Bar de la Place. There's a black Safrane parked just outside his door. Get him to take a cup of coffee out to the driver, say it's from the guy in the Renault 5." He picked up the receiver. "And ask him to see what the guy looks like. For the last hour he's been sticking to my tail like a limpet."

"Too many jerks around these days. You been banging his wife?"

"Not that I recall."

Jo liked the idea of having a laugh at the end of the day. That didn't surprise me. It was the kind of trouble they got up to in his bar. I wasn't one of his customers. The place was a bit too *mia* for my taste. Full of vulgar, narrow-minded people. There were other bars I preferred. Chez Félix, of course. Etienne's place, at the top of the Panier, on Rue de Lorette. And Ange's, on Place des Treize-Coins, just behind the station house.

"After the coffee," Jo said, "you want us to grab him? There are eight of us in the bar."

Félix looked at me. I was holding the earpiece. I shook my head.

"Forget it," Félix answered. "Just the coffee. His wife's just cheated on him."

Fifteen minutes later, Jo called back. We'd already gotten through a Côteaux d'Aix, a red wine from the Domaine des Béates. 1988.

"Hey, Félix! You been banging this guy's wife, you better watch out."

"Why?" Félix asked.

"His name's Antoine Balducci."

Félix gave me a questioning look. I didn't know anyone of that name. Let alone his wife.

"Don't know him," Félix said.

"He's a regular at the Rivesalte in Toulon. He's got underworld connections in the Var. That's what Jeannot says. I got him to go with me when I took the coffee out. Just for a laugh, you know. Jeannot was a waiter over that way. That's where he met Balducci. Hell, it was a good thing it was dark! If he'd recognized him, things might have hotted up . . . And anyhow, there were two of them."

"Two," Félix repeated, giving me a questioning look. "You didn't know?"

"No."

"I couldn't even tell you what the other guy looks like," Jo went on. "He didn't move. Didn't say a word. Didn't even breathe. In my opinion, he's top brass, compared with Balducci . . . Hey, you in trouble, Félix?"

"No, no, it's not me . . . It's one of my customers . . . A really good customer."

"Well, tell him to make himself scarce. If you ask me, these guys are armed to the teeth."

"I'll pass it on. Look, Jo, are you sure this hasn't landed you in any trouble?"

"No, Balducci laughed. Maybe not very genuine, but he did laugh. These guys can take it, you know."

"Are they still there?"

"No, they've gone now. 'So someone bought this for me?' he asked, and pointed to the coffee. 'Yes, monsieur,' I said. He put a hundred francs in the cup. The coffee spilled all over my fingers. 'There's your tip.' You see the kind of guy."

"Yeah, I see. Thanks, Jo. Drop by for an aperitif one of these days. Ciao."

Celeste brought the *fegatelli*, grilled to a turn, together with a few potatoes sprinkled with parsley. Félix sat down and opened another bottle. With its fragrances of thyme, rosemary and eucalyptus, the wine was a small masterpiece. You couldn't get tired of it.

As we ate, we talked about the tuna fishing competition traditionally organized by the nautical club of the Vieux-Port at the end of September. It was the season for it. In Marseilles, Port-de-Bouc, Port Saint-Louis. Three years ago, just off Saintes-Maries-de-la-Mer, I'd caught a 660-pound tuna, from two hundred and eighty feet down. The battle had gone on for three and a quarter hours. I'd had my photo in the Arles edition of *Le Provençal* and I'd been made an honorary member of the Les Goudes boat club, La Rascasse.

I was getting ready for the competition, as I did every year. They'd recently changed the rules to allow fishing *au broumé*. A traditional Marseilles method. You stop your boat, and you attract the fish by throwing crushed sardines and bread into the sea. It makes a kind of oily patch, which is carried along on the current. When the fish, swimming against the current, smells it, he heads for the boat. After that, the real sport starts!

"So, you don't know much more than you did before, do you?" Félix asked, a touch worried, when Céleste went to get the cheese.

"No," I replied, laconically.

I'd forgotten all about the guys in the Safrane. It was true, I didn't know much more than I'd known before. What could I possibly be involved in, that two mobsters from the Var should be on my tail? I didn't know anyone in Toulon. I hadn't been near the place in more than thirty years. I'd done my training there, as a conscript. I'd had a really bad time. I'd wiped Toulon off my map forever. And I certainly wasn't going to change my mind now. In the last municipal elections, the city had gone over to the National Front. Maybe it was no worse than the previous administration. But it was just a matter of principle. Like with Saadna. I never drank with people who were filled with hate.

"You haven't done anything stupid, I hope?" he went on, in a fatherly tone.

I shrugged. "I'm too old for that."

"What I think is . . . Look, I know this is none of my business, but . . . I thought you were taking it easy, in your cottage. I thought Lole was treating you like a king."

"I am taking it easy, Félix. But without Lole. She left."

"I'm sorry," he said. "I just thought. Seeing the two of you together last time . . . "

"Lole loved Ugo. She loved Manu. And she loved me too. All in twenty years. I was the last."

"It's you she always loved."

"Manu told me that once. A few days before he was shot down, right there, on your sidewalk. We'd been eating *aïoli*, you remember?"

"He was scared you'd steal her from him one day. He was sure the two of you would get together eventually."

"Nobody steals Lole. Ugo couldn't live without her. Neither could Manu. But I could. At least then. Not now."

There was a silence. Félix refilled our glasses.

"Have to finish the bottle," he said, slightly embarrassed.

"Yeah . . . If I'd been the first, everything would have been different. For her and me. For Ugo and Manu too. But I'm the last. Sure, we love each other. But it's not easy to live in a museum, surrounded by memories. The people you've loved never die. They're always with you . . . It's like this city, you know, it exists because of all the people who've lived in it. All the people who've sweated, toiled and hoped in it. Out there on the streets, my mother and father are still alive."

"It's because they're exiles."

"Marseilles is a city of exiles. It'll always be the last port of call in the world. Its future belongs to those who arrive. Never to those who leave."

"Oh, and what about those who stay?"

"They're like people at sea, Félix. You never know if they're alive or dead."

Like us, I thought, as I emptied my glass and waited for Félix to refill it.

Which of course he promptly did.

# 7.

## IN WHICH IT IS SUGGESTED THAT THE BLACK THREAD BE DISTINGUISHED FROM THE WHITE THREAD

I'd gotten home late, drunk a fair amount, smoked too much and slept badly. It was sure to be a lousy day.

The weather, though, was glorious, the way it sometimes is in September, but only here. Beyond the Lubéron, or the Alpilles, it was already fall. In Marseilles, sometimes until the end of October, an aftertaste of summer lingers. All it took was a breeze, and the smells of thyme, mint and basil returned.

That was how it smelled this morning. Mint and basil. Lole's smells when we made love. I'd suddenly felt old and tired. Sad too. But I'm always that way when I've drunk too much, smoked too much and slept badly. I hadn't had the courage to take the boat out. A bad sign. It hadn't happened to me in a long time. Even after Lole left, I'd continued going out to sea.

Every day I needed to distance myself from human beings. To recharge my batteries from the silence. The fishing was incidental. Like a tribute paid to the vastness of the sea. Far out there, on the open sea, you learned to be humble again. And by the time I came back to land, I was full of goodwill toward men.

Lole knew that, and a lot of other things I'd left unspoken. She'd wait for me and we'd have lunch on the terrace. Then we'd put on some music and make love. With as much pleasure as the first time. And as much passion. It was as if our bodies had been looking forward to these celebrations since we were born. The last time, we'd started making love with *Yo no puedo vivir sin ti* playing. An album by the Gypsies of Perpignan. Cousins of Lole's. It was when we'd finished that Lole announced her intention to leave. She needed to be "somewhere else" the way I needed the sea.

A cup of scalding hot coffee in my hand, I sat down facing the sea, and let my gaze wander into the distance. Out there where even memories are obsolete. Where everything is turned upside down. Out as far as the Planier lighthouse, twenty miles from the coast.

Why hadn't I left, never to return? Why was I letting myself grow old in this two-bit cottage, watching the freighters sail away? Of course, Marseilles had a lot to do with it. Whether you were born here or landed here one day, you soon grew feet of lead. Travel was something you'd rather see in other people's eyes. In the eyes of those who came back after confronting the worst that life could throw at them. Like Ulysses. We liked Ulysses here. And over the centuries, the people of Marseilles had weaved and unraveled their own history, like poor Penelope. The tragedy these days was that Marseilles no longer looked toward the East, but saw only the reflection of what she was becoming.

I was just like her. And what I was becoming was nothing, or almost. With fewer illusions and more of a smile, maybe. I was sure I'd never really understood anything that had happened in my life. And anyhow, the Planier no longer lighted the way for ships. It was disused. But it was my only belief, that there was something out there, beyond the sea. I remembered a line by Louis Brauquier, my favorite Marseilles poet.

*I shall return to run aground in the midst of the ships.*

Yes, I told myself, when I'm dead, I'll embark on a freighter and set sail for my childhood dreams. Finally at peace. I finished my coffee and went out to see Fonfon.

Nobody had been waiting for me by my car, when I'd left Chez Félix at one in the morning. Nobody had followed me either. I don't scare easily but, once past the Madrague de Montredon, in the far south east of Marseilles, the road that leads to Les Goudes can be quite hair-raising at night. The landscape is as empty as the surface of the moon. The houses stop near the *calanque* of Samena. After that, there's nothing. The road is narrow, twisting and turning alongside the sea just a few dozen feet above the rocks. Those two miles had never seemed so long. I was anxious to get home.

Gélou was asleep, with the bedside lamp still on. She must have waited for me. She was rolled in a ball, her right hand clutching the pillow like a life preserver. In her sleep, I imagined, she was shipwrecked. I switched off the lamp. That was all I could do for her right now.

I'd poured myself a glass of Lagavulin and had settled down for a night on the couch with Conrad's *Within the Tides*. A book I constantly reread at night. It calms me down and helps me get to sleep. Just as the poems of Brauquier help me live. But my mind was elsewhere. In the land of men. I had to find Guitou and bring him back to Gélou. As simple as that. Then I'd have to have a talk with her, even though I was sure she'd already realized the most important thing. If you have a child, you should go all the way with him, because he deserves it. No woman had ever given me the opportunity to be a father, but I was convinced of that. I didn't suppose it was ever easy to raise a child. There was always pain involved. But it was worth it. If love had a future.

I'd fallen asleep and woken again almost immediately. My anxiety went deeper. I was thinking about Serge's death. And all the things it had brought back to the surface. Like Arno, and Pavie, lost somewhere in the night. All the things it had set in motion too. Why had two mobsters been tailing me? It had to be because of that. Because of what Serge had been up to. I couldn't see what connection there was between fanatical Islamists and the Var underworld. But on this coast, from Marseilles to Nice, anything was possible. You wouldn't believe the things that had happened. And it was always easy to imagine the worst.

It seemed strange to me that I hadn't come across an address book, a notebook, anything like that. Or even just a sheet of paper. Maybe, I'd told myself, Balducci and his pal had gotten there before me. I'd arrived too late. But I couldn't remember seeing or passing a Safrane on my way to the old mill. All that literature about the Islamists must mean something.

I'd poured myself a second glass of Lagavulin and started reading the newspapers and press cuttings I'd brought with me. The gist of what I read was that there were several paths that Islam could take these days in its relationship with Europe. The first was the Dar al-Suhl, literally, the "land of contract," in which Muslims had to conform to the laws of the country. The second was the Dar al-Islam, in which Islam had to become the majority religion. This was the theme of an article by Habib Mokni, an activist of the Tunisian Islamist movement who'd sought refuge in France. That was in 1988.

Since then, the fundamentalists had rejected the Dar al-Suhl. Europe, and especially France, had become a base from which they could launch actions intended to destabilize their countries of origin. The terrorist attack on the hotel Atlas Asni in Marrakesh in August 1994 had been planned in a housing project in La Courneuve. This conjunction of aims had led us, the Europeans, and them, the fundamentalists, to a third path, that of the Dar al-Harb, "the land of war," as the Koran put it.

Since the wave of attacks in Paris in the summer of '95, it had become impossible to hide our heads in the sand anymore. A war had started on our soil. A dirty war. The heroes of which, like Khaled Kelkal, had grown up in the suburbs of Paris or Lyons. Could North Marseilles also be a breeding ground for "holy warriors"? Was that the question Serge had been trying to answer? But why? And on whose behalf?

On the last page of Habib Mokni's article, Serge had written in the margin: "Its most visible victims are those killed in terrorist attacks. Others fall without any apparent connection." He had also underlined with a yellow marker a quotation from the Koran: "Until you can clearly distinguish the white thread from the black thread." That was all.

Exhausted, I'd closed my eyes. And was immediately swallowed by a vast web of black and white threads. Next, I was lost in the craziest maze you could imagine. A real hall of mirrors. But it wasn't my own image that the mirrors reflected back to me. It was images of friends I'd lost, women I'd loved. I was pushed from one to the other. There was a blackboard covered with names and faces. I was moving forward like a ball in a pinball game. I was inside a pinball machine. I'd woken up in a sweat. I was being shaken energetically.

I came to.

Gélou was standing there in front of me, with sleepy eyes.

"Are you all right?" she'd asked anxiously. "You were shouting."

"I'm all right. I was having a nightmare. It always happens when I sleep on this damn couch."

She'd looked at the bottle of whisky and my empty glass. "And when you've had a few too many."

I'd shrugged and sat up. My head felt heavy. I was returning to earth. It was four in the morning.

"I'm sorry."

"Come and sleep with me. It'll be better for you."

She'd pulled me by the hand. As gentle and warm as when she was eighteen. Sensual and maternal. Guitou must have learned gentleness from those hands touching his cheeks, those lips kissing him on the forehead. Why had those two grown apart? Why, dammit?

In bed, Gélou had turned away and immediately fallen asleep again. I hadn't dared move, for fear of waking her again.

I must have been twelve the last time we'd slept together. It often happened, when we were children. Almost every Saturday night in summer, the whole family gathered here in Les Goudes. We children were put to sleep on the floor, on mattresses. Gélou and I were the first to go to bed. We'd fall asleep holding hands, listening to our parents laughing and singing *Maruzzella, Guaglione* and other Neapolitan songs made popular by Renato Carosone.

Later, when my mother fell ill, Gélou started coming to the house two or three times a week. She'd do the washing and ironing and make dinner. She was almost sixteen. As soon as we were in bed, she'd huddle against me and we'd tell each other horror stories and scare each other to death. Then she'd slide her leg between mine, and we'd hug each other even tighter. I'd feel her breasts, already well developed, the hard nipples against my chest. It got me really aroused, and she knew it. But of course we never talked about it, because these were things that still belonged to the adult world. And we'd fall asleep like that, feeling tender and confident.

I'd turned gently, to dismiss these memories, which were as fragile as crystal. To repress the desire to place my hand on her shoulder and take her in my arms. Like before. Just to chase away our fears.

I should have.

Fonfon said I looked terrible.

"Yeah," I said, "you don't always choose the way you look."

"Oh, I see monsieur slept badly too."

I smiled, and sat down on the terrace. In my usual place. Facing the sea. Fonfon returned with a coffee and *Le Provençal*.

"Here! I made it strong. I don't know if it'll wake you up, but at least it may make you more civil."

I opened the newspaper and looked to see if there was anything about Serge's murder. There was only a small item, which didn't go into detail and didn't make any comment. There wasn't even any mention of the fact that Serge had been a youth worker in the projects for several years. He was described as "unemployed" and the item ended with the laconic words: "The police are inclined to the theory of a gang slaying." Pertin's report must have been extremely brief. If this was a gang-related murder, it meant there wouldn't be an investigation. And that Pertin was keeping the case for himself, like a dog chewing a bone. The bone in question could well be me.

As I stood up to fetch *La Marseillaise*, I automatically turned the page. The headline at the top of page 5 rooted me to the spot. "Double Murder in the Panier: The Half-Naked Body of an Unidentified Young Man." In the center of the article, in a box, was a picture of the owner of the house: "The architect Adrien Fabre, deeply distressed."

I sat down, stunned. Maybe it was just coincidence, I told myself. That was the only way I could read the article without shaking. I'd have given anything not to see those lines spread out in front of me. Because I knew what I was going to find. A shiver went down my spine. The Algerian historian Hocine Draoui, an expert on the ancient Mediterranean, had been staying for the past three months in the house of the well-known architect Adrien Fabre. Threatened with death by the Islamic Salvation Front (FIS), Draoui, like a large number of Algerian intellectuals, had fled his country. He had recently asked for political asylum.

Naturally, suspicion had initially fallen on the FIS. But the investigators now thought this unlikely. So far, the FIS had only claimed responsibility—officially, at any rate—for one murder, that of Imam Sahraoui, in Paris on July 11 1995. Dozens of people like Hocine Draoui lived in France. Why him and not someone else? Besides, as Adrien Fabre stated, Draoui had never mentioned to him any immediate threat. He had only been worried about the fate of his wife, who had stayed behind in Algeria, and who was due to join him as soon as his status was decided.

Adrien Fabre talked about his friendship with Hocine Draoui. They had met for the first time in 1990, at a major conference on the theme of "Greek Marseilles and Gaul." Draoui's work on the location of the port—first Phoenician, then Roman—was, according to Fabre, a major contribution to our knowledge of the city's history, and would help it to at last recover its memory. Under the title "In the Beginning Was the

Sea," the newspaper published extracts from Hocine Draoui's speech at the conference.

For the moment, the police were working on the theory that this was a burglary that had gone wrong. Burglaries were common in the Panier. Clearly a major obstacle to the policy of redeveloping the neighborhood. The newcomers, the majority of them middle class, were targeted by criminals, mostly young Arabs. Some houses had even been burglarized two or three times, at regular intervals, forcing the new owners to leave the Panier in disgust.

This was the first time the Fabres' house had been burglarized. Were they going to move? He and his wife and son were still too shocked to think about that.

There was still the mystery of the second body.

The Fabres did not know the young man, aged about sixteen, who had been found dead on the first floor, outside the door of their son's studio apartment, dressed only in his underwear. The investigators had searched the whole house and had found his clothes—a pair of jeans, a T-shirt, a jacket—and a small rucksack with toiletries and a change of clothes, but no wallet, not even any identity papers. His neck bore the marks of a chain that had been violently torn off.

According to Adrien Fabre, Hocine Draoui would never have brought someone into the house without telling them. Even a relative passing through, or a friend. If he'd had to do so, for whatever reason, he'd have phoned to Sanary first. He was very respectful of his hosts.

Who was the young man? Where was he from? What was he doing there? According to Chief Inspector Loubet, who was in charge of the investigation, the answers to these questions would be a great help in solving this tragic case.

I had those answers.

"Fonfon!"

Fonfon appeared with two cups of coffee on a tray.

"No need to shout, the coffee's ready! Look, I told myself you could probably use another coffee, a strong one. Here."

He put the tray down on the table. Then he looked at me. "Are you feeling all right? You've gone white!"

"Did you read the paper?"

"Haven't had time yet."

I slid the newspaper toward him.

"Read this."

He read it, slowly. I didn't touch my coffee. I couldn't move. Every inch of my body, down to my fingertips, was shaking.

"So?" he said, looking up.

I told him the story. Gélou. Guitou. Naïma.

"Shit!"

He looked at me, then went back to the article. As if reading it a second time could cancel out the awful truth.

"Give me a cognac."

"There are lots of Fabres—" he began.

"In the phone book, I know. Just get me a cognac!"

I needed to melt the ice in my veins.

He came back with the bottle. I drank two glasses, straight down. With my eyes closed, holding on to the table with one hand. The world's corruption was moving faster than us. You could forget it, deny it, it always caught up with you in the end.

I drank a third cognac, and retched. I ran to the end of the terrace and threw up over the rocks. It was the world I was vomiting. Its inhumanity, and its pointless violence. A wave broke on the rocks, swallowing my vomit. I watched the white foam lick the crevices of the rocks and then withdraw. My stomach hurt. I wanted to vomit all my bitterness. But there was nothing left in me. Just an immense sadness.

Fonfon had made me another coffee. I drank another cognac, then the coffee. Then I sat down.

"What are you going to do?"

"Nothing. I won't tell her. Not for the moment. He's dead, it makes no difference. And it makes no difference if she goes through hell tonight or tomorrow. I'm going to check it out. I have to find the girl. And the boy, Mathias."

"Yeah," he said, shaking his head skeptically. "You don't think—"

"You see, Fonfon, there's something I don't understand. This kid spent his vacation with Guitou, they went to parties together, almost every night. Why does he say he doesn't know him? In my opinion, Guitou and Naïma had planned to spend the weekend in that studio apartment. Guitou slept there on Friday night, expecting to see the girl the next day. He needed a key to get in, or someone to let him in."

"Hocine Draoui."

"That's right. And the Fabres know who Guitou is. I'd swear to it, Fonfon."

"Maybe the police wanted to keep it secret."

"I don't think so. If it was anyone else other than Loubet, maybe. He's not as devious as that. If he knew Guitou's identity, he'd have said so. He himself says that identifying the body will help solve the case."

I knew Loubet well. He was on the anti-crime squad. He'd seen plenty of dead bodies. He'd tackled the most complicated cases and had managed to shine a light into areas that might otherwise have remained dark. He was a good cop. Honest and upright. The kind of cop who thought the police were there to maintain the order of the Republic. To serve the citizen, whoever that citizen might be. He didn't believe in very much anymore, but he stood fast. And when he was in charge of an investigation, anyone who trod on his toes had better watch out. He always went all the way. I often wondered how he'd managed to keep his position. And stay alive.

"Well?"

"Well, there's something that's not right."

"You don't think it was a burglary?"

"I don't think anything."

Yes, I'd thought it was going to be a lousy day. But it was worse.

# 8.

## IN WHICH HISTORY IS NOT
## THE ONLY FORM OF DESTINY

The door opened, and I didn't know what to say. In front of me there stood a young Oriental woman. Vietnamese, I thought. But I might be wrong. She was barefoot, and traditionally dressed in a thigh-length scarlet silk tunic buttoned on the shoulder and a pair of short midnight blue pants. Her long black hair was gathered at the side and partly covered her right eye. Her face was grave and unsmiling, and there was a look of reproach in her eyes because I'd rung her doorbell. I supposed she belonged to that category of women who never like to be disturbed, whatever the hour. Right now, it was only just after eleven o'clock.

"I was hoping to talk to Monsieur and Madame Fabre."

"I'm Madame Fabre. My husband is at his office."

Once again, I was speechless. I'd never for a moment imagined that Adrien Fabre's wife was Vietnamese. Or so young. She must be about thirty-five. I wondered how old she'd been when she'd had Mathias. But maybe she wasn't his mother.

"Hello," I managed to say at last. All the time, my eyes were on her, devouring her.

I was being quite brazen. But it was more than the fact that she was beautiful. She was casting a spell over me. I felt it in my body. It was like an electric current. Like when you're walking along the street and your eyes meet a woman's, and you turn around, hoping to see that look a second time. Not even thinking about whether the woman is beautiful, what her body is like, how old she is. Just wanting to see again what she has in her eyes at that moment: a dream, an expectation, a desire. Her whole life, maybe.

"What's this about?"

She'd hardly moved her lips, and her tone of voice was like a door being slammed in your face. But the door was still open. With a nervous gesture, she pushed back her hair, letting me see her face.

She looked me up and down. I was wearing navy blue cotton pants, a blue shirt with white polka dots—a present from Lole—and white espadrilles. I stood there, all five feet eight of me, with my hands in the pockets of a petroleum-gray jacket. Honorine had said I looked very elegant. I hadn't told her what I'd read in the newspaper. As far as she and Gélou were concerned, I was going out to look for Guitou.

Our eyes met, and I couldn't take mine off hers. I didn't say anything. Her face tensed.

"I'm listening," she said, curtly.

"Wouldn't it be better to talk inside?"

"What's this about?"

She gave the impression of someone who was usually self-confident, but right now she was on the defensive. Finding two dead bodies in your house when you came back from a weekend away didn't exactly encourage you to be welcoming. And for all the effort I'd made with my clothes, my black, slightly curly hair and sallow, almost ashen skin made me look like a wop. Which is what I was.

"About Mathias," I said, as gently as I could. "And a friend he made on vacation this summer. Guitou. The boy who was found dead in your house."

Her whole body clammed up. "Who are you?" she asked, stammering as if the words were hurting her throat.

"A relative."

"Come in."

She pointed to a staircase at the end of the hall, and moved aside to let me pass. I took a few steps, then stopped at the bottom of the stairs. The stone—a white Lacoste stone—had absorbed Guitou's blood. There was a dark patch on the step, like black crepe. Even the stone was in mourning.

"Was this where you found him?" I asked.

"Yes," she said in a low voice.

Before making up my mind to leave home, I'd smoked several cigarettes, looking out to sea. I knew what I was going to do, and in what order, but I felt as heavy as lead. Like a little lead soldier waiting for a hand to set it in motion. And the hand was destiny. Life, death. You couldn't escape that hand. Whoever you were. Wherever it led.

In my experience, it usually led somewhere bad.

I'd called Loubet. I knew his habits. He was a hard worker and an early riser. It was eight-thirty and he'd answered at the first ring.

"Montale here."

"Ah! The ghost returns. This is a pleasure."

He'd been one of the few to buy me a drink when I was dismissed. I'd been grateful to him for that. Whether or not to toast my departure had been as revealing of the splits within the police force as the union elections. Except that this wasn't a secret ballot.

"I have the answers to your questions. About the boy in the Panier."

"What are you talking about, Montale?"

"Your investigation. I know who the kid is. Where he's from, everything."

"How do you know that?"

"He's my cousin's son. He ran away from home on Friday night."

"What was he doing there?"

"I'll tell you. Can we meet?"

"Sure! How soon can you be here?"

"I'd rather meet you at Ange's bar. The Treize-Coins. OK with you?"

"OK."

"About twelve, twelve-thirty."

"Twelve-thirty! What the hell have you got to do before that, Montale?"

"Go fishing."

"You're a damn liar."

"That's true. See you later, Loubet."

I really was planning to go fishing. Fishing for information. Bass and bream could wait. They were used to it. I wasn't a real fisherman, just an amateur.

Cûc—that was her first name and she was indeed Vietnamese, from Dalat, in the south, "the only cold town in the country"—turned to look at me, her eyes again hidden by a lock of hair, which she didn't push back. She had sat down on a couch, her legs folded beneath her buttocks.

"Who else knows?"

"No one," I lied.

I was sitting with my back to the light, in an armchair to which she'd motioned me. From where I was, her jade eyes were like two slits, dark and shiny. She'd regained her self-confidence. Or at least enough strength to keep me at a distance. Beneath her apparent calm, I sensed her potential energy. She moved like a sportswoman. Cûc was not only on her guard, she was ready to pounce. She must have had a lot to protect since she arrived in France. Her memories, her dreams. Her life. Her life as the wife of Adrien Fabre. Her life as the mother of Mathias. Her son. She'd been very clear about that. "My son."

I was on the verge of asking her a lot of prying questions. But I kept to the basics. Who I was. My relationship to Gélou. I told her about Guitou and Naïma. How he'd run away, come to Marseilles. What I'd read in the newspaper and how I'd made the connection.

"Why didn't you tell the police?"

"Tell them what?"

"That the young man was Guitou."

"I just heard it from you. We didn't know."

I found that hard to believe. "But Mathias . . . He knew him, he—"

"Mathias wasn't with us when we got back on Sunday

evening. We dropped him in Aix, with my parents-in-law. He's going to college this year, and he still had a few formalities to take care of."

It was a plausible story, but I wasn't convinced.

"And of course," I couldn't help saying in an ironic tone, "you didn't call him. He doesn't know anything about the terrible thing that happened. He doesn't know one of his vacation pals was killed here."

"My husband called him. Mathias swore he hadn't lent his key to anyone."

"And you believed him?"

She moved aside her lock of hair. It was a gesture that was intended to make her look sincere. I'd gathered that much from the start.

"Why wouldn't we have believed him, Monsieur Montale?" she said, leaning forward slightly, and looking straight at me.

I was falling increasingly under her spell, and that was setting my nerves on edge. "Because if someone was in your house, Hocine Draoui would have told you," I replied, more harshly than I'd intended. "That's what your husband said in the newspaper."

"Hocine is dead," she said softly.

"So is Guitou," I cried. I stood up, nervously. It was noon. I had to know more before meeting with Loubet. "Can I use your phone?"

"Who are you calling?"

She had leaped to her feet. She stood facing me, very upright, completely still. She seemed taller, her shoulders broader. I could feel her breath on my chest.

"Chief Inspector Loubet. It's time he learned Guitou's identity. I don't know if he'll buy your story. But I'm sure it'll help him with the investigation."

"No. Wait."

She pushed back her hair with both hands and looked closely at me. She was ready to do anything. She'd even fall into my arms if she had to. And I didn't really want that.

"You have beautiful ears," I heard myself whisper.

She smiled, almost imperceptibly, and placed her hand on my arm. This time, the electric current went through, and it was really strong. Her hand was burning hot.

"Please."

I arrived late at the Treize-Coins. Loubet was drinking a *mauresque*, in a large glass. When Ange saw me come in, he brought me a *pastis*. Old habits die hard. For years, I'd been a regular here, in this bar behind the station house. Away from the other cops, who had their haunts on Rue de l'Évêché or Place des Trois-Cantons. Where the waitresses flirt with you to get tips.

Ange wasn't the talkative type. He didn't chase after customers. When the band IAM decided to shoot the video for their new album in his bar, he'd said, "Oh, why my place?" With a touch of pride, all the same.

His great interest was history. He read everything he could get hold of—Decaux, Castellot—and whatever he could find in secondhand booksellers: Zevaes, Ferro, Rousset. Over a drink, he'd fill in the gaps in my knowledge. The last time I'd dropped by to see him, he'd buttonholed me and launched into a detailed account of Garibaldi's triumphal entry into the port of Marseilles on October 7, 1870. "At exactly ten o'clock in the morning." By my third *pastis*, I'd told him I rejected the idea that history was the only form of destiny. I didn't know what I meant by that, and I still don't know, but it seems right. He'd looked at me in stunned silence.

"We've been waiting for you," he said, pushing the glass toward me.

"Good catch, Montale?"

"Not bad."

"Are you eating here?" Ange asked.

Loubet looked at me.

"Later," I said, wearily.

I wasn't too crazy about the morgue. But Loubet said there was no way around it. Only Mathias, Cûc and I knew that the boy who'd been found dead was Guitou. I didn't like the idea of telling Loubet that I'd met Cûc. He wouldn't have appreciated it, and he'd have immediately rushed off to see her. And I'd promised Cûc I'd give her some time, until after lunch. Enough time for her, her husband and Mathias to concoct a true version of a lie. I'd promised her that much. It didn't cost anything, I'd told myself, though I was a little ashamed, all the same, to have let myself be seduced so easily. But I'll never change, I'm susceptible to female beauty.

I emptied my glass like a condemned man.

I'd set foot in the morgue only three times in my career. The icy atmosphere gripped me as soon as we walked through the door into the reception area. You went straight from sunlight to neon. White, pale. Damp. This was what hell was like. Death was cold. Here or at the bottom of a hole in the summertime, it was always the same.

I tried not to think about the people I'd loved that I'd already buried. When I'd thrown the last handful of earth on my father's coffin, I'd said to myself, "There, now you're alone." It had been hard afterwards, dealing with other people. Even with Carmen, the woman who was living with me at the time. I'd become taciturn. Unable to explain why it was that this man, who wasn't around anymore, had suddenly become more important to me than she was, even though she was there and she loved me. It was stupid, I knew. But my father had been a real father. Like Fonfon and Félix. Like many others. Like I might have been. It would have come naturally to me.

What really wore me down was death itself. I'd been too young when my mother left us. Now, for the first time, when my father died, death had started eating away at me, like a rodent. At my head, my bones. My heart. The rodent had continued on its way, inexorably. Ever since Leila had died so horribly, my heart had been an open wound, a wound that would never heal.

I concentrated my attention on a big African woman who was mopping the floor. She looked up and I smiled at her. After all, you needed guts to work in a place like this.

"No. 747," Loubet said, showing his police ID.

There was a metallic click and the door opened. The morgue was in the basement. That unmistakable hospital smell grabbed me by the throat. Daylight filtered in, as yellow as the water in the bucket where the cleaning woman was dipping her mop.

"Are you OK?" Loubet asked.

"I'll be fine," I replied.

Guitou arrived on a chrome gurney, pushed by a small bald man with a cigarette hanging from the corner of his mouth.

"Is this yours?"

Loubet nodded. The guy parked the gurney in front of us and left without saying another word. Loubet slowly lifted the sheet and moved it down to the neck. I'd closed my eyes. I breathed in, opened them again and finally looked down at the body of Gélou's precious son Guitou.

He looked the same as he had in the photo. But now he was clean, bloodless, frozen. He was like an angel who'd fallen from heaven to earth. Had he and Naïma had time to make love? Cûc had told me they'd arrived on Friday evening. She'd phoned Hocine around eight. My head buzzed with questions. Where could Naïma have been when Guitou was killed? Had she already gone? Or was she with him? What had she seen? I'd have to wait until five to get some answers, maybe. Mourad was supposed to be taking me to see his grandfather.

The first thing I'd done after calling Loubet was to visit Naïma's mother. She hadn't been pleased that I'd come, especially so early. Redouane might have been there, and she was determined to keep him out of this. "Life is already complicated enough without that," she'd said. I'd taken the risk because

I didn't have much time. I was determined to get a head start over Loubet. It was stupid, but I wanted to *know* before he did.

She was a good woman, worried about her children. That was what persuaded me to give her a scare.

"Naïma may be involved in something bad. Because of the boy."

"The French boy?"

"My cousin's son."

She'd sat down slowly on the edge of the couch, and put her face in her hands. "What has she done?"

"Nothing. To be honest, I don't really know. She was the last person to see the boy."

"Why don't you leave us alone? I have enough worries with the children right now." She turned to look at me. "The young man may be home by now. Or else he'll be back soon. Redouane also ran away. We didn't hear from him for three months. Then he came back. He's here for good now. He's a serious boy."

I crouched in front of her. "I believe you, Madame. But Guitou will never come back. He's dead. He was killed. And Naïma was with him that night."

I saw panic in her eyes. "Dead? And Naïma . . . "

"They were together. Both of them, in the same . . . the same house. I need to talk to her. If she was still there when it happened, she must have seen something."

"My poor girl."

"I'm the only person who knows all this. If she wasn't there, nobody needs to know. There's no way the police will find out about her. They don't even know she exists. You understand? That's why I can't wait any longer."

"Her grandfather doesn't have a phone. It's true, you must believe me, monsieur. He says people use the phone these days as an excuse not to see each other anymore. I was planning to go there, as I promised you. He lives a long way from here, in Saint-Henri. You have to go by bus. It isn't easy."

"I'll take you, if you like."

"It's not possible, monsieur. Me in your car. People would know. People know everything here. And Redouane would make a fuss again."

"Give me the address."

"No!" she said, categorically. "Mourad finishes his classes at three o'clock this afternoon. He'll go with you. Wait for him at the bus station on Cours Joseph Thierry at four."

"Thanks," I'd said.

I jumped. Loubet had taken hold of my arm. He wanted me to take a closer look at Guitou's body. He'd moved the sheet down to the stomach.

"He was shot with a .38 special. A single bullet. At point blank range. No way he could have survived. With a good silencer on a gun like that, it's as quiet as a fly. The guy was a pro."

My head was spinning. It wasn't what I was seeing. It was what I was imagining. Guitou naked, and the other guy with a gun in his hands. Had he looked at the boy before shooting him? Because he hadn't fired blindly while escaping. No, they'd been face to face. I hadn't met that many guys in my life capable of doing something like that. A few in Djibouti. Legionnaires, paras. Survivors of Indochina and Algeria. Even on the nights when they got drunk, they didn't talk about it. They'd saved their skins, that was all. I could understand that. You could kill in a fit of jealousy, in a sudden rage, out of despair. I could understand that too. But this, no.

I was overcome with hate.

"The arch of the eyebrows," Loubet went on, pointing to it. "He lost that when he fell." Then he moved his finger down to the neck. "Now this is interesting. They tore off the chain he was wearing."

"Why? Because it was valuable? You think they needed a gold chain?"

He shrugged. "Maybe the chain could have helped to identify him?"

"Why should that bother these guys?"

"They wanted to gain time."

"You'll have to explain that. I don't get it."

"It's just a guess. Maybe the murderer knew Guitou. Hocine Draoui had a superb gold chain bracelet on his wrist. It's still there."

"Where does that lead us?"

"Nowhere. I know. I'm just making an observation, Montale. It's a hypothesis. I have a hundred of them. They don't lead anywhere either. Which means they're all as good as each other." He pointed at Guitou's shoulder. "Look at this bruise. It's not all that recent. About two or three weeks old, I'd say. A big bruise. That's as much of a distinguishing feature as a chain, and it still doesn't lead us anywhere."

Loubet covered Guitou's body, then looked at me. I knew I'd have to sign the register on the way out. That wasn't the difficult part.

# 9.

## IN WHICH THERE IS NO SUCH THING
## AS AN INNOCENT LIE

In the middle of Rue Sainte-Françoise, outside the Treize-Coins, a man named José was washing his car, a Renault 21 painted in the Olympique Marseilles colors. Blue at the bottom, white on top. With a matching pennant, attached to the rear view mirror, and a supporters' scarf on the back shelf. Music in the background. The best of the Gypsy Kings. *Bamboleo, Djobi Djoba, Amor, Amor . . .*

Sicard the roadmender had opened the gutter water point for him. José had as much water as he wanted, all to himself. From time to time, he'd walk over to Sicard's table, sit down and have a *pastis*, without taking his eyes off his car. As if it was a collector's item. But maybe he was dreaming about the bimbo he was planning to take for a spin to Cassis. It was clear, at any rate, from his contented smile, that he wasn't thinking about the tax man. And he was taking his time.

That was the way the things happened in the neighborhood, when you wanted to wash your car. The years passed, but there was always a Sicard who'd let you use the water if you bought him a *pastis*. Only an asshole from Saint-Giniez would go to the car wash.

If another car came along, it would have to wait until José had finished. Until he'd slowly polished the bodywork with a shammy. Hoping that a pigeon wouldn't come and shit on it at that moment.

If the driver was from the Panier, he'd calmly have an aperitif with José and Sicard and talk about the soccer championships, making the usual sarcastic remarks about how badly Paris Saint-Germain were playing. The remarks had to be sarcastic, even though the Parisians were riding high at the top of the league. If the driver was a tourist, he might sound his horn a few times. They might even come to blows. But that was rare. If you aren't from the Panier you don't make trouble when you're here. You keep quiet and wait patiently. But there weren't any cars, and Loubet and I were able to eat in peace. Personally, I had nothing against the Gypsy Kings.

Ange had seated us on the terrace, with a bottle of Puy-Sainte-Reparade rosé. On the menu, little *farcis* filled with tomatoes, potatoes, courgettes and onions. I was hungry and they were delicious. I love to eat. Especially when I'm in trouble, or when I'm rubbing shoulders with death. I need to get as much food down me as I can: vegetables, meat, fish, dessert or candy. To let the tastes overwhelm me. It was the best way I knew to refute death. To protect myself from it. Good food and good wine. It was a survival skill. It hadn't worked too badly so far.

Loubet and I were silent. We'd exchanged small talk over our starter of cold meats. He was brooding over his hypotheses. And I had plenty to brood over too. Cûc had offered me tea, black tea. "I think I can trust you," she'd started by saying. I'd replied that, for the moment, it wasn't a question of trust, but of truth. The truth they had to tell the cop in charge of the investigation. Guitou's identity.

"I'm not going to tell you my whole life story," she said. "But there are a few things that will help you understand. I came to France in 1977, when I was seventeen. Mathias had just been born. My mother had decided it was time to leave. The fact that I'd just had a baby may have influenced her decision. I can't remember."

She threw me a furtive glance, then picked up a pack of Craven A and lit one nervously. She stared into the distance through a wreath of smoke. As she spoke, her sentences sometimes trailed off into long silences. Her voice grew thinner. Some of her words hung in the air and she seemed to dismiss them with the back of her hand as she brushed away the cigarette smoke. She didn't move her body, but from time to time she bent her head as if searching for a forgotten detail, and when she did so, her long hair swung.

I listened carefully. I didn't dare suppose that I was the first person she'd told the story of her life. I knew that when she finished she'd want something from me in return. This sudden intimacy was a way of seducing me. And that was fine by me.

"My mother, my grandmother, my three younger sisters and the child and I all returned to France. My mother was a brave woman. We were what they called repatriates. My family had been naturalized since 1930. In fact, I have double nationality. We were considered French. But there was nothing romantic about our arrival in France. From Roissy, we were taken to a workers' hostel in Sarcelles. Then we were told we had to leave, and we ended up in Le Havre.

"We lived there for four years, in a little two-room apartment. My mother took care of us until we could fend for ourselves. It was in Le Havre that I met Adrien. By chance. Without him . . . I'm in fashion. I create clothes and fabrics inspired by the Far East. My workshop and boutique are on Cours Julien. And I've just opened a boutique in Paris, on Rue de la Roquette. There'll be another one opening soon in London."

She'd sat up to say that.

Fashion was the big new thing in Marseilles. The previous administration had put a huge amount of money into the Mode-Méditerranée Center on the Canebière. In what had previously been the Thierry department store. The "Pompidou Center of haute couture," the newspapers had called it. I'd once set foot in there out of curiosity. Because I wasn't sure what was going on. In fact, nothing was going on. But, as someone had said to me, "It gives them a different image of us in Paris."

What a laugh! I was one of those people in Marseilles who don't give a damn what image they have of us in Paris or anywhere else. The image makes no difference. To Europe, we were still the first city of the Third World. The most favored, to those who have some feeling for Marseilles.

For me, the important thing was that something should be done for Marseilles. Not to impress Paris. Everything we've ever gained, we've gained in spite of Paris. That was the attitude of the old Marseilles bourgeoisie: the Fraissinets, the Touaches, the Paquets. The bourgeoisie that in 1870, as Ange had told me, had financed Garibaldi's expedition to Marseilles, to repel the Prussian invasion. But today we no longer had an active, vocal bourgeoisie. It was slowly dying in its sumptuous villas in the Roucas Blanc. Unconcerned about what Europe had in store for the city.

"Ah," I replied, evasively.

Cûc the businesswoman. That broke the spell, brought us down to earth.

"I'm just starting. It's only been two years. I got off to a good start, but I'm not yet as well-known as Zazza of Marseilles."

I'd heard of Zazza. She too had started a fashion business. Her small ready-to-wear label was becoming known around the world. Her photo was in all the magazines that sell Marseilles to the good people of France, as an example of success. The symbol of Mediterranean creativity. Maybe I wasn't objective about things like that, I'll admit. But the fact was, in Les Goudes today, there were only six professional fishermen left, not many more than that in L'Estaque. There were fewer and fewer freighters using La Joliette. The waterfront was practically deserted. Whereas La Spezia in Italy and Algeciras in Spain had seen their goods traffic increase fourfold. Given all that, I often wondered, why was a port not being used first and foremost as a port, and developed as a port? That was my idea of a cultural revolution for Marseilles. We had to keep our feet in the water, before anything else.

Cûc was waiting for me to react. I didn't. I was waiting. I wanted to understand.

"I'm telling you all this," she went on, more confident now, not stumbling over the words anymore, "to show you that I care about the things I've achieved. And all the things I've achieved, I've achieved for Mathias. He's the most important thing in my life."

"Did he ever know his father?" I said.

That threw her. Her hair fell back over her eyes, like a screen. "No . . . Why?"

"Guitou didn't know his either. Until Friday night, they had at least that much in common. And I don't suppose the relationship between Mathias and Adrien is an easy one."

"What makes you say that?"

"Because I heard Guitou's story yesterday and it was very similar. A guy who thinks he's your father. And the father you idolize. The mother you feel close to . . . "

"I don't follow you."

"Really? It's quite simple. Your husband didn't know that Mathias was lending his studio to Guitou for the weekend. It wasn't something he usually did. You were the only one who knew. And Hocine Draoui, of course. He was in on the secret. Because he was closer to you than your husband . . . "

I'd gone a little too far. She stubbed out her cigarette vigorously and stood up. If she could have thrown me out, she'd have done it. But she needed me. She stood there facing me, just as composed as she'd been before. Just as upright. Just as proud.

"You're an oaf. But you're right. Except for one thing. Hocine only agreed to it, not because he was close to me, as you seem to think, but out of friendship for Mathias. He thought the young girl in question, Naïma, who was often here, was Mathias' friend. His . . . girlfriend. He didn't know about the other boy."

"All right," I said. She was looking at me intently, and I could feel how tense she was. "You didn't have to tell me your whole life story, just to tell me that."

"So you don't understand anything."

"I don't want to understand anything."

She smiled, for the first time. Which suited her wonderfully.

"'I don't want to understand anything.' You sound like a Bogart movie!"

"Thanks. But that still doesn't tell me what you're planning to do now."

"What would you do in my place?"

"Call your husband. Then the police. As I told you earlier. Tell your husband the truth, find a plausible lie for the police."

"Can you suggest one?"

"Hundreds. But *I'm* not good at lying."

I didn't see the slap coming. I'd deserved it. Why had I said that? There was too much electricity between her and me, that was for sure. We were going to electrocute each other. And I didn't want that. We had to cut off the current.

"I'm sorry."

"I'll give you two hours. After that, Chief Inspector Loubet will come knocking at your door."

And I'd left to meet Loubet. Once outside, away from her field of attraction, I got a grip on myself. Cûc was an enigma. I sensed that there was another story behind the one she'd told me. There are no such things as innocent lies.

My eyes met Loubet's. He was looking at me.

"What do you think of this business?"

"Nothing. You're the cop, Loubet. You have all the cards, not me."

"Don't bullshit me, Montale. You always had a point of view, even when your pockets were empty. And I know the wheels are going around in your head right now."

"All right, then. As far as I can see, there's no connection between the murder of Hocine Draoui and the murder of Guitou. They weren't killed in the same way. I think Guitou just happened to be in the wrong place at the wrong time. They had to kill him, but it was a mistake on their part."

"You don't believe it was a burglary that went wrong?"

"There are always exceptions. Can I come back next week, boss?"

He smiled. "That's what I think too."

Two Rastafarians crossed the terrace, trailing a smell of marijuana. One of them had recently appeared in a movie, but he wasn't making a song and dance about it. They went inside and sat down at the bar. The smell of marijuana tickled my nose. It was years since I'd stopped smoking it. But I missed the smell. Sometimes I smoked Camels to find it again.

"What do you know about Hocine Draoui?"

"Everything we know points to the fundamentalists coming here with the express purpose of liquidating him. First of all, he was a close friend of Azzedine Medjoubi, the dramatist who was recently murdered. Secondly, for years he was a member of the PAGS, the Vanguard Socialist Party. Today, he's mainly involved with the FAIS. The Federation of Algerian Artists, Intellectuals and Scientists. His name is on a list of people planning a meeting of the FAIS in Toulouse next month.

"In my opinion, he was a really brave guy, this Draoui. He came to France for the first time in 1990. He was here for a year, though he went back and forth a lot. He came back at the end of 1994, after being stabbed in a police station in Algiers. For a while his name had been at the top of the hit list. His house is under surveillance by the army twenty-four hours a day. When he arrived in France, he lived for a while in Lille, then in Paris, on tourist visas. Then his case was taken up by various committees supporting Algerian intellectuals in Marseilles."

"And that's where he met Adrien Fabre."

"They'd already met in 1990, at a conference about Marseilles."

"That's right. He mentioned it in the newspaper."

"They got along well. Fabre has been a human rights activist for years. That must have helped."

"I didn't know he was an activist."

"Only in the human rights field. He's not known to have any other political activities. He never has. Except in 1968. He was in the March 22 movement. He must have thrown a few paving stones at the police. Like any good student at the time."

I looked at him. Loubet had taken a master's in law. He'd dreamed of being a lawyer. He'd become a cop. "I took the best paid job in the public sector," he'd joked one day. But of course I hadn't believed him.

"Were you on the barricades?"

He smiled. "I spent most of my time getting laid. How about you?"

"I was never a student."

"Where were you in '68?"

"In Djibouti. In the Colonial Army . . . Anyway, that kind of thing wasn't for us."

"You mean, you, Ugo and Manu?"

"I mean there's no revolution in the world you can point to as an example. We didn't know a lot, but that much we knew. Beneath the paving stones there was never a beach. There was only power. The real fanatics always end up in the government, and they get a taste for it. The only people power corrupts are idealists. We were just punks. We liked easy money, girls, cars. We listened to John Coltrane. We read poetry. And we swam across the harbor. Having fun and showing off. That was all we asked out of life. We didn't hurt anyone, and we enjoyed it."

"And then you became a cop."

"I didn't exactly have many choices in my life. I believed in it. And I don't regret it. But you know . . . I didn't have the right mindset."

We remained silent until Ange brought our coffees. The two Rastafarians had sat down on the terrace and were watching as José finished washing his car. As if he were a Martian, but with a touch of admiration, all the same. The roadmender looked at his watch.

"Hey! José! I'm finished here," he said, emptying his glass. "I have to turn off the water."

"I like it here," Loubet said, stretching his legs.

He lit a cigarillo and breathed in the smoke slowly. I liked Loubet. He wasn't easy to get along with, but you knew you could trust him. In addition, he loved good food, which to me was essential. I don't trust people who don't eat a lot, or don't care what they eat. I was dying to question him about Cûc. To find out what he knew. But I didn't. Asking Loubet a question was like a boomerang, it always came back in your face.

"You hadn't finished telling me about Fabre."

"Let's see . . . Middle class family. Started young. Now he's one of the most prominent architects, not only in Marseilles but all along the coast. Especially in the Var. A big practice. He specializes in major projects. Private and public. A lot of town councils call on his services."

He went on to talk about Cûc, but what he said didn't tell me much. What more would I have liked to know? Details, basically. Just enough to get a clearer idea. An objective picture. Without any emotional baggage. I hadn't stopped thinking about her during the meal. I didn't like being under anyone's spell.

"She's a beautiful woman," Loubet said, and looked at me with a smile that wasn't at all innocent. Did he somehow know I'd already met her?

"Really?" I replied, evasively.

He smiled again, looked at his watch, stubbed out his cigarillo, and leaned toward me.

"I have a favor to ask you, Montale."

"Go ahead."

"Let's keep Guitou's identity to ourselves. For a few days."

That didn't surprise me. Guitou, because he was a "mistake" on the part of the killers, was a key element in the investigation. As soon as he was officially identified, things would change. The bastards who'd done it were bound to make a move.

"And what shall I tell my cousin?"

"It's your family. You'll know."

"Easy for you to say."

To be honest, it suited me too. Since this morning, I'd decided to put off as long as possible the day when I'd have to confront Gélou. I could guess how she'd react. It wouldn't be pleasant to see. Or to live through. She'd have to identify the body. There'd be formalities to deal with. The funeral. I knew that, the moment I told her, she'd be plunged into another world. A world of grief. A world where you grow old, for good. My beautiful cousin Gélou.

Loubet stood up and put his hand on my shoulder. His grip was firm.

"One more thing, Montale. Don't make this personal. Because of Guitou. I know what you're feeling. And I know you. So don't forget, this is my case. I'm a cop, you aren't. If you find out anything, call me. I'm picking up the tab. Ciao."

I watched as he walked back along Rue du Petit-Puits. He strode resolutely, with his head held high and his shoulders thrown back. He was the living image of this city.

I lit a cigarette and closed my eyes. I immediately felt the gentle warmth of the sun on my face. It felt good. That was all I believed in. These moments of happiness. These crumbs from the world's plenty. All we had was what we could glean here and there. There were no more dreams left in this world. No more hope. And kids of sixteen could be killed for one reason or another. In the projects, coming out of a dance hall. Even in someone's house. Kids who'll never know the fleeting beauty of the world. Or the beauty of women.

No, I wasn't making this personal, because of Guitou. It was more than that. It was like a rush of blood to the head. I felt like weeping. "When you feel tears coming," my mother had said once, stroking my head, "stop just in time, and everyone else will cry." I must have been eleven or twelve. She was in bed, unable to move. She knew she was going to die soon. I guess I did too. But I hadn't understood what she meant. I was too young. Death, suffering, had no reality. I'd spent half my life crying, the other half refusing to cry. And I'd been screwed all down the line. By pain and suffering. By death.

*Chourmo* by birth, I'd learned about friendship and loyalty on the streets of the Panier, on the wharves of La Joliette. And about pride on the Digue du Large, watching a freighter move out to sea and making vows. These were basic values. Things that couldn't be explained. When someone was in the shit, you helped them as if they were your own family. It was as simple as that. There were too many anxious, suffering mothers in this affair. Too many sad, lost, bewildered kids. And Guitou was dead.

Loubet would understand. I couldn't stay on the outside. Besides, he hadn't made me promise. He'd simply given me a piece of advice. He must have known I wouldn't take it. He must have expected I'd stick my nose where he couldn't put his. At least it suited me to think so, because that was precisely what I was planning to do. I had to get involved. I had to be loyal to my youth. Before growing old, for good. We all grow old, through our indifference, our abdication of responsibility, our cowardice. And our despair at being aware of it.

"We all grow old," I said to Ange as I stood up.

He made no comment.

# 10.

## IN WHICH IT IS HARD TO BELIEVE
## IN COINCIDENCE

I had two hours to spare before meeting Mourad. I knew what I had to do. Try to find Pavie. The words she'd written Serge worried me. It was clear that her life was still hell. The risk, now that Serge was dead, was that she would hook on to me. But I couldn't abandon her. Pavie and Arno: that was something I'd believed in.

I decided to try my luck at the last address I had for her. Rue des Mauvestis, on the other side of the Panier. Maybe, I told myself, she'll be able to tell me what Serge had been up to. The fact that she'd known where to reach him must have meant they were still seeing each other.

The Panier was like one gigantic construction site. The redevelopment was in full swing. Anybody could buy a house here for next to nothing and then get it all back again in special loans from City Hall. Houses were being demolished, even parts of whole streets, to create pretty little squares, and to bring light to a neighborhood that has always been a warren of dark, narrow alleys.

Yellow and ocher were starting to be the dominant colors. Italian Marseilles. With the same smells, the same laughter, the same sounds of voices you'd find on the streets of Naples, Palermo or Rome. The same fatalistic attitude toward life too. The Panier would stay the Panier. You couldn't change its history, any more than you could change the history of the city. Throughout the centuries people had been landing here without a penny in their pockets. It was a neighborhood of exiles. Of immigrants and sailors, the persecuted and the homeless. A neighborhood of the poor. Like the Grands-Carmes, behind Place d'Aix. Or Cours Belzunce, and the alleys that climb gently toward Saint-Charles Station.

The purpose of the redevelopment was to remove the bad reputation that clung to these streets. But the people of Marseilles didn't come here for a stroll. Even those who'd been born here. As soon as they had any money coming in, they moved to the other side of the Vieux-Port. To Endoume and Vauban. To Castellane, Baille, Lodi. Or even further, to Saint-Tronc, Sainte-Marguerite, Le Cabot, La Valbarelle. The only time they ever ventured across the Canebière was when they went to the Bourse shopping mall. That was as far as they went. Beyond that, it wasn't their city anymore.

I'd grown up in these alleys, where Gélou had been "the most beautiful girl in the neigborhood." With Manu and Ugo. And Lole, who was quite a bit younger than us, and quickly became the princess of our dreams. My heart was still on that side of Marseilles. In "this melting pot where the most amazing sauce in existence is simmering," as Brauquier's friend Gabriel Audisio had called it. And nothing would change that. I belonged among the exiles. Three quarters of the inhabitants of this city could have said the same. But they didn't. Not enough of them to my taste. And yet that's what it meant to be a citizen of Marseilles. Knowing that you weren't born here by chance.

"If you have a heart," my father said to me one day, "you never lose anything, wherever you go. You only find." He'd been lucky enough to find Marseilles. And we'd stroll happily around the harbor. Surrounded by men talking about Yokohama, Shanghai or Diégo-Suarez. My mother would give him her arm and he'd hold my hand. I was still in short pants, with a fisherman's cap on my head. It was the beginning of the sixties. The happy years. Everyone was there in the evening, strolling along the embankment. With a pistachio ice cream. Or a pack of almonds or salt peanuts. Or—joy of joys—a cone of jujubes.

Even later, when life became harder, and he had to sell his beautiful Dauphine, he still thought the same. How often had I doubted him? His immigrant attitudes. Narrow and unambitious, I'd thought. Later, I'd read Dostoevsky's *The Brothers Karamazov*. Near the end of the novel, Alyosha says to Krassotkin, "You know, Kolia, you will be very unhappy in your life. But you will bless life on the whole, all the same." Words that echoed in my heart, as if my father had spoken them. It was too late to thank him.

I was holding on to the railings around the construction site in front of the Vieille-Charité. A big hole, where Rue des Pistoles and Rue Rodillat had been. An underground parking garage had been planned but, as always happened when they dug around the Vieux-Port, the contractor had come across vestiges of ancient Phocea. This had once been the center of the walled city. The Greeks had built three temples on each of the *buttes*: the Moulins, the Carmes and Saint-Laurent. With a theater right next to the last temple, and an agora where Place de Lenche now is.

At least that was what Hocine Draoui had claimed in the extract from his speech at the conference on Marseilles that *Le Provençal* had reprinted next to the interview with Adrien Fabre. Draoui had backed up his theories with ancient sources, especially the writings of a Greek geographer named Strabon. Very little of these monuments has ever been unearthed. But as the newspaper commented, the start of excavations on Place Jules Verne, near the Vieux-Port, appeared to confirm his theories. All the area from there to the Vieille-Charité was like a cross-section through almost a thousand years of history, which underlined what a major city Massilia had been, and challenged the idea that it had declined after Caesar's conquest.

Work on the parking garage had immediately been suspended. Of course, the contractors hadn't been pleased. Something similar had already happened in the center of town. When the Bourse shopping mall was under construction, there had been long, tough negotiations. The excavations had revealed the walls of Massilia for the first time. Even so, the ugly concrete bunker had been given the go-ahead, in return for an area to be designated as a "garden of ruins." So it was unlikely that anything or anybody could stop the parking garage from being built on Place du Général de Gaulle. As for the site in front of the Vieille-Charité, there must be a real trial of strength going on between the various parties.

Four young archeologists, three boys and a girl, were working in the hole. They weren't in any hurry. A few old stones had been extricated from the yellowish earth: the wall of the original city. The archeologist didn't even have shovels or pickaxes. All they were doing was drawing up plans, marking the position of each stone. I was ready to bet my shirt that here too, the eventual winner would be concrete. As had happened in other places, once they'd finished the layout, they'd toast the site with a can of Coke or Kronenbourg and move on. Everything would be lost, except memory. The people of Marseilles will be happy enough. They all know what's under their feet, and they carry the history of their city in their hearts. It's their secret, and no tourist will ever be able to steal it.

Lole had also lived here, until she came to live with me. On the side of Rue des Pistoles that hadn't been demolished. The front of her building was as decayed as ever, covered with graffiti up to the second floor. The building seemed abandoned. All the shutters were closed. As I looked up at her windows, the billboard in front of the parking garage construction site caught my eye. Especially a name. The name of the architect. Adrien Fabre.

A coincidence, I told myself.

But I didn't believe in coincidence. Or in chance, or any of those things. When things happen, there's always a meaning, a reason. What could the architect of the parking garage and the lover of the Marseilles heritage possibly have to talk about? I wondered as I walked back along Rue du Petit-Puits. Did they get on as well as Fabre had claimed?

The floodgates had opened, and the questions poured out. The last of them was one I couldn't avoid. Had Fabre killed Hocine Draoui, and then Guitou because he could have identified him? It fitted. And confirmed my hunch that Fabre didn't know the kid had been in the house. Yet, even without knowing him, I couldn't imagine him killing Draoui, then Guitou. That didn't fit. Pulling the trigger once was hard enough, but then shooting again, at point blank range, and at a kid this time, that was something else. That was the kind of thing real killers did. Hitmen.

In any case, the house had been ransacked, which meant there must have been several people involved. That was obvious. Fabre may only have opened the door to them. That was more likely. But he had a cast-iron alibi, which Cûc and Mathias would confirm. They were together in Sanary. Of course, at night, in a good car, the journey took less than two hours. Even supposing that, why would Fabre have done it? It was a good question. But I couldn't see myself asking him directly. Or any other question, for that matter. Not yet, anyway.

Pavie's name was still on one of the mailboxes. The building was as run-down as the one where Lole had lived. The walls were flaking and there was a smell of cat piss. On the second floor, I knocked at the door. No reply. I knocked again, and called her name.

"Pavie!"

I turned the handle. The door opened. There was a smell of Indian incense. No light from outside. The room was in complete darkness.

"Pavie," I said more softly.

I found the light switch, but it didn't work, so I used my cigarette lighter. I noticed a candle on the table, lit it, and raised it in front of my face. I was relieved. Pavie wasn't here. For a moment, I'd expected the worst. About a dozen candles were spread around the one room where she lived. The bed was a mattress on the floor. It had been made. There were no dirty dishes, either in the sink or on the small table near the window. Everything looked clean. I was even more relieved. Pavie might not be well, but she was holding out. For an ex-junkie, keeping things clean and tidy was a good sign.

These were only words, I knew. Sentimental platitudes. Ex-junkies often go through periods of depression. Worse, or almost worse, than when they were hooked. Pavie had been clean once before, when she met Arno. She'd wanted Arno. She'd run after him. For months. Wherever he went, she'd show up. He couldn't have a beer at the Balto in peace. One evening, there was a whole bunch of them, at a table. She was there, dogging his footsteps as usual. He'd finished his beer, and said, "Even with a condom, I don't fuck a girl who shoots up."

"Then help me."

That was all she'd said in reply. There were just the two of them left in the world. The others no longer mattered.

"Is that what you want?" he asked.

"I want you. That's what I want."

"OK."

He took her by the hand and led her out of the bar. He took her to his place, behind Saadna's scrap yard, and kept her there. For one month. Two months. He abandoned everything to take care of her. Even the bikes. He didn't leave her alone for a second. Every day he'd take her to the *calanques* along the Côte Bleue. Carry, Carro, Ensues, La Redonne. He'd force her to walk from one inlet to the next, to swim. He loved his Pavie. As she'd never been loved before.

But afterwards, she'd gone back to her old ways. After his death. Because life was shit after all.

Serge and I had found her in the Balto. Having a coffee. We'd been searching for her for two weeks. A boy had tipped us off. "She's turning tricks in cellars. She'll go with anybody for three hundred francs." Barely the price of a bad fix.

In the Balto, that day, it was if she'd been waiting for us, in a way. We were her last hope. A last effort before the final plunge. In two weeks, she'd aged at least twenty years. She was watching TV, slumped over the table. Hollow cheeks, a glum expression. Her curly hair lank. Her clothes filthy.

"What are you doing here?" I asked her, stupidly.

"As you can see, watching TV. I'm waiting for the news. They say the Pope's dead."

"We've been looking for you everywhere," Serge said.

"Oh, yeah. Can I have your sugar?" she asked him when Rico, the owner, brought Serge a coffee. "You're no Einsteins, you two. Especially not you, and you're a cop. We could all disappear, and you wouldn't be able to find us. All of us, you hear. But why would anyone want to look for us anyway? Right?"

"Stop!" I said.

"You want me to stop, buy me a sandwich. I haven't eaten anything since yesterday. I'm not like you. Nobody feeds me. You've got the State to feed you. If we weren't here, screwing up, you'd all starve to death."

The sandwich came, and she stopped talking. Serge went on the attack.

"There are two solutions, Pavie. Either you go back to the Édouard-Toulouse psychiatric clinic of your own free will. Or Fabio and I have you admitted to hospital. On medical grounds. You know how it works. We can always find a reason."

We'd been discussing it for several days. I wasn't crazy about the idea. But I couldn't think of anything better to counter Serge's arguments. "For decades, psychiatric clinics have been used as retirement homes for old people without money. Right? Well, now they're the only places that'll welcome twenty-year-old down and outs. Alcoholics, junkies, people with AIDS . . . It's the only kind of safe refuge they have. You follow me?"

Sure I followed him. But it only made me more aware of our limitations. He and I together weren't Arno. We didn't have enough love. We couldn't be there for her all the time. There were thousands of Pavies, and we were just bureaucrats, enforcing the lesser of two evils.

I said amen to the priest.

"I saw Lily again," Pavie said, with her mouth full. "She's expecting a baby. She's getting married. She's really happy, she is." There was a gleam in her eyes, like in the old days. It was as if she were expecting that baby herself. "Her guy's great. He owns a GTI. He's handsome. He has a mustache. He looks like . . . "

She burst into tears.

"It's all right, it's all right," Serge said, putting his arm around her shoulders. "We're here."

"I know," she murmured. "Without you, I'd go off the rails completely. And Arno wouldn't like that, would he?"

"No, he wouldn't like that," I'd said.

Yes, they were only words. Only ever words.

Since then, she'd had several stays at the clinic. Every time she showed up at the Balto, Rico would call us and we'd come running. We had an arrangement with him. And Pavie knew all about it. It was her lifeline. It wasn't a solution, I knew. But we didn't have any solutions. Just throw her back into an institution. Every time.

The last time I'd seen Pavie was just over a year earlier. She was working in the fruit and vegetable section of the Géant Casino supermarket in La Valentine, in East Marseilles. She seemed to be better. In good shape. I'd suggested we go for a drink the next day. She'd jumped at the idea. I'd waited for her around three. She hadn't showed up. If she doesn't want to see you, I'd told myself, that's fine. But I hadn't gone back to the supermarket to make sure. My days and nights were taken up with Lole.

With the candle in my hand, I was searching every nook and cranny of the room. I felt a presence behind me. I turned.

"What are you doing here?"

A tall black guy was standing in the doorway. He looked like a nightclub bouncer. Not much more than twenty. I felt like replying that I'd seen a light and come in. But I wasn't sure he'd think that was funny.

"I've come to see Pavie."

"Who are you, man?"

"A friend of hers. Fabio."

"Never heard of you."

"A friend of Serge's too."

He relaxed. Maybe I still had a chance of getting out the door on both legs.

"The cop."

"I thought I'd find her here," I said, without picking him up on that. For a lot of people, I'd be "the cop" for the rest of my life.

"Tell me your name again, man."

"Fabio. Fabio Montale."

"Montale, that's right. That's what she calls you. The cop, or Montale. My name's Randy. I live upstairs."

He held out his hand. I gave him mine and found it being crushed in a vise.

I told Randy that I had to talk to Pavie. Because of Serge. He was in trouble, I said, without going into details.

"Don't know where she is, man. She didn't come home today. She usually comes upstairs to our place in the evenings. I live with my parents, my two brothers and my girlfriend. We have the floor to ourselves. There's just us in the building. Us, Pavie, and Madame Gutierrez on the first floor. But she never goes out. She's afraid they'll evict her. She wants to die here, she says. We do her shopping for her. Even when Pavie doesn't stay to eat, she always comes up to say hello. To let us know she's home."

"And does it often happen that she doesn't come home?"

"Not in a while."

"How is she?"

Randy looked at me. He seemed to be sizing me up.

"She's making an effort, you know, man. We help her all we can. But . . . She got hooked again, a few days ago, if that's what you're asking. Stopped work and everything. My girlfriend Rose slept with her the other night, then cleaned the place up a little. It needed it."

"I see."

The pieces were coming together in my head. As an investigator, I still wasn't worth a dime. I rushed into things, on pure intuition, without taking the time to think. In my haste, I'd skipped a lot. Chronology, timetable. That kind of thing. The ABC of cops.

"Do you have a phone?"

"No. There's one at the end of the street. A booth, I mean. You don't need coins. You just pick up the phone and it works. Even for the States!"

"Thank, Randy. I'll be back."

"What if Pavie comes home?"

"Tell her to stay here. Or better still, to stay with you."

But if my hunch was right, this was the last place Pavie would come. Even when she was completely shot up. The proximity of death prolongs the expectation of life.

# 11.

## IN WHICH THERE'S NOT MUCH THAT'S PLEASANT TO SEE

Mourad broke the silence.
"I hope my sister's here."
That was all he said.

I'd just left Rue de Lyon, and was cutting across North Marseilles to get to Saint-Henri, where his grandfather lived. Saint-Henri is just before L'Estaque. Twenty years ago, it was still a village. With a view of the northern outer harbor and the Mirabeau basin.

I grunted a slightly irritated "Me, too." My head was humming. It was a real mess in there! Since he'd gotten in the car, Mourad had barely opened his mouth. I'd asked him questions. About Naïma and Guitou. His answers had consisted of "yes" and "no" and—mostly—"I don't know." I'd thought at first that he was jerking me around. But he wasn't, he was worried. I could understand that. I was worried too.

"Yes, me too," I said again, more gently this time. "I hope she's there."

He looked at me out of the corner of his eye. As if to say, OK, we're on the same wavelength. We both hope, but we're not sure. And it gives us the creeps, not knowing. He was a great kid.

I put on a Lili Boniche cassette. He was an Algerian singer of the thirties, who'd mixed musical styles. The whole of North Africa had danced to his rumbas, paso dobles and tangos. I'd come across a set of his recordings at the Saint-Lazare flea market. Lole and I liked to go there on Sundays around eleven. Then we'd go and have an aperitif in a bar in L'Estaque before ending up at Larrieu's, eating seafood.

That Sunday, she'd found a lovely long skirt, red with white

polka dots. A gypsy skirt. That night, I was treated to a "flamenco" fashion parade. With Los Chunguitos in the background. *Apasionadamente*. A really hot album. The night turned
out pretty hot too.

Lili Boniche had been the musical accompaniment after
that, until sleep overcame us. It was on the third record of the
set that we'd discovered *Ana Fil Houb*. A version, in Arabic, of
*Mon histoire, c'est l'histoire d'un amour*. Whenever I whistled,
that was the tune that most often came into my head. That and
*Besame mucho*. Songs my mother was always humming. I
already had several versions. Lili Boniche's was as fine as the
version by the Mexican-American singer Tish Hinojosa. And a
hundred times better than the one by Gloria Lasso. It was fantastic. A real joy.

Still whistling, I started thinking about what Rico, the owner
of the Balto, had told me. Hearing certain things clearly, I
could have kicked myself. Since the beginning of the week,
Pavie had been coming into the Balto every afternoon. She'd
have a beer and pick at the crumbs of the ham sandwich she'd
asked for. She looked as if she was going through a rough time,
Rico said. So he'd phoned Serge. At Saadna's. But Serge had-
n't come the next day. Or the day after.

"Why didn't you call me?" I'd asked.

"I don't know where to reach you these days, Fabio. You're
not even in the phone book."

I'd been unlisted for a while. It was bad enough with
Minitel. For every friend who might be looking for you, there
were five million bozos who might show up at your door. I like
my peace and quiet, and the few friends I still had all knew my
phone number. I'd simply forgotten about emergencies.

Serge had showed up yesterday. Because of Pavie's letter. I
was sure of that.

"What time?"

"Around two-thirty. He looked worried. Didn't talk much.
He wasn't really himself. They had a coffee. Stayed—what?—

fifteen, twenty minutes. They were talking low, but Serge seemed to be bawling Pavie out. She kept her head bowed, like a child. Then I saw him puffing. Like he was exhausted. He stood up, took Pavie's hand and they went out."

That was the sore point. I'd forgotten all about Serge's car. How else could he have gotten to La Bigotte? Only immigrants went there by bus. And I couldn't even remember right now whether there was a bus that went all the way up there or if you had to climb the slope on foot!

"Did he still have his old Ford Fiesta?"

"Sure."

I couldn't remember seeing it in the parking lot. But then I couldn't remember much. Except the hand holding the gun. And the shots. And Serge falling without saying goodbye to life.

Without even saying goodbye to Pavie.

Because she must have been there, in the car. Not far from where it happened. Nor far from me either. And she must have seen everything. They'd left the Balto together. Heading for La Bigotte, where Serge was supposed to meet someone. I supposed he'd promised to drive her to the psychiatric clinic afterwards. And he'd left her in the car.

She'd waited for him. She'd sat there quietly, feeling safe because he was there. As usual. He'd take her to the clinic. He'd help her, once again, to take a step in the direction of hope. One more step. The right one, this time. Of course it was the right one! This time, she'd come through. She must have believed that. Yes, sitting there in the car, she believed it really strongly. She believed that, afterwards, she'd get her life back. Friends. Work. Love. A love that would cure her of Arno. And of all the dirty tricks life played on you. A guy with a nice face, a nice car, and a bit of cash too. Who'd give her a really beautiful baby.

But there was no afterwards.

Serge had been killed. And Pavie had taken off. On foot, or

in the car? No, she didn't have a license. Or maybe she had one now. My God! Was the damn car still up there? And where was Pavie now?

Mourad's voice cut into my questions. His tone surprised me. He sounded sad.

"My father used to listen to this. My mother liked it."

"Used to? Doesn't he listen to it anymore?"

"Redouane says it's sinful."

"This singer? Lili Boniche?"

"No, music. He says music is like alcohol, cigarettes, girls, that kind of thing."

"But you listen to rap?"

"Not when he's home. He . . . "

*Oh, God, have pity on me*
*let me see those I love*
*let me forget my sorrow . . .*

Lili Boniche was singing *Alger, Alger*. Mourad fell silent again. I drove around the church of Saint-Henri.

"On the right," Mourad said. "Then first on the left."

His grandfather lived on Impasse des Roches, a street of little one- or two-story houses facing the sea. I switched off the engine.

"You didn't see an old Ford Fiesta in the parking lot, did you? A dirty blue color."

"I don't think so. Why?"

"Nothing. We'll take a look later."

Mourad rang once, twice, three times. Nobody came to open the door.

"Maybe he went out," I said.

"He only goes out twice a week. To go to the market."

He looked at me, worried.

"Do you know the neighbors?"

He shrugged. "Not me. But he does, I think."

I went down the street to the next house. I rang the doorbell a few times, quickly. It wasn't the door that opened, but the window. Behind the bars, a woman's head appeared. A big head, covered in rollers.

"What is it?"

"Hello, Madame," I said going up to the window. "I'm here to see Monsieur Hamoudi. I'm with his grandson. But there's no answer."

"That's strange. I saw him at noon, in the garden. We had a chat. Then he always takes an afternoon nap. So he must be there."

"Maybe he's sick."

"No, no, no. He's in very good health. Wait, let me open the door."

She let us in a few seconds later. She'd put a scarf on her head, to hide the rollers. She was huge. She walked slowly, puffing as if she'd just run up six flights of stairs.

"I'm always careful before I open my door. With all the drugs and all these Arabs around, they can attack you in your own home."

"You're right," I said, though I couldn't help smiling. "You have to be careful."

We followed her into the garden. Hers and the old man's were separated only by a low wall about three feet high.

"Monsieur Hamoudi!" she called. "Monsieur Hamoudi, you have a visitor!"

"Can I climb over?"

"Yes, go on! Holy mother of God, I hope nothing's happened to him."

"Wait for me," I said to Mourad.

It wasn't difficult to get over the wall. The garden was identical, and as well tended as the other one. I'd hardly reached the steps when Mourad joined me. He got into the living room before me.

Grandpa Hamoudi was on the floor, his face covered in blood. He'd been beaten up. Before they'd left, the bastards had stuffed his military medal into his mouth. I took it out, and felt his pulse. He was still breathing. He was just woozy from being knocked out. It was a miracle. But maybe his attackers hadn't wanted to kill him.

"Let the lady in," I said to Mourad, who'd kneeled beside his grandfather. "And phone your mother. Tell her to take a taxi and get here as soon as she can."

He didn't move. He was paralyzed.

"Mourad!"

He stood up, slowly. "Is he going to die?"

"No. Now go! Hurry up!"

The neighbor arrived. Fat as she was, she moved fast. "Jesus, Mary and Joseph!" she cried.

"Didn't you hear anything?"

She shook her head.

"You didn't hear a scream?"

She shook her head again. She seemed to have lost the power of speech. She was standing there, wringing her hands. I took the old man's pulse again, then felt him all over. I noticed a sofa bed in the corner of the room. I lifted him. He didn't weigh much more than a sack of dead leaves. I laid him down, and put a cushion under his head.

"Get me a bowl and a washcloth. And some ice. And see if you can make something hot. Coffee. Or tea."

By the time Mourad came back, I was cleaning his grandfather's face. He'd been bleeding from the nose, there was a cut on his upper lip, and his face was covered in bruises. But apart from his nose, maybe, nothing was broken. Apparently, they'd only hit him on the face.

"My mother's on her way."

He sat down next to his grandfather and took his hand.

"It's all right," I said. "It could have been worse."

"Naïma's satchel is in the hall," he stammered, weakly.

Then he burst into tears.

What a fucking life, I said to myself.

I was anxious for the old man to come to his senses and tell us what had happened. A beating up like that didn't seem like a random act of criminality. It was the work of a pro. The old man had Naïma staying with him. Naïma had spent Friday night with Guitou. Guitou had been killed. And so had Hocine Draoui.

I was sure Naïma had seen something. She was in danger. Wherever she was.

The old man was going to be all right. The doctor I'd sent for confirmed that there was nothing broken. Not even the nose. All he needed was rest. He wrote a prescription, and advised Mourad's mother to go to the police. Yes, of course, she said. Marinette, the neighbor, offered to go with her. "It's not right, to come and attack people in their own houses." This time, she didn't say anything about all those Arabs who went around killing people. It wasn't appropriate right now. And she was a good woman.

While the old man was having a cup of tea, I had a beer Marinette offered me. I drank it quickly, trying to get my thoughts back on an even keel. Marinette went back to her house. If we needed her, we knew where to find her.

I moved a chair close to the bed. "Do you feel like talking a little?" I asked the old man.

He nodded. His lips were swollen. His face was turning purple, in places blood-red. The man who'd beaten him had been wearing a huge signet ring on his right hand, he'd said. He'd used only that hand to hit him.

The old man's face looked familiar to me. An emaciated face. High cheekbones. Thick lips. Curly, graying hair. He looked the way my father would have looked if he were alive today. When my father was young—I'd seen photos of him— he'd looked like a Tunisian. "We come from the same womb," he used to say. From the Mediterranean. So, inevitably, we're all a bit Arab, he'd say when people teased him about it.

"Did they take Naïma?"

He shook his head. "They were hitting me when she walked in. She'd just come back from school. She surprised them. She screamed and ran out. One of them ran after her. The other hit me hard, on the nose, and I passed out."

On these narrow streets, a car stood no chance against a young girl running. She must have gotten away. For how long could she keep running? Where could she have gone? That was another story.

"So there were two of them?"

"Yes, right here. One of them held me down on the chair. The other one asked questions. The one with the signet ring. He'd stuffed my medal in my mouth. If I cried out, he said, he'd make me eat it. But I didn't cry out. I didn't say anything. I was ashamed, monsieur. For them. For this world. I think I've lived long enough."

"Don't say that," Mourad whined.

"God can take me now. There's not much that's pleasant to see on earth these days."

"What did these men want to know?"

"If Naïma came back here every evening. Where she went to school. If I knew where she'd been on Friday night. If I'd ever heard of someone named Guitou . . . But I didn't know anything. Apart from the fact that she lives here with me. I don't even know where her school is."

My worst fears were confirmed.

"Didn't she tell you anything?"

The old man shook his head. "When she came back on Saturday . . . "

"What time was it?"

"Around seven in the morning. I'd just gotten up. I was surprised, because she'd told me she'd be back on Sunday evening. Her hair was in a mess. Her eyes were wild. She wouldn't look at me. She went up to her bedroom and locked herself in. She stayed there all day. In the evening, I knocked at the door, and asked her to come downstairs and eat something. But she wouldn't. 'I'm not feeling well,' she said. But she came down later and went out to phone. I asked her what was happening. 'Just leave me alone,' she said. 'Please!' She came back fifteen minutes later, and went back upstairs, without saying a word.

"The next morning, she got up late. She came down and had something to eat. She was more civil. She apologized for the day before. She said she was sad because of a friend. A boy she really liked. But it was over. Everything was fine now. And she gave me a nice kiss on the forehead. Of course, I didn't believe a word of it. You could see it in her eyes that things weren't fine. That she wasn't telling the truth. But I didn't want to upset her any more than she already was. I could tell it was serious. An unhappy love affair, I thought. She'd broken up with her boyfriend, that kind of thing. You know how they are at that age. So all I said was, 'You can talk to me if you like, OK?' She gave me a little smile, but I could see how sad she was. 'You're sweet, Grandpa. But I'd rather not.' She was almost crying. She kissed me again and went back to her room.

"In the evening, she came down to make another phone call. This one was longer than the day before. So long, in fact, that I was worried when she didn't come back. I even went out on the street to keep a lookout for her. She ate just a little, then went to bed. Then yesterday morning, she left for school and—"

"She doesn't go to school anymore," Mourad cut in.

We all looked at him.

"Doesn't go to school!" his mother almost cried out.

"She doesn't want to. She told me she feels too sad."

"When did you see her?" I asked.

"Yesterday. Outside school. She was waiting for me. We were supposed to be going to a concert together in the evening. To see Akhénaton. The singer from IAM. He was doing a solo concert."

"What did she tell you?"

"Nothing, nothing . . . What I told you last night. That she and Guitou were over. That he'd gone. That she was sad."

"And she didn't want to go to the concert anymore?"

"She had to see a friend of Guitou's. It was urgent. Because of Guitou and all that. It made me think maybe it wasn't all over between the two of them after all. That she still cared about the guy."

"And she hadn't been to school?"

"That's right. She said she wouldn't be going for a few days. Because of all that. She said she really wasn't in the mood to listen to the teachers."

"This other friend, do you know him?"

He shrugged. It had to be Mathias. Worst case scenario: She'd seen Adrien Fabre. And he'd told everything to Mathias. I could imagine the state they both must have been in. What had they done then? Who had they talked to? Cûc?

I turned to the old man. "Do you always open the door like that, when someone rings?"

"No. I look through the window first. Like everyone here."

"So why did you let them in?"

"I don't know."

I stood up. I'd have liked another beer. But Marinette had gone. The old man must have read my thoughts.

"I have some beer in the fridge. I drink one, from time to time. In the garden. It's good. Mourad, go get a beer for monsieur."

"Don't worry," I said. "I'll get it."

I needed to stretch my legs. In the kitchen, I took a big swig directly from the bottle. It relaxed me a little. Then I took a glass, filled it, and came back into the room. I sat down next to the bed and looked at the three of them. Nobody had moved.

"Listen to me. Naïma is in danger. Mortal danger. The people who came here will stop at nothing. They've already killed two people. Guitou wasn't even seventeen. Do you understand? So, I ask you again, why did you let these men in?"

"Redouane—" the old man began.

"It's my fault," Mourad's mother cut in.

She looked at me with those beautiful eyes. In them, instead of the gleam of pride mothers usually have when they talk about their children, I could see only an infinite sorrow.

"Your fault?"

"I told Redouane everything. Last night. After your visit. He knew you'd been there. He always knows everything that happens. I get the feeling we're always watched. He wanted to know who you were, why you'd come. If there was a connection with the other man who'd asked after him in the afternoon, and . . . "

Suddenly, it was all falling into place.

"What other man, Madame Hamoudi?"

She'd said too much. I sensed her panic.

"What other man?"

"The one they killed. I think he was a friend of yours. He was looking for Redouane."

I wondered whether to stop or go on.

The screen in my head was flashing *Game over*. What was it I'd said to Fonfon yesterday? "As long as you're betting, you're still alive." So I bet again.

Just to see.

# 12.

## IN WHICH GHOST SHIPS PASS IN THE NIGHT

All three of them were looking at me, in silence. My eyes went from one to the other.

Where could Naïma be? And Pavie?

Both of them had witnessed death first hand, for real, not on a screen, and both had disappeared, both were on the run.

The old man's eyes were closing. The sedatives would soon take effect. He was struggling against sleep. Yet he was the one who resumed talking first, anxious to say what he had to say so that he could sleep afterwards.

"I thought the man who talked to me through the window was a friend of Redouane's. He said he wanted to see Naïma. I told him she wasn't back yet. He said he wasn't in any hurry and asked if he could come in and wait for her. He didn't seem . . . He impressed me. He was well dressed, in a suit and tie. So I opened the door."

"Does Redouane have friends like that?"

"He once visited me with two men who were well dressed like that. Older than him. I think one of them has a car dealership. The other one owns a store near Place d'Aix. They got down on their knees in front of me and kissed my hand. They wanted me to take part in a religious meeting. To talk to our young people. They said it was Redouane's idea. The young people would listen to me if I talked about religion. I'd fought for France. I was a war hero. So I could explain to them—the young people—that France wasn't their salvation. That it actually took away their self-respect. With the drugs and the alcohol and all those things . . . And even the music they all listen to these days . . . "

"Rap," Mourad said.

"Yes. Too noisy for me, that music. What about you, do you like it?"

"It's not my favorite kind of music. But it's like jeans, it suits them."

"You're right, it must be their age . . . In my day . . . "

"This guy listens to old Arab songs," Mourad said, indicating me. "What's the name of that singer of yours?"

"Lili Boniche."

"Oh!" The old man smiled. For a moment he was lost in thought, lost, I was sure, in a place where life was good. Then his eyes focused on me again. "What was I saying? Oh, yes. According to Redouane's friends, we had to save our children. It was time our young people came back to God. Time they learned our values again. Tradition. Respect. That was why they were asking me."

"You mustn't blame Redouane for turning to God," Mourad's mother cut in. "That's his path." She looked at me. "He did a lot of stupid things before. So I'd rather he said his prayers than kept bad company."

"That's not what I'm saying," the old man replied. "You know that. Taking things to extremes is always bad. Too much alcohol, or too much religion, it's the same thing. It makes you sick. And it's always the ones who did the worst things before who want to impose their views, their way of life. I don't mean Redouane. Although lately . . . "

He took a deep breath.

"In our country," he went on, "in our country, he'd kill your daughter. That's what it's like now, down there. I read about it in the newspapers. As soon as a girl there is happy, as soon as she sings, they rape her. I'm not saying Redouane would do something like that, but the others . . . That's not what Islam's all about. And Naïma's a good girl. Just like this boy's a good boy," he added, indicating Mourad. "I have nothing against God. What I'm saying is that it's not religion that should tell you how to live, but your heart." He turned to look at me.

"That's what I told those men. And I said it again to Redouane, when he came here this morning."

"I didn't tell you the truth, when you came before," Mourad's mother said. "Last night Redouane told me not to get involved with these things. He said it was up to the men how his sister should behave. It was up to him. My daughter, can you imagine?"

"He threatened her," Mourad said.

"I was afraid for Naïma. Redouane left first thing this morning. He was out of his head. He wanted to bring her back home. This business with the young man was like the last straw. Redouane said he'd had enough. He was ashamed of his sister. She deserved to be punished. Oh, I don't know what's going on anymore . . . "

She put her head in her hands. It was all too much for her. She was torn between her role as a mother and an upbringing that had taught her obedience to men.

"And what happened with Redouane?" I asked the old man.

"Nothing. Naïma didn't sleep here last night. I was very worried. It was the first time she'd done that. Left without telling me where she was going. On Friday, I knew she was spending the weekend with friends. She'd even left a phone number where I could reach her, in case anything was wrong. I've always trusted her."

"Where has she gone? Do you have any idea?"

I had my own idea, but I needed to hear it from someone else.

"She called, this morning. Telling me not to worry. She'd stayed in Aix. With the family of an old school friend, I think. Someone she'd been on vacation with."

"Does the name Mathias mean anything to you?"

"That might have been the name."

"Mathias!" Mourad said. "He's a really nice guy. Vietnamese."

"Vietnamese?" Mourad's mother said.

She was out of her depth. Her children's lives had slipped away from her. Redouane, Naïma. Mourad too, most likely.

"On his mother's side," Mourad said.

"Do you know him?" I asked.

"A little. He and my sister were going out together for a while. I used to go to the movies with them."

"The same story," the old man resumed. "She was having problems. That's why she wasn't feeling too good. I had to understand her." He paused for a few moments to think. "I wasn't to know. That terrible thing. Why . . . why did they kill that boy?"

"I don't know. Naïma's the only person who can tell us what happened."

"How sad life is."

"What happened with Redouane this morning?"

"I told him his sister had already left. Of course he didn't believe me. He wouldn't have believed anything I told him. Only what he wanted to believe. Only what he wanted to hear. He wanted to go up to his sister's room. Make sure she really wasn't there. Or see if she'd really slept there. But I wouldn't let him. So he started shouting at me. I reminded him that Islam teaches us to respect our elders. That's the first rule. 'I don't respect you anymore,' he said. 'You're just an infidel! Worse than the French!' I took my stick and I showed him. 'I can still punish you!' I cried. And I threw him out."

"And yet you let that other man in."

"I thought if I talked to him, he could make Redouane see reason."

"Had you ever seen them together?"

"No."

"Was he Algerian?"

"No. Looking at him, with his dark glasses, I thought he was a Tunisian. So I wasn't suspicious . . . "

"But was he an Arab?"

"I don't know. He didn't speak Arabic."

"My father was Italian, and when he was young people thought he was Tunisian."

"Yes, he might have been Italian. But from the south. Naples. Sicily. That's possible."

"What did he look like?"

"About your age. A good-looking man. A bit shorter than you, and heavier. Not fat, but stronger-looking. Graying temples. A salt-and-pepper mustache . . . And . . . he had this big gold signet ring."

"He must have been Italian," I said, smiling. "Or Corsican."

"No, not Corsican. The other man, yes. The one who jumped on me when I opened the door. All I saw of him was his gun, which he stuck under my chin. He pushed me backwards, and I fell. He definitely had a Corsican accent. I'll never forget it."

His strength was fading.

"I'll let you sleep now. I may be back to ask you some more questions if I need to. Don't worry. It'll all work out."

He smiled contentedly. That was all he wanted right now. A little comfort. The assurance that everything would work out for Naïma. Mourad leaned toward him and kissed him on the forehead.

"I'll stay with you."

In the end, it was Mourad's mother who stayed with the old man. I suppose she was hoping Naïma would come back. But mainly, she didn't much want to find herself face to face with Redouane again. "She's a little afraid of him," Mourad said as we drove back.

"He's gone crazy. He forces my mother to wear a veil when he's there. And at mealtimes, she has to serve him with her eyes lowered. My father doesn't say a word. He says it'll pass."

"How long has he been like that?"

"Just over a year. Since he got out of jail."

"How long was he in for?"

"Two years. He held up a hi-fi store in Les Chartreux. With two friends. High as kites, they were."

"And you?"

He looked me in the eyes. "I'm on the team with Anselme, if you're interested. Basketball. We don't smoke, we don't drink. It's the rule. Nobody on the team does that kind of thing. If we did, Anselme would throw us out. I often go to his place. To eat and sleep. It's cool there."

He fell silent. The thousands of lighted windows in North Marseilles looked like the lights of ships. Ghost ships lost in the darkness. It was the worst time of day. The time when people come home to these concrete slabs. The time when they know they're really a long way from everything. And forgotten.

My thoughts were all over the place. I needed to absorb all the things I'd been hearing, but I couldn't. What bothered me most was these two guys who were after Naïma and who'd beaten up her grandfather. Were they the ones who'd killed Hocine and Guitou? Were they the ones who'd followed me last night? A Corsican. The driver of the Safrane? Balducci? No, impossible. How could they have known I was looking for Naïma? And so quickly? How had they been able to identify me? It was unbelievable. Obviously, the guys last night were connected with Serge. They'd followed me when the cops had taken me in. The fact that I was there meant I was a friend of Serge's. And his accomplice in whatever he was involved in. As Pertin had assumed too. If that was the case, then logically, they might want to kill me. Or just see what I was made of. Right.

At Notre Dame-Limite, I braked hard, jolting Mourad out of his thoughts. I'd just noticed a phone booth.

"I'll be two minutes."

Marinette answered at the second ring.

"Sorry to bother you again," I said, after telling her who I was. "But this afternoon, did you by any chance notice a car that was a little out of the ordinary?"

"The one that belonged to Monsieur Hamoudi's attackers, you mean?"

She certainly didn't beat around the bush. In a neighborhood like hers, just like in the projects, people noticed everything. Especially a new car.

"No, not me. I'd just had my hair done. So I didn't go out on the street. But Emile, my husband, he saw it. I told him what had happened, and he told me that when he went out, he saw a big car. Around three o'clock. It was coming down the street. He was on his way to Pascal's. That's the bar on the corner. Emile plays *belote* there every afternoon. It keeps him occupied, poor man. Naturally, he took a good look at the car. You don't see a car like that every day. And I don't mean just in this neighborhood! It was the kind of car you only see on TV."

"Was it black?"

"Hold on a minute. Emile!" she called to her husband. "Was the car black?"

"Yes! A black Safrane," I heard him reply. "And tell monsieur it wasn't from around here. It was from the Var."

"It was black."

"I heard."

Yes, I'd heard. I felt a chill run down my spine.

"Thanks, Marinette."

I hung up, mechanically.

I was stunned.

I didn't understand what was going on, but there couldn't be any doubt now, it was definitely the same people. Since when had those two bastards been tailing me? A good question. Answering it would explain a lot. But I didn't have the answer. What I did know was that I'd led them to the Hamoudis'. Yesterday. Before or after the time I'd spent at the station house. They'd let me go last night, but it wasn't because they'd thought I was cleverer than they were. No, they'd assumed, correctly, that I wouldn't go anywhere when I left Chez Félix . . . Shit! Did they know where I lived too? I dismissed that question as soon as I'd asked it. The answer was likely to give me the creeps.

OK, I told myself, let's start again. This morning, they'd gone to La Bigotte and waited for things to start moving. And the one who'd moved was Redouane. He'd gone to see his grandfather. How did they know it was him? Easy. You slip a hundred francs to any kid who's hanging around, and it's done.

"We'll go straight to your place," I said to Mourad. "Pack enough things for a few days and I'll take you back to your grandfather's."

"What's going on?"

"Nothing. I'd just rather you didn't sleep there, that's all."

"What about Redouane?"

"We'll leave him a note. It'd be better for him if he did the same."

"Couldn't I go to Anselme's place instead?"

"If you want to. But phone Marinette. So your mother knows where you are."

"Are you going to find my sister?"

"Yes, I want to."

"But you're not sure, eh?"

What could I be sure of? Nothing. I'd set off to find Guitou like someone going to do the shopping. Hands in my pockets. Taking my time. Looking around. The only reason I'd wanted to find him quickly was because Gélou was worried. Not because I'd intended to put an end to the two kids' love affair. And now Guitou was dead. Shot at point blank range by a couple of hitmen. At the same time, an old pal of mine had been shot down by a different bunch of killers. And two girls were on the run. Both in mortal danger.

There was no doubt about it anymore. And the boy too. Mathias. I had to see him. Put him somewhere safe too.

"I'll go with you," I said to Mourad, when we reached La Bigotte. "I have a few calls to make."

"I was starting to worry," Honorine said. "You haven't called all day."

"I know, Honorine. I know. But—"

"You can talk to me. I read the newspaper."

Damn!

"Oh!"

"How are such horrible things possible?"

"Where did you read the newspaper?" I asked, evading her question.

"At Fonfon's. I went there to invite him. You know, for Sunday. To eat *poutargue*. You remember, don't you? He told me not to mention Guitou. To let you do what you think is right. But do you know what you're doing? Eh?"

I didn't know much of anything anymore, to tell the truth.

"I talked to the police, Honorine," I said, to reassure her.

"And did Gélou read the paper too?"

"Oh no! I didn't even switch on the local twelve o'clock news."

"Isn't she worried?"

"Well . . ."

"Put her on, Honorine. And don't wait for me. I don't know what time I'll be back."

"I've already eaten. But Gélou isn't here anymore."

"She's not there? You mean she left?"

"No, no. I mean, she's not at your place. But she's still in Marseilles. He phoned her this afternoon, her . . . friend."

"Alexandre."

"That's it. Alex, she calls him. He'd just gotten back to their house in Gap. He saw the note on the boy's bed. So he put two and two together, got back in his car, and drove to Marseilles. They met in town. Around five, it must have been. They've gone to a hotel. She called me to tell you where to reach her. The Hotel Alizé. That's on the Vieux-Port, isn't it?"

"Yeah. Just past the New York."

All Gélou had to do was open a newspaper and she'd find out Guitou was dead. Just the way I had. There couldn't be many Fabres with a son named Mathias. And even fewer who owned a house where a sixteen-and-a-half-year-old boy had been killed.

Alexandre being around changed a few things. I could think what I wanted of the guy, but he was the man Gélou loved. The man she wanted to keep. They'd been together for ten years. He'd helped her to raise Patrice and Marc. And Guitou, in spite of everything. They had their life, and just because they were racists it didn't give me the right to deny them that. Gélou depended on the man, and I had to as well.

They had to know about Guitou.

Well, maybe.

"I'll call her, Honorine. So long."

"Hey."

"What?"

"Are you OK?"

"Sure. Why?"

"Because I know you, that's why. I can tell from your voice you're not too good."

"I'm a bit irritable, that's all. But don't worry."

"Of course I worry. Especially when you talk to me like that."

"So long."

What a woman! I loved her. The day I die, I'm sure that when I'm in my hole, she's the one I'll miss the most. It was more likely to be the other way around, but I preferred not to think about that.

Loubet was still in his office. The Fabres had admitted lying about Guitou. They had to be believed now. They'd had no idea the young man was in their house. It was their son, Mathias, who'd invited him and lent him his key. On Friday, before leaving for Sanary. They'd met this summer. They'd gotten on well, and exchanged telephone numbers . . .

"And when they got back, Mathias wasn't with them, he was in Aix. And they didn't want to upset him with what had happened . . . They were spinning me a line, I know. But it's progress."

"You don't think it's the truth?"

"This thing of 'Now we're telling you the truth' always puzzles me. When you lie once, it's because there's something going on. Either they haven't told me everything, or Mathias is still hiding something."

"What makes you say that?"

"Because your Guitou wasn't alone in the apartment."

"Oh," I said, innocently.

"There was a condom in between the sheets. And it wasn't that old. The kid was with a girl. She may have been the reason he ran away from home. Mathias must know something about it. I think he'll tell me when I see him tomorrow. Eyeball to eyeball, a kid and a cop, I don't think he'll hold out on me for long. And I'd like to know who the girl was. Because she must have a few things to tell, eh? What do you think?"

"Yeah, sure . . . "

"Imagine it, Montale. They're both in the sack. Can you see the girl going home after that? At two or three in the morning? Alone? I can't."

"Maybe she had a moped."

"Stop kidding!"

"No, you're right."

"Maybe—" he went on.

I didn't let him finish. I knew I had to appear really dumb here. "She could still have been there, hiding. Is that what you're saying?"

"Yeah. Something like that."

"A little unlikely, don't you think? The guys whack Draoui. Then a kid. Surely they'd have checked to see if there was anyone else there."

"Even pros screw up sometimes, Montale. I think this was one of those times. They were planning on killing Hocine Draoui, nice and easy. But they hit a snag. Guitou. What he was doing in the hall butt naked, God alone knows. The noise, I guess. He was scared. And everything got out of hand."

"Hmm," I said, as if I was thinking about it. "Do you want me to ask my cousin about Guitou? Whether he had a girlfriend in Marseilles. She's his mother. She should know."

"You know something, Montale? I'm surprised you haven't already done that. If I were in your shoes, that's where I'd have started. A boy runs away from home, there's often a girl behind it. Or a close friend. You should know that. Or did you forget you used to be a cop?"

I said nothing.

"I still don't see how you managed to find out it was Guitou," he said.

Montale in the role of village idiot!

That's the problem when you lie. Either you take your courage in both hands and tell the truth. Or you persist until you find a solution. My solution was to get Naïma and Mathias somewhere safe. A hideout. I already had an idea where. Until I had a clearer idea of what was going on. I trusted Loubet, but not the police force in general. The cops and the underworld had been in bed together for a long time. Whatever anyone said, the lines of communication were still open.

Loubet had put me on the spot. I sidestepped by asking, "Do you want to question Gélou?"

"No, no. You do it. But don't keep the answers to yourself. They may help me gain time."

"OK," I said, seriously.

Then I remembered Guitou's face. His angelic face. It was like a red flash in front of my eyes. His death had sullied me, as if I'd been spattered by his blood. How could I close my eyes now, without seeing his body? His body in the morgue. The thing that was on my mind wasn't whether or not I should tell Loubet the truth. It was the killers. I wanted those two scumbags for myself. I wanted to have the one who'd killed Guitou in front of me. Face to face. I hated him enough to shoot first.

That was the only thing in my head. Just that one thing.

The desire to kill.

*Chourmo*, Montale! *Chourmo*!

Dammit, that's life!

"Hey, are you still there?"

"I was thinking."

"Best not to, Montale. You might get the wrong idea. If you want my opinion, this case stinks. Don't forget, there must have been a reason they killed Hocine Draoui."

"I was thinking that myself."

"That's what I meant. Best to keep out of it. OK, will you be home if I need to reach you?"

"You know me. I never leave the house. Except to go fishing."

# 13.

## In which we've all dreamed of living like kings

Mourad was ready. He stood there, stiffly, with a ruck-sack on his back and a satchel in his hand. I hung up. "Did you call Four Eyes?"

"No, why?"

"But you were talking to a cop."

"I was a cop myself, as I'm sure you know. They aren't all like Four Eyes."

"Never met one who wasn't."

"They do exist."

He looked at me, fixedly. As he'd already done several times. He was trying to find a reason to trust me. It wasn't easy. I knew that kind of look pretty well. Most of the kids I'd met in the projects didn't know what an adult was. A real adult.

Thanks to the economic downturn, unemployment, racism, these kids thought of their fathers as losers. Men who'd lost their authority. Who lowered their eyes and their arms. Who refused to argue. Who didn't keep their word. Not even to give them the fifty francs they'd promised them for the week-end.

So these kids went out on the street. Abandoned by their fathers. With nothing to believe in. Their only rule was not to be what their fathers had been.

"Are we going?"

"I still have something to do," I said. "That's why I came up here. Not just to phone."

It was my turn to look at him. Mourad put down his satchel. His eyes filled with tears. He'd guessed what I was planning to do.

As I'd listened to the old man talking about Redouane, the

idea had gradually grown in my mind. Especially when I remembered what Anselme had told me. Redouane had already been seen with the guy who was driving the BMW. The car the shots had come from. And Serge had been coming out of the Hamoudis'.

"Is this his room?" I asked.

"No, it's my parents' room. His is at the end."

"I have to do this, Mourad. There are some things I need to know."

"Why?"

"Because Serge was my friend," I said, opening the door. "I don't like it when the people I like are killed, just like that."

He still stood there, stiffly. "My mother isn't allowed in there. Not even to make the bed. Nobody is."

The room was tiny. A little desk, with an old typewriter, a Japy. Various publications, in neat piles. Issues of *Al Ra'id* and *Le Musulman*—a monthly published by the Association of Islamic Students in France—and a pamphlet by Ahmed Deedat, *How Salman Rushdie Deceived the West*. A sixties corner unit with a single bed. A few shirts and pairs of jeans on hangers. A bedside table, with a copy of the Koran.

I sat down on the bed, to think. I leafed through the Koran. One of the pages was marked with a sheet of paper folded in four. I read the first line on the page: "Every people has its end, and when its end arrives, it will be able neither to postpone it nor to hurry it by a single moment." A pleasant prospect, I thought. Then I unfolded the paper. It was a leaflet. A National Front leaflet. Shit! It was a good thing I was sitting! That was the last thing I'd have expected to find here.

The text was taken from a National Front statement that had appeared in *Minute-la-France*, No. 1552. "Thanks to the FIS, the Algerians are more and more like Arabs and less and less like Frenchmen. The FIS is in favor of the rights of blood. So are we! The FIS is against the integration of immigrants into French society. SO ARE WE!" The conclusion said: "The victory of the FIS is an unexpected opportunity to have another Iran on our doorstep."

Why was Redouane keeping this leaflet inside the Koran? Where had he picked it up? I couldn't imagine extreme right-wing activists pushing them through letter boxes in the projects. But maybe I was wrong. The electoral setbacks suffered by the Communists in these neighborhoods had left the field wide open to all kinds of demagogues. The National Front had demagogues to spare, and it seemed they were even reaching out to immigrants now.

"You want to read this?" I asked Mourad, who'd sat down next to me.

"I read it over your shoulder."

I folded the leaflet and put it back inside the Koran, on the same page. In the drawer of the bedside table, there were four five-hundred franc bills, a pack of condoms, a ballpoint pen, and two ID photos. I closed the drawer. Then I noticed some rolled prayer mats in a corner of the room. I unrolled them. Inside, there were more leaflets. About a hundred of them. They had a heading in Arabic, followed by a short text in French: "Demonstrate that your brains haven't turned to mush! Throw a stone, prime a bomb, lay a mine, hijack a plane!"

It wasn't signed, of course.

I knew enough. For the moment.

"Come on. Let's go."

Mourad didn't move. He put his right hand behind the mattress, under the corner unit, and brought out a blue plastic bag. A garbage bag, rolled up.

"Don't you want to see this?"

Inside there was a .22 long rifle and a dozen bullets.

"Shit!"

I don't know how much time passed. No more than a minute, I suppose. But the minute felt like several centuries. Centuries before prehistory. Before fire. When there was nothing but darkness, menace, fear. An argument broke out on the floor above. The woman had a shrill voice. The man's voice was rough but weary. Echoes of life in the projects.

Mourad broke the silence. He sounded weary too.

"It's like that almost every night. He's unemployed. Long term. All he does is sleep. And drink. So she shouts at him." Then he turned to me. "You don't think he killed him, do you?"

"I don't think anything, Mourad. But you have your suspicions, right? You're telling yourself it's possible."

"No, I didn't say that! I can't believe it. My brother, doing that. But . . . Well, the fact is, I'm afraid for him. Afraid he'll get involved in things that are over his head, and one day he'll . . . use something like this."

"I think he's already involved. Up to his neck."

The pistol was between us, on the bed. I've always hated firearms. Even when I was a cop. I always hesitated to take my service pistol. I knew that all you had to do was pull the trigger. Death was at your fingertips. One shot, and another person's life might be over. One bullet for Guitou. Three for Serge. When you've fired once, you can fire three times. Or more. And start over again. Kill again.

"That's why as soon as I get home from school, I check to see if it's there. As long as it is, I tell myself he can't do anything stupid. You ever killed anyone?"

"Never. Not even a rabbit. Never fired at anyone either. The only time I ever fired a gun, apart from at fairs, was in training. In fact, I scored high marks. I was a pretty good shot."

"But not when you were a cop?"

"No, not when I was a cop. I'd never have shot anyone. Not even a real scumbag. Well, yes, maybe a scumbag. In the legs. My colleagues knew it. My bosses too, of course. The others, I don't know. I never had to save my skin. By killing, I mean."

I wasn't lacking, though, in the desire to kill. But I didn't say that to Mourad. It was bad enough knowing I had that in me sometimes. That madness. Because, goddammit, I wanted to kill the man who'd killed Guitou with a single bullet. It wouldn't change anything, of course. There'd be other killers. There always were. But it'd make me feel better. Maybe.

"You should take this thing away," Mourad said. "You must know where to get rid of it. I'd prefer it if I knew it wasn't here anymore."

"OK."

I put the gun back in the plastic bag. Mourad stood up and started pacing, his hands in his pockets.

"Anselme says Redouane's not a bad person. But he may become dangerous. That he's only like this because he has nothing else to hold on to. He flunked the technical school certificate, and then he did little jobs. The electricity board, for example, but in that job he didn't have any . . . what do they call it?"

"Job security."

"Yes, that's it, job security. No prospects."

"It's true."

"Then he sold fruit, on Rue Longue. He also distributed *Le 13*. You know, the free newspaper. Just jobs like that. In between jobs, he'd hang around on the stairs, smoking, listening to rap. He used to dress like MC Solaar! That's when he started doing stupid things. Getting into drugs. At first, when my mother went to see him at Les Baumettes, he forced her to bring him dope. Right there in the visitors' room! And she did it, can you imagine? He said if she didn't, he'd kill all of us when he got out."

"Don't you want to sit down?"

"No, I'm better standing." He threw me a sidelong look. "It's hard to talk about Redouane. He's my brother, and I love him. When he first started working and had a bit of money, he'd blow it all on us. He'd take Naïma and me to the movies. At the Capitole, you know, on the Canebière. He'd buy us popcorn. And we'd come home by taxi! Like kings."

He clicked his fingers as he said that, and smiled. It must have been great, those times. The three kids, strolling along the Canebière. The older brother and the younger brother, with their sister in the middle. Proud of her, of course.

Living like kings. That had been our dream too, Manu, Ugo and I. Tired of working for nothing plus a few centimes an hour, while the guy you worked for made a packet out of your hard labor. "We aren't whores," Ugo would say. "We're not going to let those jerks screw us over." The thing that drove Manu crazy was the centimes in the hourly rate. The centimes were like an extra bone to chew on. I was like them, I didn't want a bone, I wanted meat.

How many drugstores and gas stations had we held up? I couldn't remember. But we had quite a tally. We knew the ropes. At first in Marseilles, then all over the region. We weren't trying to break any records. Just enough to live an easy life for two or three weeks. And then we'd start again. We enjoyed throwing our money around and showing off. We liked to dress well. We even went to Cirillo's, an Italian tailor on Avenue Foch, and had suits made to measure. Choosing the material, the style. Going for fittings. With a straight crease in the pants. And Italian shoes, of course. Class!

One afternoon, I could still remember, we decided to drive down to San Remo. Just to buy new clothes and shoes. A mechanic friend of ours, José, who was crazy about racing cars, had lent us an Alpine coupé. Leather seats and wooden dashboard. A masterpiece. We stayed three days. We gave ourselves the works. A good hotel, girls, restaurants, nightclubs, and in the early hours of the morning, as many chips as possible at the casino.

The good life. The belle époque.

It wasn't the same these days. Stealing a thousand francs from a supermarket without getting collared three days later was quite an achievement. That was why the drug trade had prospered. It offered a bigger return for less risk. Becoming a dealer was a must.

Two years ago, we'd caught a dealer named Bachir. His big dream had been to open his own bar. To finance that, he'd sold heroin. "I'd buy a gram for eight, nine hundred francs," he'd told us. "I'd cut it, and resell it for almost a million. Sometimes, I was making four thousand profit a day . . . "

He'd soon forgotten all about the bar, and had started working for a big shot. A top dealer. The split was fifty-fifty, but he was the one who took all the risks. Walking around with the packs, waiting. One night, he refused to hand over the take, to get the guy to agree to a seventy-thirty split. The next day, feeling pleased with himself, he was drinking an aperitif at the Bar des Platanes, in Le Merlan. A guy had come in and fired two bullets into his legs. One in each leg. That was where we'd come to pick him up. We booked him, and managed to get him sent down for two and a half years. But he hadn't squealed about his suppliers. "I'm from around here," he'd said. "I can't squeal. But I can tell you my life story, if you like . . . " I hadn't wanted to listen. I knew his life story.

Mourad was still speaking. Redouane's life was like Bachir's and hundreds of others.

"When Redouane got into drugs, he didn't take us to the movies anymore. He'd just give us money. 'Here, buy whatever you like.' Five hundred francs, a thousand. Once, I bought some Reeboks with what he gave me. They were great. But deep down, I didn't really like the idea. It wasn't like they were a gift from him. Knowing where the money came from wasn't so great. The day Redouane was arrested, I threw them away."

How was it, I wondered, that children from the same family could go in such different directions? The girls, I could understand. They wanted to succeed because it was their way of gaining their freedom. Of being independent. Marrying who they wanted to marry. Getting out of North Marseilles one day. Their mothers helped them. But the boys? When had the gulf opened up between Mourad and Redouane? How? Why? Life was full of questions like that, questions without answers. And precisely in those cases where there were no answers, there was sometimes room for a little happiness. It was like thumbing a nose at the statistics.

"What happened, for him to change like that?"

"Prison. At first, he played the big shot. He got into fights. 'You gotta be a man,' he'd say. 'If you're not a man, you're fucked. They walk all over you. It's dog eat dog.' Then he met Saïd. A prison visitor."

I'd heard about Saïd. An ex-convict who'd become a preacher. An Islamist preacher belonging to the Tabligh, a movement originating in Pakistan, which recruited mainly in poor suburban areas.

"I know him."

"Well, after that, he didn't want to see us anymore. He wrote us crazy things. Like . . . " He thought about it, searching for the exact words. "'Saïd is like an angel who appeared to me.' And 'His voice is as sweet as honey, and as wise as the voice of the Prophet.' Saïd had kindled a light in him, that's what he wrote. He started learning Arabic and studying the Koran. And he didn't cause any more trouble in jail.

"They reduced his sentence for good behavior. When he came out, he was different. He didn't drink or smoke anymore. He'd grown a little goatee beard and refused to say hello to anyone who didn't go to the mosque. He spent his days reading the Koran. He'd recite it out loud, like he was learning whole sentences by heart. He'd lecture Naïma about modesty and dignity. Whenever we went to see Grandpa, he'd bow to him and recite some sacred words. Which made Grandpa laugh, because it must be a long time since he last went to the mosque! He even tried to lose his accent . . . Nobody in the project recognized him.

"Then some guys came to see him. Fundamentalists, in djellabas, with big cars. He'd leave with them in the afternoon, and come back late at night. Then there were other guys, wearing white abayas and turbans. One morning, he packed his bags and left. To follow the teachings of Muhammad, he told my mother and father. To me, he said—I can remember it word for word—that he was leaving to take up arms, to liberate our country. 'When I come back,' he added, 'I'll take you with me.'

"He was away more than three months. When he came back, he'd changed again, but he didn't bother with me anymore. All he ever said to me was, you mustn't do this, you mustn't do that. And he also said, 'I don't want anything more to do with France, Mourad. It's a country of idiots. Put that in your little head! Soon, you'll see, you'll be proud of your brother. He's going to do things people will talk about. Great things. *Insh'Allah!*'"

I could imagine where Redouane had gone.

In among Serge's papers, there was a big file about the "pilgrimages" organized by the Tabligh—though not only by them—for its new recruits. Mainly to Pakistan, but also Saudi Arabia, Syria, Egypt . . . Visits to Islamist centers, study of the Koran, and most important of all, initiation into the armed struggle. That mostly took place in Afghanistan.

"Do you know where he went during those three months?"

"Bosnia."

"Bosnia!"

"With a humanitarian association called Merhamet. Redouane joined the Islamic Association of France, which champions the Bosnians. They're Muslims, you know. They're fighting to defend themselves against the Serbs, and against the Croats too. Redouane explained it all to me. At first, anyway. Afterwards he hardly ever talked to me. I was just a dirty little kid. I couldn't find out anything more. About the people who came to see him. Or the money he brought home every week. All I know is that one day he and some others went to beat up some dealers in Le Plan d'Aou. Not marijuana dealers, heroin dealers. Some of my friends saw him. That's how I found out."

We heard the front door open, then voices. Mourad rushed to the dining room, to bar the way to the corridor.

"Get out of my way, kid, I'm in a hurry!"

I walked out of the bedroom, the plastic bag in my hand. Behind Redouane was another young guy.

"Shit!" Redouane cried. "Let's get out of here!"

There wouldn't have been any point in running after them. Mourad was shaking all over.

"The other guy's name is Nacer. He's the guy who was driving the BMW. It's not just Anselme who thinks so. We all know. We've already seen him around here in that car."

And he started crying. Like a kid. I went up to him and hugged him. He only came up to my chest. His sobs increased in intensity.

"It's nothing," I said. "It's nothing."

Nothing, except that there was too much shit in this world.

# 14.

## IN WHICH YOU CAN'T BE SURE THINGS ARE ANY BETTER ELSEWHERE

I'd lost all sense of time. In my head, my thoughts were shooting off in all directions. I'd left Mourad outside Anselme's building. He'd slipped the plastic bag with the gun in the glove compartment, and said, "Ciao." He didn't even look back, didn't even make a sign. I knew he was upset. Anselme would know what to say to him. How to cheer him up. In fact, I was happy to know he was with Anselme rather than with his grandfather.

Before leaving La Bigotte, I'd looked all over the parking lot for Serge's car. I wasn't under any illusions. So I wasn't disappointed when I couldn't find it. Pavie must have driven off in it. I hoped she really had a license, and hadn't done anything stupid. The usual pious wishes. Like believing she was somewhere safe right now. At Randy's, for example. I didn't believe it, but it had given me an incentive to get back in my car and drive back down to the center.

Now Art Pepper was playing *More for Less*. A real gem. Jazz had always had the effect on me of putting the pieces back together. At least as far as feelings were concerned. Affairs of the heart. But this was a whole other ball game. There were too many pieces. Too many opinions, too many leads. And too many memories coming back to the surface. I needed a drink badly. Maybe two.

I drove past the quays, past the basin of La Joliette, as far as the Quai de la Tourette, then drove around the Butte du Parvis Saint-Laurent. The Vieux-Port was there, girdled with lights. Immutable and magnificent.

I remembered some lines of Brauquier:

*The sea,*
*Half asleep, took me in her arms,*
*As if welcoming a stray fish . . .*

I slowed down in front of the Hotel Alizé. That was my destination. But I didn't have the courage to stop. To see Gélou. Meet Alex. I couldn't handle it right now. I had a thousand excuses not to get out of the car. There was nowhere to park, they must be out somewhere having dinner, that kind of thing. I promised myself I'd call later.

A drunkard's promise! I was already on my third whisky. My old Renault 5 had led me with my eyes closed to the Plaine. To Hassan's bar, Les Maraîchers. Where you're always welcome. A bar popular with young people, the friendliest in the neighborhood. Maybe in the whole of Marseilles. I'd been hanging out there for years. Since before all the little streets between the Plaine and Cours Julien filled up with bars and restaurants and clothing stores. The neighborhood had become quite hip these days. But everything was relative. You still didn't parade around in Lacoste, and you could drink *pastis* until dawn.

One night, a few months earlier, Hassan's bar had been torched. Because, it was said, the draft beer was the cheapest in Marseilles. Maybe it was true. Maybe it wasn't. People say all kinds of things. In this town, there always had to be something behind anything that happened. Some mystery. Some secret. Otherwise, it would be an ordinary news item, without any interest.

Hassan had repaired the bar. The paintings, everything. Then, calmly, as if nothing had happened, he'd hung on the wall the photo of Brel, Brassens and Ferré together at the same table. To Hassan, that photo was a symbol and a testimonial. You didn't listen to just any old crap in his bar. The music he played had to be meaningful, and it was only meaningful if it had heart. When I'd entered, Ferré was singing:

*Oh Marseilles it seems the sea has wept*
*Words that once walked arm in arm*
*That once were so ardently kept*
*On lips that now have lost their charm*
*Oh Marseilles . . .*

I'd found a seat at a table, in the middle of a group of young people I knew a little. Regulars. Mathieu, Véronique, Sébastien, Karine, Cédric. I'd bought a round when I sat down, and it had been followed by other rounds. Now Sonny Rollins was playing *Without a Song*. With Jim Hall on guitar. From his best album, *The Bridge*.

It was doing me a lot of good, being here, in a normal world. With young people who felt good about themselves. Hearing that frank laughter. That talk, flying happily on fumes of alcohol.

"You mustn't hit the wrong target, dammit!" Mathieu was yelling. "Why do you want to screw the Parisians? It's the State we should be screwing! Who are the Parisians? The most affected, that's who. They live next to the State, that's why. We're far away, so of course we get along better."

The other Marseilles. The Marseilles with a tradition of being a touch libertarian. This was a city where the black flag had flown over the prefecture for forty-eight hours during the 1871 Commune. Five minutes from now, they'd suddenly change the subject. They'd start talking about Bob Marley, and Jamaicans, and how if you have two cultures, you're more likely to understand other people and the world around you. They could spend the whole night talking about that.

I stood up and pushed my way to the bar to find a phone. She answered at the second ring, as if she'd been waiting for a call.

"Montale here," I said. "I hope I didn't wake you?"

"No," Cûc said. "I was thinking you'd call. Sooner or later."

"Is your husband there?"

"He's in Fréjus, on business. He'll be back tomorrow. Why?"

"I wanted to ask him something."

"Maybe I could give you the answer?"

"I'd be very surprised."

"Ask it anyway."

"Did he kill Hocine?"

She hung up.

I dialed the number again. She answered immediately.

"That wasn't an answer," I said.

Hassan placed a glass of whisky in front of me. I winked at him in gratitude.

"It wasn't a question."

"I have another one, then. Where can I get in touch with Mathias?"

"Why?"

"Do you always answer a question with another question?"

"I don't have to answer you."

"I'm sure Naïma is with him!" I cried.

The bar was full to bursting. Around me, people jostled. B. B. King's *Rock Me Baby* was playing so loudly the sound was distorted, and everyone was screaming along with it.

"What of it?"

"What of it? Stop screwing around with me! You know what's going on. She's in danger. So is your son. It's obvious! It's obvious!" I repeated, shouting now.

"Where are you?"

"In a bar."

"I can hear that. Where?"

"Les Maraîchers. In the Plaine."

"I know it. Don't move, I'll be right there."

She hung up.

"Everything OK?" Hassan asked.

"I don't know."

He served me again, and we clinked glasses. I went back to the table where my young friends were.

"You've gotten a head start on us," Sébastien said.
"Old people are like that."

Cûc made her way through the crowd to my table. All eyes converged on her. She was wearing tight-fitting black jeans, an equally tight-fitting black T-shirt, and a denim jacket. I heard Sébastien say, "Wow! What a looker!" I'd done a stupid thing, letting her come here, but I was no longer in a fit state to think clearly about anything. Except her. And how beautiful she was. Even Jane March might as well put her clothes back on and go home.

She found an empty seat, as if by magic, and sat down facing me. The young people were trying to keep out of it, sounding each other out about going somewhere else. How about the Intermédiare, nearby, where a blues singer named Doc Robert was performing? Or the Cargo, a new venue on Rue Grignan, where the Mola-Bopa quartet played jazz? They could spend hours like that. Talking about places where they might finish the night, and not moving.

"What are you drinking?"
"The same as you."
I signaled to Hassan.
"Have you eaten?"
She shook her head. "A snack, around eight."
"We'll have a drink, and then I'm taking you to dinner. I'm hungry."

She shrugged, then pushed her hair back behind her ears. The gesture that got me every time. Her face, now revealed, was turned toward me. She'd painted her lips, discreetly. She smiled and looked into my eyes. Her own eyes were like those of a wild animal that knows it will get its prey in the end. Cûc seemed to exist on that border where a human being takes on a kind of animal beauty. I'd known it since the first time I'd seen her.

Now, it was too late.

"Cheers," I said.

Because I didn't know what else to say.

Cûc liked to talk about herself, and she didn't hold back during the meal. I'd taken her to Chez Loury, on Carré Thiars, near the harbor. The food is excellent, whatever Gault and Millau say. And they have the best selection of Provençal wines. I chose a Château-Sainte-Rosaline. Definitely the greatest of Provençal reds. The most sensual.

"My mother came from an important family. Well-educated and aristocratic. My father was an engineer who worked for the Americans. In 1954, when the country was partitioned, they left the North. For him, it was like being uprooted. He was never happy again after that. His relationship with my mother deteriorated. He became more and more withdrawn. They should never have gotten together . . .

"They weren't from the same world. In Saigon, the only people who came to our house were friends of my mother. The only things we ever talked about were things that came from the United States or France. By that time, everyone knew the war was already lost, but . . . It was strange, but we weren't really aware of the war. Later, yes, during the big Communist offensive. I mean, there was an atmosphere of war, but not the war itself. It was like being suffocated. A lot of nighttime visits and searches."

"Did your father stay in Vietnam?"

"He was supposed to join us. That's what he said. I don't know what he really wanted. He was arrested. We found out he'd been interned in a camp called Lolg-Giao, about forty miles from Saigon. That was the last we heard of him. Any more questions?" she said, finishing her glass.

"You might find them indiscreet."

She smiled. Again, she made the gesture of pushing her hair back behind her ears. Every time she did that, my defenses crumbled. I was at the mercy of that gesture. I waited for it, hoped for it.

"I've never loved Adrien, if that's what you want to know. But I owe him everything. When I met him, he was full of enthusiasm, full of love. He gave me a chance to escape. He gave me security and helped me to finish my studies. Suddenly, thanks to him, I was able to hope again. For me, and for Mathias. I had a future."

"A future that included Mathias' father?"

There was a lightning flash of anger in her eyes. But the thunder didn't follow. She was silent for a few moments, and when she resumed it was in a more solemn voice.

"Mathias' father was a friend of my mother's. A French teacher. He gave me Hugo, Balzac and Céline to read. I got along well with him. Better than with the girls at school, who didn't think about anything but boys. I was fifteen and a half. I was quite wild, and bold too . . .

"One evening, I provoked him. I'd drunk some champagne. Maybe two glasses. We were celebrating his thirty-fifth birthday. I asked him if he was my mother's lover. He slapped me. The first time in my life anyone had hit me. I threw myself on him. He took me in his arms . . . He was my first love. The only man I've ever loved. The only man who ever possessed me. Can you understand that?" she said, leaning toward me. "He took my virginity, and put a child inside me. His name was Mathias."

"Was?"

"He was supposed to stay in Saigon until the end of the school year. He was stabbed on the street, as he was on his way to the embassy to see if there was any news of us. That's what the principal of the school told us later."

Cûc had trapped my knee between hers, and I felt her warmth flow into me. Her electricity. Heavy with emotion and regret. And desire. Her eyes were fixed on mine.

I refilled our glasses and raised mine in front of her. I had another question to ask her. A question I couldn't avoid.

"Why did your husband have Hocine killed? Why was he there that night? Who were the killers? Where did he meet them?"

I knew that, or something like it, was the truth. I'd turned it over and over in my head all evening. Drinking one whisky after another. And everything fitted. I didn't know how it had happened that Naïma had seen Adrien Fabre that night. But she had seen him. She knew him, because she'd been at the Fabres' house several times. To see Mathias, her ex-boyfriend. And she'd told Mathias all about the terrible thing that had happened. Mathias who didn't love this "father" that even his mother didn't love.

"Shall we talk about this at your place?"

"Just one thing, Cûc."

"Yes," she said, without hesitation. "Yes, I already knew when you came to the house. Mathias had called me." She placed her hand on mine. "Right now, the two of them are in a safe place. Really. Believe me."

I had no choice but to believe her. And hope it was true.

She'd come in a taxi, so I took her in my old car. She made no comment about the state of the vehicle, inside or out. It was full of old smells: stale tobacco, sweat and fish, I think. I opened a window and put on a cassette by my favorite blues singer, Lightnin' Hopkins. *Your Own Fault, Baby, to Treat Me the Way You Do.* And we were off. Like in 14. Like in 40. Like all the stupid things men are capable of.

I went via the Corniche. Just to get an eyeful of the bay of Marseilles, strung out like a Christmas garland. I needed to convince myself that it existed. And to convince myself that Marseilles is a destiny. My destiny and the destiny of all those who live there and never leave it. It wasn't a question of history or traditions, geography or roots, memory or beliefs. No, that's just the way it was.

You belonged *here*, as if everything had been decided in advance. And because, in spite of everything, we can't be sure it isn't worse elsewhere.

"What are you thinking?"

"That it must be worse elsewhere. I'm not even sure the sea is more beautiful."

Her hand, which had been moving along my thigh since I'd started the car, paused when it reached my crotch. Her fingers were burning hot.

"What I know about elsewhere makes me want to throw up. I heard last week about an uprising of four thousand Vietnamese boat people in a refugee camp in Sungai Besi, in Malaysia. I don't know how many people died . . . But what does it matter, eh?"

She took her hand away. She lit two cigarettes and handed me one.

"Thanks."

"Collectively, death doesn't exist. The more dead there are, the less it matters. Too many dead, it's like elsewhere. It's too far away. It isn't real. Only the death of individuals has any reality. When it touches us personally. Directly. When you see it with your own eyes, or in someone else's eyes."

She fell silent. She was right. That was why there was no question of letting Guitou's death pass. I couldn't. Nor could Gélou. Or Cûc. I understood what she was feeling. She'd seen Guitou. When she came home. His angel face. Beautiful, as Mathias must be. As all boys of that age were. Whoever they were, of whatever race. Everywhere.

Cûc had seen death in his eyes. So had I, at the morgue. The world's corruption had caught us by the throat. One death, as unjust and senseless as this one, and all the atrocities on this earth screamed too. No, I couldn't abandon Guitou to the profit and loss account of this rotten world. And leave these mothers to weep forever.

*Chourmo*! Whether I liked it or not.

When we reached the Pointe-Rouge, I turned right onto Avenue d'Odessa, alongside the new marina. Then I turned left onto Boulevard Amphitrite, and left again onto Avenue de Montredon. Toward the center of town.

"What are you doing?" she asked.

"Just checking," I replied, glancing in the rear view mirror.

But nobody seemed to be tailing us. All the same, I kept my eyes open as far as Avenue des Goumiers, dodged into the warren of little streets in Vieille-Chapelle, then drove back onto Avenue de la Madrague de Montredon.

"You live in the middle of nowhere," she said, when I turned onto the little road that leads to Les Goudes.

"That's my home. The middle of nowhere."

She put her head on my shoulder. I'd never been to Vietnam, but all its smells greeted me. As soon as there is desire, I thought, there are different smells. Always pleasant ones. That was my way of justifying whatever might be about to happen.

And I needed to justify it. I hadn't called Gélou. I'd even forgotten that I was driving with a gun in my glove compartment.

By the time I returned with the two glasses and the bottle of Lagavulin, Cûc was standing there naked in the dim light of the little blue lamp I'd lit when we came in.

She had a perfect body. She took a few steps toward me. She seemed marked for a destiny of love. There was a contained sensuality, subdued and intense, in every move she made. I could hardly bear to look at her.

I put the glasses down but didn't let go of the bottle. I really needed a drink. She was less than two feet from me. I couldn't take my eyes off her. I was spellbound. There was a look of absolute indifference in her eyes. Not a muscle moved in her face. The mask of a goddess. Dull and smooth. Like her skin, its texture so even, so delicate, that it cried out, I told myself, to be both caressed and bitten.

I took a swig of whisky, straight from the bottle. A long swig. Then I tried to look beyond her. Behind her, toward the sea. The open sea. The horizon. Searching for the Planier, as if it could show me which direction to take.

But I was alone with myself.

And with Cûc at my feet.

She had kneeled, and her hand followed the outline of my cock. She moved a single finger along its length. Then she undid the buttons, one by one, unhurriedly. The tip of my cock burst out of my underwear. My pants slid down my legs. I felt Cûc's hair on my thighs, then her tongue. She grabbed hold of my buttocks, digging her nails into them, hard.

I wanted to cry out.

I took another long swig of whisky. I was feeling dizzy. The alcohol was burning the pit of my stomach. A dribble of sperm appeared on the tip of my cock. She was about to take it in her mouth, which was hot and moist, like her tongue, and her tongue . . .

"And with Hocine . . . "

The nails moved away from my buttocks. Cûc's whole body went limp. Mine started to shake. From the effort of stammering those words. I drank again. Two short swigs. Then I moved my leg. Cûc laid her now flaccid body on the tiled floor. I pulled up my pants.

I heard her crying, weakly. I walked around her and picked up her things. Her weeping increased in intensity when I crouched next to her. She was shaken with sobs. She was like a dying caterpillar.

"Here, get dressed, please."

I said it tenderly.

I didn't touch her. Even though all the desire I'd felt for her was still there. It hadn't let go of me.

# 15.

## In which regrets are also part of happiness

Day was breaking as I drove Cûc back to the nearest taxi stand, which wasn't as near as all that. We had to go all the way to Vieille-Chapelle to find one.

We'd driven in silence, smoking. I liked that dark hour before the break of day. It was a moment of purity, a moment that no one person could lay claim to, that no one person could use.

Cûc turned to face me. Her eyes still had that jade brilliance that had attracted me from the start, though slightly tarnished by fatigue and sadness. The most important thing, though, was that, free now of lies, they were no longer indifferent. They'd become human. Full of pain, but also full of hope.

We'd talked for a good two hours, and in all that time I hadn't stopped drinking. The bottle of Lagavulin was gone. Cûc had broken off in the middle of a sentence and asked, "Why do you drink so much?"

"I'm afraid," I replied, without any further explanation.

"I'm afraid too."

"It's not the same fear. The older you get, you see, the greater the number of irreparable acts you can commit. I avoid them, as I just did with you. But those aren't the worst ones. There are others that you can't get around. If you do get around them, in the morning you can't look at yourself in the mirror."

"And that wears you down?"

"That's right. A little more every day."

She'd fallen silent, lost in thought. Then she'd said, "Is avenging Guitou one of them?"

"Killing someone is an irreparable act. But killing the piece of shit who killed Guitou seems to me one of those things I can't get around."

I'd said those words wearily. Cûc had placed her hand on mine. To share that weariness.

I parked behind the only taxi in the stand. The driver was just starting his day. Cûc gave me a fleeting kiss. The last one. The only one. We both knew that what hadn't happened would never happen. Regrets were also part of happiness.

I saw her get in the taxi, without looking back. Like Mourad. The taxi moved out and drove off, and when I lost sight of its sidelights I turned and went back home.

To sleep, at last.

I was being shaken gently, by the shoulders. "Fabio . . . Fabio . . . Hey, hey! . . . " I knew that voice. It sounded familiar. It was my father's voice. But I didn't want to get up to go to school. No. Besides, I was ill. I had a fever. That's it, yes. At least a hundred. My body was burning. What I wanted was breakfast in bed. And then to read Tarzan. I was sure it was Wednesday. The new issue of *The Adventures of Tarzan* must be out. My mother would go out and buy it for me. She couldn't refuse, because I was sick.

"Fabio."

It wasn't my father's voice. But the intonation was the same. Gentle. I felt a hand on my skull. God, it felt good! I tried to move. One arm. The right one, I think. It was heavy. Like a tree trunk. Shit! I was trapped under a tree. No. I'd had an accident. My mind was clearing. A motor accident. On the way home. That was it. I'd lost my arms. Maybe my legs too.

"No!" I yelled, turning.

"There's no point in screaming like a maniac, dammit!" Fonfon said. "I hardly even touched you!"

I felt myself all over. I seemed to be intact. Completely intact. And fully dressed. I opened my eyes.

Fonfon. Honorine. My bedroom. I smiled.

"You really scared us, you know. I thought something had

happened to you. I thought you'd had some kind of attack. Or whatever. That's why I fetched Fonfon."

"If I have to die, I'll leave you a note the day before. On the table. So as not to scare you."

"He's just woken up," Fonfon said to Honorine, "and already he's making jokes! I'm wasting my time with this nonsense. I'm too old for this!"

"Take it easy, Fonfon, please! It feels like Easter Sunday in my head! Did you bring me any coffee?"

"What else? A croissant? A brioche? Would monsieur like it on a tray?"

"Well, you know, that would have been really nice."

"Go fuck yourself!"

"The coffee'll be ready in a minute," Honorine said. "It's on the stove."

"I'm getting up."

It was an exceptional day. No clouds. No wind. Ideal weather for fishing, if you have the time. I looked at my boat. It was as sad as I was, because it wouldn't get the chance to go to sea today either.

Fonfon had followed the direction of my eyes. "Hey, will you have time to catch the fish before Sunday? Or will I have to order it?"

"The seafood you can order. But leave the fish to me. And don't make such a fuss."

He smiled, and finished his coffee.

"OK, I'm going back. The customers must be getting impatient. Thanks for the coffee, Honorine." He turned to me, with a fatherly look. "Stop by before you leave."

It was good to have Honorine and Fonfon with me. When they were around, I always knew there was going to be a tomorrow. That life would go on. Once you pass a certain age, it's as if you're immortal. You make plans for tomorrow. Then for the day after tomorrow. Next Sunday, and the one after. And the days pass, each one a victory over death.

"Maybe you'd like another coffee?"

"Thanks, Honorine. You're an angel."

She went into the kitchen. I heard her bustling about. Emptying the ashtrays, washing the glasses. Throwing out the bottles. If she went on like that, she'd be changing my sheets next.

I lit a cigarette. It tasted disgusting, but the first one always did. It was the smell I needed. I wasn't sure yet what planet I was on. I had the feeling I was swimming against the current. But that was my style.

The sky and the sea were an infinite variety of blues. To the tourists, whether they come from the North, the East or the West, blue is always blue. It's only later, when you take the trouble to look at the sky and the sea, to caress the landscape with your eyes, that you discover the gray blues, the black blues, the ultramarine blues, the peppery blues, the lavender blues. Or the eggplant blues on stormy evenings. The green blues of the swell. The copper blues of the sunset, the night before a mistral. Or the blues that are so pale they're almost white.

"Are you asleep?"

"I was thinking, Honorine. Thinking."

"With your head the way it is, there's no point. Better not to think at all than only half think, my poor mother used to say."

There was no answer to that.

Honorine sat down, brought her chair close to me, pulled on her skirt, and watched me drinking my coffee. I put down the cup.

"Ah, that's not all. Gélou called. Twice. At eight o'clock, then again at nine-fifteen. I told her you were asleep. Well, it was true. I said I couldn't wake you right away because you'd gone to bed late."

She looked at me with her a mischievous gleam in her eyes.

"What time is it now?"

"Nearly ten."

"Then I never really went to bed. Is she worried?"

"Well, the thing is . . . " She stopped, and tried to look angry. "It was bad of you not to call her. Of course she's worried. She specially ate at the New York, in case you came. She left a message for you at the hotel. You know, I don't understand you sometimes."

"Don't try, Honorine. I'll call her now."

"Yes, because her . . . her Alex wants her to go back to Gap. He says there's no point in her staying on in Marseilles, he'll look for Guitou with you."

"Uh-huh," I said, thinking about that. "Maybe he knows. Maybe he read the papers, and he's trying to let her down gently. I don't know. I don't know the man."

She gave me a long, searching look. Something was bothering her. Finally, she pulled again on her skirt and said, "Do you think he's a good man? For her, I mean."

"They're together, Honorine. They've been together for ten years. He raised the kids . . . "

"To me, a good man . . . " She thought for a moment. "OK, so he phones. But . . . I don't know, maybe I'm old-fashioned, but he could have come here, couldn't he? Introduced himself . . . You see what I'm saying? I'm not thinking about me, but about you. We don't even know what he looks like."

"He'd only just gotten here from Gap, Honorine. And besides, coming home after a few days away and discovering that Guitou had disappeared . . . Surely it was more important to him to see Gélou again. The rest of it . . . "

"Yes, maybe," she said, not convinced. "It's strange, all the same . . . "

"You see complications everywhere. Things are already complicated enough, don't you think? And besides . . . " I was searching for arguments to convince her. "He's said he wants to work with me on this, hasn't he? Anyway, what did Gélou say?"

"She doesn't want to go back. The poor woman's worried. She doesn't know what to do. I think she's starting to imagine the worst."

"Whatever she's imagining can't be anything like the reality."

"That's why she called. To talk to you. To find out what's going on. She needs you to reassure her. If you tell her to go back, she'll listen to you . . . You won't be able to hide the truth from her much longer."

"I know."

The phone rang.

"Talk of the devil . . . " Honorine said.

But it wasn't Gélou.

"Loubet here." He sounded grouchy.

"Oh! Any news?"

"Where were you between midnight and four in the morning?"

"Why?"

"I'm asking the questions here, Montale. It's in your own interests, firstly, to answer, secondly, not to bullshit. It really would be better for you. OK, I'm listening."

"At home."

"Alone?"

"Loubet, are you going to tell me what this is about?"

"Answer me, Montale. Were you alone?"

"No. I was with a woman."

"Do you at least know her name?"

"I can't, Loubet. She's married and—"

"When you pick up a woman, check first. Because afterwards it's too late, you asshole!"

"Dammit, Loubet! What is all this?"

"Listen carefully, Montale. I could pin a murder on you, if I wanted to. You, and nobody else. Do you understand? Or do you want me to come and get you? Sirens blaring and all that shit? Tell me her name. And if there are any witnesses who saw you together. Before, during and after. I'll see if it checks out, I'll hang up, and fifteen minutes later I'll see you here. Am I making myself clear?"

"Adrien Fabre's wife. Cûc."

I told him everything. The evening. The places. And the night. Well, almost everything. He could imagine the rest if he wanted.

"Perfect," he said. His voice softened. "Cûc's statement tallies with yours. We just have to check the taxi. But it'll be fine. So I want to see you here! Adrien Fabre was killed last night on Boulevard des Dames. Between two and four in the morning. Three bullets in the head."

It was time for me to come out of my coma.

God knows why, but there are days when everything gets off to a bad start. At Rond-Point de la Plage, where David—a replica of Michelangelo's statue—stood naked, facing the sea, there had just been an accident. We were diverted toward Avenue du Prado and the center of town. At the Prado-Michelet intersection, the bottleneck stretched as far as Place Castellane. I turned right onto Boulevard Rabatau, then, in a fit of pique, the Le Jarret bypass. That way you could get back to the harbor without going through the center. This circular boulevard, which covers a small watercourse that's been turned into a sewer, is one of the ugliest streets in Marseilles.

I'd just passed Les Chartreux when I saw a sign saying "Malpasse-La Rose-Le Merlan," and I suddenly it struck me where Pavie had taken refuge.

I didn't hesitate for a moment. I didn't even signal. A car honked behind me. Loubet can wait, I told myself. That was the only place she could have gone in the car. To Arno's. To that shack where she'd once been happy. Right under Saadna's nose. I should have thought of it earlier, goddammit! What a fool I was.

I cut through Saint-Jérôme, with its little villas and its large population of Armenians. I passed the school of science and technology, and came to Traverse des Pâquerettes. Just above Saadna's scrap yard. Back where I was the other day.

I parked on Rue de Muret, by the Canal de Provence, and

walked to Arno's place. I heard Saadna's transistor blaring, down in the scrap yard. The air stank of rubber. Black smoke rose into the sky. The asshole still burned his old tires. There'd been petitions, but he didn't give a damn. As if even the cops were scared of him.

Arno's door was open. A quick glance inside confirmed my fears. The sheets and blankets were rumpled. There were syringes on the floor. Good God, why hadn't she gone back to the Panier? To Randy's family. They'd have been able to . . .

I went down to the scrap yard, as unobtrusively as I could. No sign of Pavie. I saw Saadna stuffing more tires into oil drums and setting fire to them. Then he disappeared. I moved forward, hoping to surprise him. I heard the click of his switch-blade. Behind my back.

"I got you, asshole!" he said, pricking my back with the blade. "Now move."

We went into his place. He took his hunting rifle and inserted a cartridge. Then he closed the door.

"Where is she?"

"Who?"

"Pavie."

He burst out laughing. His breath stank of alcohol.

"You wanted to fuck her too, did you? I'm not surprised. You give yourself airs, but you're nothing special. Just like that other guy. Your pal Serge. Except he wouldn't have harmed Pavie. Chicks weren't his bag. He preferred boys and their cute little asses."

"I'm going to smash your face, Saadna."

"Big shot, eh?" he said, waving his rifle. "Sit down."

He indicated a dirty old brown leather armchair. Sinking into it was like sinking in shit. It was almost on the ground. Once you were in it you couldn't move.

"You didn't know that, did you, Montale? That your pal Serge was the worst kind of faggot there is. The kind that likes fucking little boys."

He pulled up a chair and sat down, some distance from me, next to a Formica table. On the table were a bottle of red wine and a sticky glass, which he refilled.

"You're talking crap."

"No, I'm well informed. I know a lot of things. What did you think? That he'd been thrown out of the district because you were hanging out together? The cop and the priest? Like hell he was!" He laughed, showing his black teeth. "There were complaints. The parents of little José Esparagas, for example."

I couldn't believe it. José Esparagas was a scrawny kid, the only child of a single mother. He had a really hard time of it at school. From all sides. He was beaten up regularly. In particular, he was bullied into coughing up money. A hundred francs here, a hundred francs there. The day he was asked to bring a thousand francs, he decided he couldn't take it anymore and tried to kill himself. I collared the two kids who'd been extorting money from him. Serge intervened and managed to get José transferred to another school. For several months, Serge went to his house, to help José catch up on the school work he'd missed. José got his high school diploma.

"That's just gossip. It still doesn't tell me where Pavie is."

He poured himself a glass of red wine, and knocked it back in one.

"So it's true, you're after that little whore. You missed each other the other night. She got here right after you left. Bad luck, huh? But I was here. I'm always here. You need anything, I'm your man. Always ready to do a good turn. That's the way I am. I aim to please."

"Cut the crap."

"You're not going to believe this. She saw you run to Serge after they whacked him. But then the cops arrived and that freaked her out. So she took off in his car. She didn't know what to do. She drove around in circles. Then she came here. She was sure you'd come. You were bound to put two and two together.

I let her talk. I thought it was funny. It cracked me up to think she took you for some kind of Zorro. So I told her you'd just left." He laughed again. "I told her you'd run away like a rabbit when you saw this." He indicated the rifle. "And that you weren't likely to be back soon. You should have seen her face!

"She just stood there. Right there in front of me. Not proud like when she was with Arno. In those days, you could see her ass but you couldn't lay a hand on her. But now, after a minute or two, she was perfectly willing. Provided I could get her a fix. I aim to please, like I said. I just had to make a phone call. I've got plenty of dough. So if it was a fix she wanted . . . "

"Where is she?" I cried, anxiety rising inside me.

He drank another glass of wine.

"I only fucked her twice, you know. It was too expensive. But all the same it was worth it. Mind you, she was a little shopworn, our Pavie. Been putting it about too much, I guess . . . But nice tits and a sweet little ass. You'd have liked her, I think. You're just an old pervert, like me, I know. Hurrah for youth! I said to myself as I banged her."

He burst out laughing again. I could feel hatred rising in me, overwhelming me. I braced myself, ready to leap at the slightest opportunity.

"Don't move, Montale," he said. "You're just a pervert, like I said. I've got my eyes on you. If you so much as move your little toe, I'll shoot you. In the balls, preferably."

"Where is she?" I asked again, as calmly as I could.

"You're not going to believe this. The little idiot was so out of it, she had a fix that sent her sky high. Can you imagine? She must have been higher than she'd ever been in her fucking life! What an idiot. She had it all here. Bed and board. As many fixes as she liked, all on the house. And me to fuck her from time to time."

"It's you she couldn't bear, you fucking asshole. Even when someone's as high as a kite, they know who the real scumbags are. What did you do with her, Saadna? Answer me, dammit!"

He laughed. A nervous laugh this time. He refilled the glass with his cheap wine and knocked it back. He was staring through the window. Then he nodded in that direction. Smoke was rising, thick and black. I felt a lump in my throat.

"No," I said, weakly.

"What did you want me to do with her, huh? Bury her in the field? And bring her flowers every evening? She was nothing but a whore, your Pavie. Good for a fuck, nothing else. That's no kind of life, is it?"

I closed my eyes.

Pavie.

I screamed like a madman. Letting out all the rage that was in me. As if a red-hot iron had been plunged into my heart. And all the most horrible images I'd ever seen paraded before my eyes. Mass graves. Auschwitz. Hiroshima. Rwanda. Bosnia. A scream of death. The scream of all the fascisms in the world.

Enough to make you throw up.

Really.

I put my head down and jumped.

Saadna didn't know what hit him. I landed on him like a cyclone. The chair toppled over and he went down with it. The rifle fell out of his hands. I seized it by the barrel, raised it, and hit him as hard as I could on the knee.

I heard it crack. And that made me feel better.

Saadna didn't even cry out. He'd fainted.

# 16.

## IN WHICH THERE IS AN APPOINTMENT
## WITH THE COLD ASHES OF TRAGEDY

I woke Saadna with a pail of water.

"You bastard!" he yelled.

But he couldn't move an inch. I grabbed him by the neck and dragged him to the armchair. He leaned his back against one of the armrests. He stank of shit. He must have crapped himself. I picked up the rifle again, by the barrel, with both hands.

"Your bad leg, Saadna, that was nothing. I'm going to shoot you in the other knee. You'll never be able to walk again. I think I'll break your elbows too. You'll be no better than a worm. All you'll want is to die."

"I've got something for you."

"It's too late to make deals."

"Something I found, in Serge's car. When I took it apart."

"Tell me more."

"Will you stop hitting me?"

I couldn't have hit him again with as much violence and hate as I had before. I felt drained. As if I was one of the living dead. Nothing circulating through my body anymore. Just vomit where the blood should have been. My head was spinning.

"Tell me, and then we'll see."

Even my voice wasn't the same.

He looked at me. He must have thought he'd hooked me. To him, life was just a succession of plots and schemes. He smiled.

"There was a notebook stuck to the spare tire. In a plastic bag. This is something big, I tell you. A lot of things written in it. I didn't read all of it. Because I don't give a shit about all that Arab stuff. Islam, that kind of thing. They can all croak, as far as I'm concerned! But there are lists of names and addresses. From all over the projects. Like some kind of network, you know. False papers. Money. Drugs. Arms. I'll give you the book and you can split. Forget everything. Forget me. No need for us to have anything to do with each other ever again."

I'd been right to think there was a notebook. I had no idea what Serge had been mixed up in, but I knew him, he was conscientious. When we worked together, he noted everything down, every day.

"Think you're clever, do you, Saadna? I just have to hit you and you'll tell me where that fucking notebook is."

"I don't think you can, Montale. You may think you've got balls because you're full of hate. But in cold blood, you're not worth shit. Go on, hit me . . . "

He offered me his leg. I avoided looking him in the eyes.

"Where is this notebook?"

"Swear. On your parents."

"What makes you think I'm interested in your notebooks anyway?"

"Man, it's like a fucking phone book. Just read it, and then you can do what you like with it. You can eat it, you can sell it. I tell you, with that book, you've got them all. Just take one page, and you can make them pay!"

"Where is it? I swear I'll split if you tell me."

"You got a smoke?"

I lit a cigarette and stuck it between his lips. He looked at me. Obviously, he wasn't sure he could trust me completely. And I wasn't sure I didn't want to throw him in one of the oil drums, along with the tires.

"Well?"

"The drawer in the table."

It was a thick exercise book. The pages were covered with Serge's fine, cramped handwriting. I read at random: "The militants make thorough use of the welfare field, which has been neglected by the local authorities. They claim to be pursuing humanitarian aims, such as leisure activities, educational support, the teaching of Arabic . . . " Farther on, I read: "The aims of these agitators far exceed the fight against drug addiction. They are preparing for urban guerilla warfare."

"Do you like it?"

The second half was like an address book. The first page opened with this comment: "North Marseilles is full of young North Africans ready to be suicide bombers. Those who manipulate them are known to the police (see Abdelkader). Above them there are others. Many others."

For La Bigotte, just one name. Redouane. What Serge had written confirmed what Mourad had told me, though there were more details. All the things Redouane hadn't told his brother.

Redouane's two sponsors in North Marseilles were Nacer and someone named Hamel. Both, according to their files, had been militants since 1993. Before that, they had been stewards for the Islamic Youth Movement. Hamel had even been responsible for security at the big pro-Bosnian demonstration at La Plaine-Saint-Denis.

An extract from an article in the *Nouvel Observateur* gave an account of this demonstration. "Among those on the platform were the cultural attaché of the Iranian Embassy and an Algerian named Rachid Ben Aïssa, an intellectual with links to the Algerian Brotherhood in France. Rachid Ben Aïssa is not a minor player. He organized many conferences, during the 1980s, at the Iranian Islamic Center on Rue Jean-Bart, in Paris. It was there that most of the members of the terrorist network led by Fouad Ali Salah, the brains behind the bomb attacks in Paris in 1986, were recruited."

Before leaving for Sarajevo, as part of the Seventh International Brigade of Muslim Brothers, Redouane had followed a number of commando survival courses at the foot of Mount Ventoux.

A certain Rachid (Rachid Ben Aïssa? Serge wondered) was responsible for organizing these courses, including the provision of accommodation in self-catering cottages in the village of Bédoin, at the foot of Mount Ventoux. "Once someone has followed these courses," Serge had written, "there is no turning back. Those who try to pull out are threatened. They are told about the fate reserved for traitors in Algeria and are shown photographs. Photographs of men who have been bled like sheep." According to Serge, these "commando courses" were held at the rate of one every three months.

"The man who went with these young recruits to Bosnia was named Arroum. This Arroum had powerful patrons. As a member of the Lowafac Foundation, whose main office is in Zagreb, he was accredited, on every one of his missions to Bosnia, by the United Nations High Commission for Refugees." In the margin, Serge had written: "Arroum arrested March 28."

Redouane's file ended with these words: "Since his return, has only taken part in operations against heroin dealers. Apparently not yet considered reliable enough. But should be watched. Very much under the wing of Nacer and Hamel, both hard liners. May become dangerous."

"What was Serge working on? Some kind of investigative article?"

Saadna gave a nervous laugh. "He'd gone over to the other side. Not exactly voluntarily, but . . . He was working for the cops. Security branch."

"Serge?"

"When he was dismissed, the security branch pounced. They had a file full of testimonies from parents. Complaints. About the kids he'd been fucking."

The bastards, I thought. That sounded like their methods. To infiltrate a network, of whatever kind, they'd stop at nothing. They were good at using people. Mobsters who'd turned state's evidence. Algerians who were in France illegally . . .

"What happened?"

"Well, I don't know if it was true, about the kids. What I do know is that the morning they showed up at his place, waving their file, he was in bed with another faggot. A boy, still in his teens. Maybe even a minor. Imagine that, Montale! It's disgusting! He could have gone down for it. Mind you, if he'd been sent to Les Baumettes, he'd have gotten himself laid every night."

I stood up and picked up the rifle again. "Another remark like that, and I'll break the other knee."

"I'm just saying," he said, with a shrug. "It doesn't exactly matter now."

"Precisely. How do you know all this, anyway?"

"Four Eyes put me in the picture. We get along well, him and me."

"Was it you who told him Serge was staying here?"

He nodded. "Not everyone was happy about Serge stirring the shit. Four Eyes isn't interested in going after the guys in that notebook. They're just doing the housekeeping, he says. Clearing out the dealers, that kind of thing. Helps to keeps the statistics down. It's to his advantage. And when the fundamentalists are in power in Algeria, he says, we'll be able to put all the Arabs in a boat and send them back to their country."

"What does that asshole know about it?"

"It's what he says. He's not completely wrong, if you ask me."

I remembered the National Front leaflet in Redouane's Koran. "I see."

"Word was out there was a squealer in the projects. Four Eyes asked me to check it out. Well, you can imagine, that wasn't too hard. He was right here . . . " He laughed.

Four Eyes had really taken me for an idiot, back there at the station house. What must have bothered him was seeing me at La Bigotte. That wasn't part of the plan. There might be something behind it, he must have thought. Serge and I might still be a team. Just like the old days.

All at once, I realized why they'd kept so quiet about Serge's death. A guy working for the security branch who gets whacked, and there's no publicity. It doesn't make any waves.

"Have you told anyone else about the notebook?"

"It's starting to hurt," he said.

I crouched beside him. Not too close. Not because I was afraid he'd jump me, but because of the foul smell coming off him. He closed his eyes. It must indeed be starting to hurt. I lightly pressed the butt of the rifle against his broken knee. The pain made him open his eyes. There was hatred in them.

"Who did you talk to, scumbag?"

"All I did was tell Four Eyes where he could hit the jackpot. A guy named Boudjema Ressaf. Expelled from France in 1992. A GIA militant. Serge spotted him in Le Plan d'Aou. It's down there in the book. Where he's staying, everything."

"Did you tell him about the notebook?"

He lowered his head. "Yes, I told him."

"He's got you by the balls, right?"

"Yeah."

"When did you call him?"

"Two hours ago."

I stood up. "I'm surprised you're still alive."

"What do you mean?"

"The reason Four Eyes isn't going after the fundamentalists, you asshole, is because he's in bed with them. You told me that yourself."

"You think so?" he spluttered, trembling with fear now. "Give me a drink, please."

Fuck, I told myself, he's going to shit himself again. I filled the glass with his foul wine and handed it to him. I had to get out of there as soon as possible.

I looked at Saadna. I wasn't even sure you could still class him as a human being. Slumped against the armchair, bent double, he looked like a boil full of pus. Saadna knew what my look meant.

"Look, Montale, you . . . You're not going to kill me, are you?"

We both heard the noise at the same time. The noise of a bottle breaking. Flames rose from a heap of old metal, on the right. Another bottle exploded. The bastards were throwing Molotov cocktails! I crouched down and walked in that position to the window, with the rifle in my hand.

I saw Redouane running toward the bottom end of the scrap yard. Nacer couldn't be very far. Was the other guy, Hamel, here too? I really had no desire to die in this rat hole.

Nor did Saadna. He crawled toward me, groaning. He was sweating profusely. He stank of death. Shit and death. The two things his life had consisted of.

"Save me, Montale," he said, sniveling now. "I have lots of money."

All at once, the scrap yard went up in flames. I saw Nacer coming. I made a dash for the front door and cocked the rifle. But Nacer didn't bother to come in. He hurled one of those damn bottles through the open window. It fell and smashed at the far end of the room. Where Saadna had been sitting a few minutes earlier.

"Montale," he cried. "Don't leave me."

His shack was on fire now. I ran to the table, grabbed Serge's notebook, and slipped it inside my shirt. I went back to the door and opened it slowly. But I wasn't expecting anyone to shoot at me. Redouane and Nacer must be some distance away by now.

The heat caught me by the throat. There was a terrible burning stench in the air. Something exploded. Gasoline, I guessed. The whole place was about to blow.

Saadna had dragged himself as far as the door. Like a worm. He caught hold of my ankle and squeezed it in both hands, with a strength I wouldn't have suspected. His eyes seemed to be popping out of his head.

He was going crazy with fear.

"Get me out of here!"

"You're going to die!" I grabbed him by his hair and forced him to raise his head. "Look! You see, this is what hell is like. Hell for scum like you! Your whole stinking life is coming to eat you up. Think of Pavie."

I struck him hard on the wrist with the rifle butt. He screamed and let go of my ankle. I jumped away and went around the outside of the house. The fire was spreading. I threw the rifle into the flames, as far as I could, and started running, without stopping.

I got to the canal just in time to see Saadna's dump disappear in the flames. I thought I heard him scream. But it was only in my head that he was screaming. Like in a plane when you've just landed and your ears are still ringing. Saadna was burning, and my ear drums were bursting with his death. But I didn't feel any remorse.

There was another explosion. A burning pine crashed down on Arno's shack. It's over now, I told myself. Soon there'll be nothing left. It'll all be razed to the ground. In a year or two, there'll be Provençal housing developments on the site of what was once Saadna's scrap yard. To everyone's great joy. Young middle managers, happy with their lot, will settle there, eager to give their wives children. And they'll live happy lives, long after the year 2000. On the cold ashes of Arno and Pavie's tragedy.

I took off as the first fire sirens were sounding.

# 17.

## IN WHICH, SOMETIMES, THE LESS YOU EXPLAIN, THE BETTER

L oubet bawled me out, of course. He was furious. He'd spent hours waiting for me. To make matters worse, Cûc had told him he couldn't see Mathias because she didn't know where he was anymore.

"Is she putting me on, or what?"

As I wasn't sure if it was a question or a statement, I didn't say anything.

"Since you're so intimate with the lady," he continued, "advise her to find her son. As soon as possible."

From where I was, I could see a thick column of black smoke rising into the sky from Saadna's scrap yard. Fire engines were appearing from all sides. I'd driven just far enough not to get caught in the middle. At the place known as Four de Buze, I'd stopped at a phone booth.

"Give me one more hour," I said.

"What!"

"Just one more hour."

He bawled me out again. He was right, but it was getting tiresome. I waited. Without listening. Without saying a word.

"Are you still there, Montale?"

"Can you do me a favor? Call me in fifteen minutes. At Pertin's station house."

"Wait. Aren't you going to explain?"

"No point. Call me. And don't worry, I'll be along to see you. Alive, I mean."

And I hung up.

Sometimes, the less you explain, the better. Right now, I felt like a wooden horse in a carousel. I was going around in circles. Not overtaking anyone. Always coming back to the same point. To the world's corruption.

I called Gélou.

"Room 406, please."

"Hold on." A pause. "I'm sorry, Monsieur and Madame Narni have gone out. Their key's here."

"Is there any message for me? Montale. Fabio Montale."

"No, monsieur. Would you like to leave one?"

"Just say I'll call back in two hours, two and a half hours."

Narni. Good, I told myself. I hadn't wasted the whole morning. I knew Alexandre's name. A lot of good it did me!

The first thing I saw when I entered the station house was a National Front poster for the police union elections. As if Solidarité Police wasn't enough.

"What we are witnessing in the field of law enforcement," said a leaflet pinned to the poster, "is a situation in which the majority of senior officers are afraid to give orders and force us to avoid confrontation as much as possible.

"This situation has led to a woefully inadequate police force and a massive increase in the number of wounded officers, whereas the criminals are free to select their targets at will.

"We must counter the nihilistic tendencies prevalent in our force. It should be the other side that feels afraid, not us. Especially as our adversaries at demonstrations are not honest members of society but scum whose main purpose is to attack the police. Give us the means to be the butchers rather than the meat."

Clearly, if you really wanted to know what was going on, a visit to the station house was essential. It was better than the eight o'clock news on TV!

"It's just come out," Babar said, behind my back.

"Roll on retirement, eh?"

"You said it. To me, that kind of thing stinks."

"Is he here?"

"Yes. But it's like he had piles. He can't keep still on his chair."

I went in without knocking.

"Don't mind me," Pertin grunted.

I didn't. I sat down and lit a cigarette. He walked around his desk, placed his two hands flat on it, and thrust his red face in my direction.

"To what do I owe this honor?"

"I did something stupid, Pertin. The other day. You know, when they killed Serge. I've thought it over, and I'd like to sign my statement."

He straightened up, surprised. "Don't jerk me around, Montale. Nobody's interested in some faggot thing. We've got enough on our hands with the Arabs and the niggers. You don't know what it's like! These kids, maybe they give the judges blow jobs. You collar one of them in the morning, by the evening he's already walked . . . So get out of here!"

"But that's just it. You see, I've been thinking maybe this wasn't some faggot thing that ended badly. Maybe Serge's death was an Arab thing after all. What do you think?"

"What did Serge have to do with the Arabs?" he asked, innocently.

"You should know, Pertin. Nothing escapes you. You told me you were really well informed, didn't you?"

"Spit it out, Montale."

"OK. Let me explain."

He sat down, folded his arms, and waited. I'd have liked to know what he was thinking about behind his Ray-Bans. But I was ready to bet at least a hundred francs he was dying to punch me in the face.

I told him a story I only half believed. But it was plausible. Serge had been "enlisted" by the security branch. Because he was a pedophile. At least that was what they'd managed to pin on him.

"Interesting."

"It gets better, Pertin. You found out the security branch had sent an informer into the projects. To defuse potential networks like Kelkal's. That was no laughing matter, with bombs going off in Paris and Lyons. But you didn't find out the informer was Serge until a few months ago. When Serge slipped out of sight, and the security branch lost track of him. Nobody knew where he was staying. I can imagine the panic."

I paused. To clear my mind a little. My thoughts were coming together. Whether Serge was gay or not, the kids in the projects were his life. He couldn't have changed like that, overnight. Become an informer. Fingered the kids. All the potential Kelkals. Passed the list to the cops. Who, when the time was right—and in the full glare of media attention, naturally—would simply have to pick everyone up in dawn raids.

There had already been some good hauls. In Paris, and in the suburbs of Lyons. There'd been a few arrests in Marseilles too. Around the harbor. And on Cours Belzunce. But nothing really serious yet. The networks in North Marseilles that supported the terrorists hadn't been touched. They were being saved till last, I supposed.

I was sure Serge would never have done such a thing. Even to avoid the shame of a trial or prison. Every name he gave to the police would become a target. And he knew perfectly well it always ended the same way. The big shots, the leaders, the people who gave the orders, always got away scot-free, while the small fry got life. Or a bullet in the head.

You could cut the silence with a knife. A thick silence. Like something decayed. Pertin hadn't flinched. He must be thinking hard. I'd heard the telephone ringing several times, but no call had come through to his office. Loubet had forgotten about me. Or else he really was angry with me. Having gotten this far, all I could do was continue.

"Shall I go on?" I asked.

"Sure, I'm fascinated."

So I resumed my story. I sensed that what I was saying was increasingly likely, and I clung to that.

Serge had gotten it into his head to do something nobody had yet attempted. To go to the young men he'd identified and talk to them. To meet with their parents, their brothers and sisters. And at the same time, to pass the message on to the other kids. So that they would get involved. So that everyone in the projects should get involved. Like Anselme. The *chourmo* principle.

That was the way Serge had worked for years, the only way he knew. It was a good method. An effective method. It had produced results. The young guys who were working for the fundamentalists were of course the very same delinquents he'd been dealing with for years. But hardened by prison, more aggressive. And given a liberating fix of the Koran. Fanatics. Like their unemployed brothers on the outskirts of Algiers.

Everyone in the projects knew Serge. They listened to him, trusted him. Anselme had said it. "He was an OK guy." He had the best arguments, because he'd patiently analyzed the way young Arabs were recruited. The war against the dealers, for example. They'd been chased out of Le Plan d'Aou and La Savine. Everyone had approved. City hall, the newspapers. "Such good young people . . . " It was like they were talking about "noble savages." But the heroin trade hadn't stopped, it had simply upped sticks and moved to the center of town. It had been restructured. And in the projects, nothing had changed. They still dealt in grass. A little prayer, a little smoke, Allah wouldn't mind.

The dealers were now being controlled by the very people who'd urged the young people to fight them. In Serge's notebook, I'd read that one of the prayer halls—the back room of a store selling fabrics, near Place d'Aix—was used as a meeting place by the dealers who supplied North Marseilles. The owner of the store was none other than Nacer's uncle. A man called Abdelkader.

"Where are you going with this?" Pertin asked at last.

"I'll tell you," I said, with a smile. He was finally rising to the bait. "Firstly, the security branch asked you to track down Serge. But you'd already done that. Thanks to Saadna. Secondly, they wanted you to find a way to stop him screwing things up. In other words, to put a bullet in him. Thirdly, you're taking me for an idiot, pretending to listen to my story. You already know it by heart. Or almost. Because you've been in on it from the start, you and a few young mobsters who've turned into Islamists. Like Nacer and Hamel. I guess you forgot to hand those two over to the judges. Maybe you're the one they're giving blow jobs to!"

"Say that again, and I'll smash your face."

"You know something, Pertin? For once, you could have said I'm not as stupid as I look."

He stood up, rubbing his hands.

"Carli!" he yelled.

I was going to get it in the neck. Carli came in, and gave me a nasty look.

"Yeah."

"Nice day, isn't it? How's about getting some fresh air? Over at the quarry. We have a guest here. The king of assholes in person."

The phone rang in the station house. Then on Pertin's extension.

"Yeah?" Pertin said. "Who is this?" A pause. "Hi. Yeah, fine." He looked at me, then at Carli. He didn't so much sit as sink onto his chair. "Yeah, yeah. I'll put him on. It's for you," he said, coldly, holding out the receiver.

The first thing Loubet asked me was what I was doing with that jerk. "I'd almost finished, old buddy," I replied. "What? Yes . . . Let's say . . . Wait. Have we finished?" I asked Pertin sarcastically. "Or are we still planning to visit the quarry?" He didn't answer. "Yeah, half an hour. OK." I was about to hang up, but I decided to add something. To impress Pertin. "Yeah,

yeah, a guy named Boudjema Ressaf. And while you're about it, see what you have on a man named Narni. Alexandre Narni. OK. I'll tell you all about it, Loubet."

He told me I was a bullshit artist, and immediately hung up. He was probably right.

I stood up. I felt great. I was smiling again. I wasn't going to sully myself spitting in the face of that scumbag.

"Leave us alone," Pertin roared at Carli.

"What gives with the performance?" he yelled when Carli had gone out.

"What performance? I don't hear anyone laughing."

"Stop being a smartass, Montale. It doesn't suit you. And Loubet won't stop a bullet for you."

"You wouldn't do that, would you, Pertin? Even sending your people to set fire to Saadna's place this morning wasn't such a good idea, if you ask me. Especially as the two kids—you know the ones I mean, don't you?—didn't even take the time to check if Saadna had burned or not. Not that I weep any tears over him."

This time, he reacted. It was like fishing for tuna. They always weakened in the end. You had to hold out till they did, then strike.

"What do you know about that?"

"I was there, you see. He called you to tip you off about Boudjema Ressaf. He thought it was a really hot tip, and you'd be eternally grateful. I can even tell you who you called immediately afterwards."

"Oh yeah?"

I was bluffing, but only just. I took out the notebook.

"It's all written down here. You just have to read it." I opened the notebook at random. "Abdelkader. Nacer's uncle. It's a mine of information, this notebook. I'd be willing to bet he owns a black BMW, this Abdelkader. Like the one that showed up at La Bigotte the other afternoon. They were so sure they wouldn't have any trouble, they used Abdelkader's car. As if they were going dancing! Except that—"

Laughing nervously, Pertin tore the notebook out of my hands and leafed through it. All the pages were blank. I'd stashed the original in my car and had bought a new one before coming in. There was no reason to do that. It was just the icing on the cake.

"You fucking son of a bitch!"

"Sorry, you lost. Loubet has the original." He threw the notebook on the desk. "Let me tell you this, Pertin. It really doesn't look good, you and your pals turning a blind eye to scumbags who manipulate kids into tearing France apart."

"What are you talking about now?"

"That I've never had any sympathy for Saddam Hussein. I prefer Arabs without beards, and Marseilles without you. Bye, Four Eyes. Keep the notebook to write your memoirs."

As I went out, I tore down the National Front poster and leaflet, rolled them into a big ball and aimed it at the trash can by the entrance. It went straight in.

Babar whistled in admiration.

# 18.

## IN WHICH YOU CAN'T FORCE THE TRUTH OUT INTO THE OPEN

I managed to persuade Loubet to meet with me at L'Oursin, near the Vieux-Port. One of the best places for oysters, sea urchins, clams and sea squirts. That's what I ordered when I went in. With a bottle of Cassis. A white wine, from Font-creuse. Not surprisingly, Loubet was in a bad mood.

"I don't care what order you tell it in," he said. "But I need to know everything you know. All right? I like you, Montale, but you're really starting to be a pain in the butt."

"Can I ask just one question?"

He smiled.

"Did you really think I'd killed Fabre?"

"No. Not you, and not her."

"Why did you do that number on me, then?"

"In her case, to scare her. In yours, to stop you jerking me around."

"Have you made any progress?"

"You said one question. That's the third. So now I'm listening. First of all, I want to know what you were doing with Pertin."

"All right, let me start with that. But it has nothing to do with Guitou, Hocine Draoui, Fabre, or any of that."

So I told him the whole story. From the time I arrived in La Bigotte—without mentioning the real reason I was there—and witnessed Serge's murder, down to the death of Saadna. And my little conversation with Pertin.

"OK," I said. "So Serge was gay, maybe even a pedophile, who knows? I don't give a damn. He was an honest guy. Non-violent. He loved people. With the innocence of a true believer. He had a real faith in mankind, without God's help. The kids were his life."

"Yeah, and maybe he loved them a just little too much, eh?"

"What of it? Even if it was true. Maybe he made them happy."

My attitude toward Serge was the same as with all the people I loved. I trusted them. I could even accept it when they did things I didn't understand. The only thing I couldn't tolerate was racism. I'd spent my childhood watching my father suffer from not being treated like a human being, but like a dog. A harbor dog. And he was only an Italian! I must admit, I don't have a whole lot of friends.

I had no desire to continue this conversation about Serge. In spite of everything, it made me uncomfortable. I wanted to forget that episode. Remember only the pain. Serge. Pavie. Arno. Another episode of my life, to be added to the already long column of losses.

Loubet was leafing through Serge's notebook. With him, there was a good chance that all these things that had been so meticulously written down wouldn't be forgotten at the back of a drawer. At least, the most important parts. Above all, there was a good chance Pertin wouldn't get away scot-free. He wasn't directly responsible for Serge's death. Or Pavie's. But he was the symbol of a police force I hated. A police force in which political ideas and personal ambitions were placed above the values of the Republic, like justice and equality. There were lots of guys like Pertin. Guys who'd stop at nothing. If the suburbs exploded one day, it would be down to them. Their contempt. Their xenophobia. Their hate. And all their shabby little schemes to become, one day, "a great cop."

Pertin I knew. For me, he wasn't just an anonymous cop. He had a face. He was fat and red, with Ray-Bans hiding his piggy eyes and an arrogant smile. I wanted to bring him down. But I didn't have any illusions.

"There is one way I can safeguard this investigation," Loubet said, thinking hard. "By linking it to the other one."

"But there isn't any link."

"I know. Unless we can pin Hocine Draoui's death on the FIS or the GIA. I make a beeline for this Abdelkader, and see what comes out. See if I can implicate Pertin."

"A bit unlikely, isn't it?"

"Let me tell you something, Montale. You take what you can get. You can't force the truth out into the open. Not always. If I can get to the truth in one case, that's good enough for me."

"But what about the others? The men who killed Draoui and Guitou?"

"Don't worry. I'll get them, trust me. However long it takes. Shall we have another dozen oysters and sea urchins?"

"Fine by me."

"Did you sleep with her?"

If anyone else had asked me that question, I wouldn't have answered. Or if he'd asked me in other circumstances. But right now, it was a question of trust. Of friendship.

"No."

"Do you regret it?"

"You bet!"

"What stopped you?"

Loubet was a great interrogator. He always knew exactly the question to ask to get a suspect to open up.

"Cûc is a man eater. Because the only man she ever loved, the first one and the only one, was Mathias' father, and she couldn't keep him. He died. And you know, Loubet, when you've lost something once, even if it's vanished entirely, you keep losing it over and over. I know. I've never been able to hold on to the women I've loved."

"Have you eaten many women?" he asked, smiling.

"Too many, I suppose. I'm going to tell you a secret, and then we can get back to the matter at hand. I can't seem to grasp what it is I'm searching for, when it comes to women.

And as long as I don't know what I need, all I do is hurt them. One after the other. Are you married?"

"Yes. With two children. Both boys."

"Are you happy?"

"Yes, I think so. I don't often have time to ask myself the question. Or I don't take the time. Maybe because it's the kind of question you don't ask."

I finished my glass and lit a cigarette. I looked at Loubet. He was a solid, dependable man. His job was no bed of roses, but he exuded confidence. A man who knew what he was doing. The opposite of me.

"Would you have slept with her?"

"No," he said, laughing. "But I have to admit there is something irresistible about her."

"Draoui couldn't resist Cûc. She needed him. The same way she needed Fabre. And when she needs a man, she knows how to get him."

"Did she need you?"

"She wanted Draoui to help her save Fabre," I said, without answering his question.

Because it hurt me to say yes. Yes, she'd tried to play with me, as she had with Hocine Draoui. Yes, she knew she could use me. In my head, I preferred to continue thinking that she'd desired me, without any ulterior motive. It didn't hurt my male pride so much. I wasn't a Latin for nothing!

"Do you think she loved her husband?" he asked, without reacting to the way I'd evaded his earlier question.

"You know, I really couldn't tell you if she loved him or not. She says she didn't. But she owes him everything she is today. He gave her a name. He helped her to raise Mathias. Thanks to him, she had a comfortable life. Not all Vietnamese refugees have been as lucky."

"You said she wanted to save Fabre. Save him from what?"

"Wait. Cûc is also a woman with an urge to create, to build, to win, to succeed. Like a lot of people who've lost everything.

Jews, Armenians, *pieds noirs*, they're all the same. They aren't immigrants. Do you know what I mean? An immigrant hasn't lost anything, because he didn't have anything in the place where he was living before. His only motivation is to survive, maybe just a little better than before.

"Cûc wanted to start a fashion business. Fabre got her the money. A lot of money. It gave her the means to establish her label in a very short time, not only in France but all over Europe. She had enough talent to convince the people putting up the money. Except that they would have put up the money for anything, or almost. The important thing was for the money to find a home. A safe home."

"You mean it was dirty money?"

"Cûc's business is a limited company. The shareholders are Swiss, Panamanian and Costa Rican banks. She's the director but she doesn't own anything, not even her own brand name. She didn't realize what was going on at first. Until the day some big orders arrived, and her husband told her there was no point in meeting them. As long as she invoiced them. And let the money be paid into another company account rather than her current account. A Swiss account for which she can't even sign. You see what I'm saying?"

"If I've got this right, we're talking about the Mafia?"

"It's a word that scares people so much, no one in France even dares to mention it. What makes the world go round, Loubet? Money. And who has the most money? The Mafia. You know how much the worldwide drug traffic is worth? 1,650 billion francs a year. That's more than oil! Almost double."

My journalist friend, Babette, had explained the whole thing to me one day. She knew a lot about the Mafia. She'd been in Italy for the last few months, working with a Roman journalist on a book about the Mafia in France. It was dynamite, she'd said.

According to her, within two years France would be in the

same boat as Italy. Black money, the kind that, by definition, has no need to state where it comes from, had become the commodity most popular among politicians. Things had reached such a point, Babette had recently told me over the phone, that we had moved imperceptibly from a Mafia-style political society to a Mafia-style system.

"So Fabre had Mafia connections?"

"Who was Fabre? You've been looking into that, haven't you?"

"An architect, talented, left-wing sympathies, successful."

"Extremely successful, you mean. Cûc told me his practice has been strongly tipped for the Euroméditerranée port development."

Euroméditerranée was supposed to be the "new order" for Marseilles. A way for it to return to the international stage, through its port. I had my doubts. The Brussels technocrats who'd concocted the project were hardly likely to have the future of Marseilles at heart. They were only interested in regulating port activity. In changing the face of the Mediterranean between Genoa and Barcelona. But in Europe as a whole, the ports of the future were already Antwerp and Rotterdam.

We were being tricked, as always. The only future being mapped out for Marseilles was to be the leading port for fruit in the Mediterranean. And for international cruises. That's what the current project was basically looking toward. A huge construction site was rising in the eastern harbor basin, an area of half a square mile. A business park, an international communications center, a teleport, a tourism college . . . a godsend to the construction industry.

"Lots of money for Fabre! A whole different heap of shit than Serge and the fundamentalists."

"Not really. It may be different, but the stink is the same. Let me tell you, in Serge's papers, I found some documents from the Federation of Algerian Intellectuals. You told me Draoui was a member. According to them, Algeria has gotten into the same Mafia-style political system. The war the Islamists are waging on the current government isn't a holy war. It's just a struggle for a share of the cake. That's why Boudiaf was murdered. Because he was the only one to come out and say it."

"Here," he said, refilling our glasses. "We need this."

"It's the same in Russia right now. Not much hope there either. It'll be the death of us all." I raised my glass. "Cheers."

We remained silent for a moment, holding our glasses and thinking our thoughts. The second helping of seafood came as a relief.

"You're a strange guy, Montale. To me, you're like an hourglass. When the sand has gone down completely, there's always someone who comes and turns it over. Cûc must have had quite an effect on you!"

I smiled. I liked that image of the hourglass. Time draining away. In that interval of time you lived your life. Until nobody came to turn the hourglass over. Because you'd lost the taste for living.

"It wasn't Cûc who turned the hourglass over, as you put it. It was death. The closeness of death. The fact that it's all around us. I still believe in life."

This conversation was taking me farther than I wanted to go. To places I usually feared to tread. As time went on, I found fewer and fewer reasons to carry on living. So I preferred to keep to the simple things. Like eating and drinking. Going fishing.

"To get back to Cûc," I went on, "all she did was start the ball rolling. By urging Fabre to break with his Mafia friends. She'd started looking into his business affairs. The contracts. The people he met. What she found made her panic. She felt threatened. All the things she'd built up were at risk. The goals she'd set herself, one night, in a shabby two-room apartment in Le Havre. Her life itself, and her life was Mathias. The fruit of her lost love. A love destroyed by violence, hatred, war.

"She begged Fabre to stop. She wanted the three of them to

go to Vietnam and start a new life. But Fabre was tied hand and foot. The classic bind. Like those politicians who take kickbacks to climb the ladder and think that once they get to the top, they'll have so much money they'll be able to make a clean sweep. Break with their old habits, their dubious connections. But they can't. It's impossible. Once you accept that first envelope, you're done for. Or even a tie as a gift.

"Fabre couldn't draw a line under all that. So long, guys, thanks for everything. He didn't want to go under. To end up in prison, the way others have lately. It made him bad-tempered. He started drinking. He became impossible to live with. He'd come home later and later at night. Sometimes he wouldn't come home at all. That was the only reason Cûc seduced Hocine Draoui. To humiliate her husband. To tell him she didn't love him. That she was going to leave him. It was a desperate kind of blackmail. A cry for love. Because deep down, I think she loved him.

"But Fabre didn't understand that. Or didn't want to. Anyway, he couldn't bear it. Cûc was his whole life. He loved her more than anything, I think. Maybe she was the reason he'd done what he had. I don't know. We'll never know. What's certain is that he felt betrayed by her. And by Hocine Draoui . . . Especially as Draoui's work threatened the plans for the parking garage in the Vieille-Charité . . . It's Fabre's practice that has the job. I read that on the billboard outside the construction site."

"I know, I know, but . . . The thing is, Montale, the Vieille-Charité excavations are really nothing special. And being a friend of Hocine Draoui, Fabre must have known that. His sales pitch to the authorities in support of the parking garage project was perfectly straightforward. It didn't give anything away to the archeologists. But Draoui had no great interest in the site. I read his speech at the 1990 conference. The most exciting site is the one on Place Jules Verne. The excavations there date back six hundred years before Christ. They may even unearth the landing stage of the port of Liguria. The one where Protis landed. I'd bet my bottom dollar we'll never see a parking garage there . . . As far as I can see, Draoui and Fabre really respected each other. Which explains why Fabre, as soon as he found out that Draoui was in trouble, offered to let him stay in his house.

"From what I've been able to find out about him," he went on, "Fabre was a cultivated man. He loved his city. His heritage. The Mediterranean. I'm sure the two of them had a lot in common. After they met in '90, they started writing to each other frequently. I read a few of Draoui's letters to Fabre. They're fascinating. I'm sure they'd interest you."

"This story doesn't make sense," I said, not knowing what else to say. I guessed where he was going with this, and I knew I'd be caught out. I couldn't keep playing the idiot. I couldn't keep quiet forever about what I knew.

"Yes, a beautiful friendship," he resumed, in a lighter tone. "Which goes wrong. The kind of thing you read about in the papers every day. The friend who sleeps with the wife. The deceived husband who takes his revenge."

I thought about that for a moment. "But it doesn't tally with what you know about Fabre, is that what you're thinking?"

"Especially as the deceived husband gets killed himself soon afterwards. She didn't kill him. Neither did you. He was killed by hitmen. So was Draoui. And so was Guitou, who was unlucky enough to find himself in the wrong place at the wrong time."

"So you think there was another motive."

"Yes. Draoui's death had nothing to do with the fact that he'd slept with Cûc. It's more serious than that."

"So serious that two hitmen came all the way from Toulon just to kill Hocine Draoui."

Dammit, I had to tell him in the end!

He didn't blink. He looked straight at me. I had the strange feeling that he already knew what I'd just told him. The number of hitmen. Where they came from. But how could he have known?

"Ah. How do you know they came from Toulon?"

"They tailed me the first day, Loubet. They were looking for the girl. The one who was in bed with Guitou. Her name is Naïma. I knew that, and—"

"That's why you went to La Bigotte."

"That's right."

The look on his face was angrier than I'd ever known it to be. He stood up.

"A cognac," he called to the waiter.

And he headed for the toilet.

"Make that two," I said. "And another coffee."

# 19.

## IN WHICH ONCE DEATH HAS ARRIVED IT'S TOO LATE

L oubet came back from the toilet. He'd calmed down. "You're lucky you're in solid with me, Montale," he said. "Because I could happily have smashed your face!"

I spilled it all, everything I knew. Guitou, Naïma, the Hamoudi family. Plus all the things Cûc had told me the other night that I hadn't yet told him. In detail. Like a good pupil.

Naïma had gone to see Mathias, in Aix. On Monday evening. She'd already told him the gist of it the night before, on the phone. Mathias had called his mother. He was in a panic, and at the same time really angry. Cûc, of course, went straight to Aix. Naïma told them both what had happened on that tragic night.

Adrien Fabre had been in the house that night. She hadn't seen him, but she'd heard his name being called. After they'd killed Guitou. "Fuck, what was the kid doing here? Fabre!" a man had yelled. "Come here!" She remembered the words. She'd never be able to forget them.

She'd hidden in the shower.

She'd huddled there in terror. The only way she'd managed not to scream was by concentrating on the water dripping on her left knee. Seeing how far she could count before the next drop hit her knee.

An argument had started up between the men, outside the door of the apartment. Three voices, including Fabre's. "You killed him! You killed him!" he was crying. Almost in tears. The one who was clearly the ringleader called him an idiot. Then there was a dull sound, like a slap. After that, Fabre really started blubbering. One of the men, who had a strong Corsican accent, asked what they should do. The ringleader told him he had to get a van. With three or four removal men. To empty the place of the biggest things. The most important things. He'd take "the other guy" away before he drove them crazy.

Naïma didn't know how long she spent in the shower, counting the drops of water. The only thing she remembered was that at a particular moment everything fell silent. No more noise. Except the sound of her own sobbing. She was shivering. The cold had penetrated her skin. Not from the water. From the horror around her, the horror she could imagine.

She'd saved her own skin, that much she realized. But she stayed where she was, in the shower, her eyes closed. Motionless, unable to move. Sobbing, shivering, hoping the nightmare would end. Hoping Guitou would kiss her on the lips and she'd open her eyes and he'd say gently, "Come on, it's all over now." But the miracle didn't happen. Another drop of water hit her knee. That was real. Everything she'd just lived through was real. She stood up, with difficulty. She was resigned. She got dressed. The worst thing of all, she thought, was waiting for her outside the door. She would have to step over Guitou's body. She walked with her head turned away, in order not to see him. But she couldn't do it. This was *her* Guitou. She crouched by him, to take one last look at him. To say goodbye. She stopped shaking. She wasn't afraid anymore. Nothing else would ever matter now, she told herself, as she stood up and . . .

"And where are they now, she and Mathias?"

I assumed my most angelic expression. "That's the problem. I don't know."

"Are you bullshitting me, or what?"

"I swear."

He looked at me, with a wicked gleam in his eyes. "Maybe two or three days in the can would help."

"Quit kidding!"

"You've jerked me around long enough! And I don't want you under my feet anymore."

"Even if I pick up the tab?" I said, trying to look as dumb as I could.

Loubet burst out laughing. A good honest laugh. A man's laugh. A laugh that could stand up to all the meanness in the world.

"I got you scared, didn't I?"

"You sure did! Everyone would have come to see me. Like an animal in the zoo. Even Pertin would have brought me peanuts."

"We'll share the tab," he went on, in a more serious tone. "I'm going to put out a wanted poster, for Balducci and the other guy. Narni." He said the name slowly. Then he looked me in the eyes. "How did you manage to finger him?"

"Narni. Narni," I repeated. "But . . . "

A door had opened, and there was the worst, the most unthinkable thing of all. I felt a knot in my stomach. I retched.

"What is it, Montale? Are you sick?"

Hold on, I told myself. Hold on. Don't throw up all over the table. Keep it in. Concentrate. Breathe. Go on, breathe. Slowly. As if you were walking in the *calanques*. Breathe. There, that's better. Breathe again. Breathe out. That's good. Yeah, that's it . . . You see, you can digest anything in the end. Even pure shit.

I wiped my forehead, which was covered in sweat.

"It's all right, it's all right. Something in my stomach."

"You look scary."

I couldn't see Loubet anymore. All I could see in front of me was the other man. A handsome man with graying hair and a salt-and-pepper mustache. And a big gold signet ring on his right hand. Alexandre. Alexandre Narni. I retched again, but the worst was over. How could Gélou have shared her bed with a hitman? For ten years, dammit!

"It's nothing, really. It'll pass. How about another quick cognac?"

"You're sure you're all right?"

I'd be all right.

"I don't even know who Narni is," I resumed, in a jocular tone. "It was just a name that came into my head. Boudjema Ressaf, Narni . . . I was trying to impress Pertin. To make him believe you and I were in cahoots."

"Uh-huh," he said, not taking his eyes off me.

"So who is this Narni?"

"That name didn't just come into your head. You must have heard of Narni. I'm sure you have. One of Jean-Louis Fargette's strong arm men." He smiled ironically. "I hope you remember Fargette at least? Eh? The Mafia and all that . . . "

"Yes, of course."

"For years, this Narni of yours was best known for being in charge of the extortion racket on the coast. Then his name was mentioned when Fargette got whacked in San Remo. He may even have done the job himself. Shifting alliances between families, you know how it goes. Since then, he's kept a low profile."

"So what's he been doing since Fargette died?"

Loubet smiled. The smile of someone who knows he's about to impress the other person. I braced myself for the worst.

"He's financial adviser to an international economic marketing company. The company that handles the second account for Cûc's fashion business. And the second account for Fabre's architectural practice. Others too . . . I haven't had time to go through the whole list . . . The Neapolitan Camorra is behind it, I got confirmation of that before coming here. You see, Fabre was in it up to his neck. But not in the way you think."

"Right," I said, evasively.

I wasn't really listening. There was a knot in my stomach. Everything was going up and down inside me. The sea urchins, the sea squirts, the oysters. The cognac hadn't helped. And I felt like crying.

"What do you think economic marketing means, for guys like these?"

I knew. Babette had explained it to me.

"Loan sharking. They lend money to businesses in difficulty. Dirty money, obviously. At crazy rates. Fifteen, twenty percent. A lot, anyhow. The whole of Italy already functions like that. Even some banks!"

Now the Mafia had started making inroads in the French market. The recent Schneider affair, with its Belgian connections, had been the first example.

"Well, the guy who runs all that is called Antonio Sartanario. Narni works for him. His specialty is dealing with people who are having problems with their payments. Or who try to change the rules of the game."

"Was that the case with Fabre?"

"He'd started borrowing to get his practice off the ground. Then a large amount to help Cûc get started in the fashion world. He was a regular client. But these last few months, he'd needed a little more persuasion. When we went through his accounts, we discovered he'd been transferring a lot of money into a savings account. An account he'd opened in Mathias' name. So you see, Hocine Draoui was a warning to Fabre. The first warning. That's why they killed him, right there in front of him, in his own house. On Monday morning, Fabre withdrew a large sum."

"But they killed him all the same."

"The kid's death must really have had an effect on Fabre. What was he planning to do instead of handing over the money? Spill the beans? Blackmail them into leaving him alone? . . . Are you listening to me, Montale?"

"Yeah, yeah."

"You see what a mess this whole thing is. Balducci, Narni. Guys like that don't fool around. Do you hear, Montale?" He looked at his watch. "Shit, I'm late."

He stood up. I didn't. I wasn't steady on my legs yet. Loubet put his hand on my shoulder, like the other day in Ange's bar.

"A word of advice. If you hear anything about the two kids, don't forget to call me. I wouldn't like anything to happen to them. I don't think you would either."

I nodded. "Loubet," I heard myself saying, "I like you."

He leaned toward me. "So do me a favor, Fabio. Go fishing. It's healthier . . . for what you've got in your stomach."

I asked for a third cognac, and drank it straight down. It gave me the kick I'd been hoping for. A kick to unleash the storm in my belly. I stood up, with difficulty, and headed straight for the toilets.

On my knees, holding the toilet bowl in both hands, I threw up. Everything. Down to the last clam. I didn't want to keep any of that damn meal inside me. My stomach twisted with pain, I sobbed softly. Things always end like this, I told myself. Out of balance. They can't end any other way. Because that's how they started. You'd like everything to be balanced in the end. But it never happens.

Never.

I stood up and pulled the chain. Like someone pulling an alarm bell.

Outside, the weather was glorious. I'd forgotten the sun existed. It was flooding Cours d'Estiennes-d'Orves. I let myself be borne along by its gentle warmth. I walked with my hands in my pockets as far as Place aux Huiles. In the Vieux-Port.

A strong smell rose from the sea. A mixture of oil, grease and salt water. It really wasn't a pleasant smell. Any other day, I'd have said it stank. But right now that smell did me a whole lot of good. It was real, it was human. It was a whiff of happiness. It was like Marseilles catching me by the throat. In my mind, I could hear the chugging of my boat. I saw myself at sea, fishing. I smiled. Life was resuming its rightful place in me. Through the simplest things.

The ferry arrived. I bought a return ticket for the shortest and most beautiful of all journeys. Across the bay of Marseilles. Quai du Port to Quai de Rive-Neuve. There weren't many passengers at this hour. A few old people. A mother giving her baby the bottle. I found myself humming *Chella lla*. An old

Neapolitan song by Renato Carosone. I was finding my bearings again. And the memories that went with them. My father had sat me down at the window of the ferry and said, "Look, Fabio. Look. That's the entrance to the harbor. See? The Saint-Nicolas fort. The Saint-Jean fort. And there's the Pharo. Look. And after that, there's the sea. The open sea." I could feel his big hands holding me under my armpits. How old was I? No more than six or seven. That night, I dreamed I was a sailor.

At Place de la Mairie, some of the old people got off and others got on. The woman with the baby looked at me before leaving the ferry. I smiled at her.

A schoolgirl got on. The kind that flourish better in Marseilles than anywhere else. West Indian father or mother, maybe. Long curly hair. Firm breasts. Ankle-length skirt. She came and asked me for a light, because I'd glanced at her. She gave me an unsmiling Lauren Bacall look. Then she went and took up position on the other side of the cabin. I didn't have time to say thank you, just for the pleasure of looking in her eyes again.

After I got off the ferry, I walked along the embankment, on my way to see Gélou. I'd called the hotel before leaving L'Oursin. She was waiting for me at the New York. I didn't know what I'd do if Narni was there. Strangle him on the spot, maybe.

But Gélou was alone.

"Isn't Alexandre here?" I said, as I kissed her.

"He'll be here in half an hour. I wanted to see you without him. For the moment. What's happening, Fabio? About Guitou."

Gélou had shadows under her eyes. She bore all the signs of anxiety. The wait was wearing her down. But she was my cousin, and she was beautiful. Still. I wanted to take advantage of her face, as it was right now, while I still could. Why hadn't life been kind to her? Had she hoped for too much? Expected too much? But aren't we all like that? As soon as we open our eyes and see the world? Are there people who ask nothing of life?

"He's dead," I said, softly.

I took her hands. They were still warm. Then I looked up at her, trying to put in my look all the love I kept in reserve for the winter months.

"What?" she stammered.

I felt the blood drain from her hands.

"Come," I said.

I forced her to stand up, to walk out. Before she broke down. I put my arm around her shoulders, like a lover. She slipped her arm around my waist. We crossed in the middle of the flow of traffic. Cars braked, horns honked, drivers shouted insults. But we ignored them. There was only us now. The two of us. And this pain we shared.

We walked along the embankment. In silence. Holding each other tight. I wondered for a moment where that bastard Narni was. He couldn't have been far. Spying on us. Wondering when he could finally put a bullet in my head. He must be dying to do that. Me too. The gun I'd been carrying in my car since last night would be for that. And I had an advantage over Narni. I knew now what a scumbag he was. I felt Gélou's shoulder shaking. The tears were coming. I stopped, turned Gélou to face me, and embraced her. She clung to me, pressing her body close to mine. Anyone seeing us would have thought we were two lovers, unable to contain their desire. Behind the bell tower of Les Accoules, the sun was already going down.

"Why?" she asked through her tears.

"The questions don't matter anymore. Or the answers. It's the way it is, Gélou. It's just the way it is."

She lifted her face to me. A ravaged face. Of course, her mascara had run, leaving long blue trails. Her cheeks seemed cracked, like the ground after an earthquake. I saw her eyes turn inward. Forever. Gélou was leaving. For another place. A land of tears.

In spite of everything, she still clung to me, desperately, with her hands and her eyes. Trying to stay in the world. Trying to hold on to everything that had united us since childhood. But I was no help to her. I hadn't brought a child into the world out of my own belly. I wasn't a mother. Not even a father. The only words I could say came from the dictionary of human stupidity. There was nothing to say. I had nothing to say.

"I'm here," I whispered in her ear.

But it was too late.

Once death has appeared, it's always too late.

"Fabio . . ."

She fell silent, and rested her forehead on my shoulder. She was calming down. The worst would come later. I stroked her hair gently, then put my hand under her chin and lifted her face to look at me.

"Do you have a Kleenex?"

She nodded. She freed herself from me, took out a Kleenex and a little mirror. She wiped away the mascara trails. That was all she did.

"Where's your car?"

"In the parking garage behind the hotel. Why?"

"Don't ask any questions, Gélou. What level? One? Two?"

"Level one. On the right."

I put my arm around her shoulders again, and we walked back toward the New York. The sun was disappearing behind the houses on the Butte du Panier, leaving a beautiful light that turned the houses pink on Quai de Rive-Neuve. It was magnificent. And I needed that, needed to cling to these moments of beauty.

"Talk to me," she said.

We were in front of one of the entrances to the Vieux-Port metro station. There were three. This one. One at the bottom of the Canebière. The third on Place Gabriel-Péri.

"Later. Go to your car. Get in and wait for me. I'll be there in less than ten minutes."

"But—"

"Can you do that?"

"Yes."

"Good. I'll leave you here. Start walking as if you're going back to the hotel. When you get there, hesitate for a few moments. As if you'd just thought of something. Something you've forgotten, for example. Then go to the parking garage, but without hurrying. OK?"

"OK," she said, mechanically.

I kissed her, as if I was saying goodbye. I clasped her to me, tenderly. "You must do exactly as I say, Gélou," I said, gently but firmly. "Have you got that?" She put her hand in mine. "Go on now."

She went. Walking stiffly, like an automaton.

I watched her as she crossed the street. Then I took the escalator down into the metro. Without hurrying. When I reached the corridor, I broke into a run. I ran the whole length of the station as far as the Gabriel-Péri exit. I climbed the stairs two by two, and found myself on the square. I turned right to get back onto the Canebière, in front of the Palais de la Bourse. The parking garage was opposite me.

If Narni or the other guy, Balducci, had been watching me, I'd gotten a head start on them. Where Gélou and I were going, we didn't need anyone. I crossed without waiting for the little green man and walked into the parking garage.

Lights flashed and I recognized Gélou's Saab.

"Move over," I said, opening the door. "I'll drive."

"Where are we going, Fabio?" she cried. "Please tell me!"

"We're just going for a drive," I said, gently. "We have to talk, right?"

We didn't talk until we got onto the highway leading north. I'd zigzagged across Marseilles, looking constantly in the rearview mirror. But we weren't being tailed. Once I was sure of that, I'd told Gélou what had happened. I'd told her the inspector who was on the case was a friend of mine and we could trust him. She'd listened, without asking any questions.

"It doesn't make any difference now." That was all she'd said.

I left the highway at the Les Arnavaux fork and drove through the streets that climb toward Sainte-Marthe.

"How did you meet Narni?"

"What?"

"Alexandre Narni. Where did you meet him?"

"At the restaurant I had with Gino. He was a customer. A good customer. A regular. Sometimes he brought friends, sometimes he came alone. He liked Gino's cooking."

So did I. I still remembered his *lingue di passero* with truffles. The best I'd ever eaten. Even in Italy.

"Did he flirt with you?"

"No. Well, he'd make compliments . . . "

"The kind a handsome man makes to a beautiful woman."

"If you like . . . But I treated him like all the other customers. No better, no worse."

"Hmm. And how did he treat you?"

"What do you mean, how did he treat me? Fabio, what's this all about? Why are you asking me all these questions? Is there a connection with Guitou's death?"

I shrugged. "There are things I need to know about your life. I'm trying to understand."

"Understand what?"

"How my dear cousin Gélou met a Mafia hitman named Alexandre Narni. And how, in the ten years she slept with him, she never suspected a thing."

I braked quickly. I wanted to park before she slapped me.

# 20.

## IN WHICH A LIMITED VISION OF THE WORLD IS PROPOSED

The restaurant had only been open a few months when Narni became one of its best customers. Whenever he came, he'd bring well-known people with him. Mayors, deputies. Regional representatives. Ministers. People from show business, the movies.

These are my friends, he seemed to be saying. You're lucky that I like your cooking. And that we're fellow countrymen. Like Gino, Narni was from Umbria. Almost certainly the region with the best cuisine in Italy. Even better than Tuscany. That really was lucky. You had to admit it. The restaurant was always full. Some people came just to catch a glimpse of a celebrity or two.

The walls were soon covered with framed photos of the customers. Gélou posed with all of them. Like a star. In this restaurant, she was the biggest star. An Italian director, she couldn't remember which one now, had even wanted her for his next movie. That had made her laugh a lot. She loved the movies, but she'd never imagined appearing in one. And besides, Guitou had just been born. So movies were out.

Plenty of money was coming in. It was a happy time. Even if it meant going to bed at night exhausted. Especially on weekends. Gino had hired an assistant cook and two waitresses. Gélou didn't wait on tables anymore. She'd greet the important guests, drink an aperitif with them, that kind of thing. Narni would get her invited to official receptions and galas, as well as several times to the Cannes Film Festival.

"Did you go alone?" I'd asked.

"Without Gino, yes. The restaurant had to carry on. And you know he wasn't crazy about socializing. The only thing that turned his head was me," she said, with a sad little smile. "He wasn't impressed by money, or honors. He was a real peasant, with his feet firmly planted on the ground. That's why I loved him. He kept me balanced. He taught me to tell the difference between what was real and what was fake and flashy. You remember the way I was when I was as a girl? The way I used to run after all the boys who flashed their daddies' money?"

"You even wanted to marry the son of a Marseilles shoe manufacturer. That would have been a good match."

"He was ugly."

"But Gino . . . "

She was lost in thought. We were still parked on the street where I'd braked suddenly. Gélou hadn't slapped me. She hadn't even moved. As if stunned. Then she'd turned to me, slowly. Her eyes were sending out distress signals. I hadn't dared look at her right away.

"Is that how you've been spending your time?" she'd said. "Prying into my life?"

"No, Gélou."

And I'd told her the whole story. Well, not quite the whole story. Only what she had every right to know. Then we'd sat in silence, smoking.

"Fabio," she resumed.

"Yes."

"What are you trying to find out?"

"I don't know. It's like when a piece is missing from a jigsaw puzzle. You can see the picture, but the missing piece screws everything up. Do you understand?"

Night had fallen. Even though the windows were open, the car was filled with smoke.

"I'm not sure."

"Gélou, this guy lives with you. He helps you raise the kids. Patrice, Marc and Guitou. He saw Guitou grow up . . . He must have played with him. There must have been birthdays. Christmases."

"How could he do it? Is that what you're saying?"

"Yes, how could he do it? And how could . . . ? Supposing we'd never found out, right? Supposing you hadn't come to see me. Narni kills this guy, Hocine Draoui. Then he kills Guitou because he was in the wrong place at the wrong time. He slips through the police net. As usual. He comes back to Gap . . . How could he . . . ? I mean, he puts on his pajamas, all clean and ironed, he gets into bed with you and . . . "

"Even supposing that, I don't think . . . With Guitou dead, I don't think I could have stood having a man in my bed anymore. Alex or anyone else."

"Ah," I said, thrown.

"I had the kids to raise. Especially Guitou. That was why I needed a man. A father. Yes, I needed a father for them." Gélou was increasingly nervous. "Oh, Fabio, it's all so mixed up! There are the things a woman expects from a man, you know. Kindness. Affection. Pleasure. Pleasure matters too, you know. But there are all the other things. The things that make a man a real man. The stability he can give you. The confidence. The sense of authority. Someone to rely on . . . A single mother, with three children. I wasn't brave enough to face it. That's the truth." She lit another cigarette, mechanically. She was pensive. "None of this is simple."

"I know, Gélou. Tell me, didn't he ever want a child with you?"

"Yes. *He* did. Not me. Three was enough for me. Don't you think so?"

"Have you been happy these last few years?"

"Happy? Yes, I think so. Everything was going well. You've seen the car I drive."

"I've seen it. But that's not what being happy is about."

"I know. But what do you want me to say? Switch on the TV . . . When you see the things that are happening here, and in other places . . . I can't say I've been unhappy."

"What did Gino think of Narni?"

"He didn't really like him. At first, maybe, yes. They got along quite well. They'd talk about the old country. But Gino, you know, was never good at making friends with people. For him, only the family mattered."

"Was he jealous? Was that it?"

"A little. Like any good Italian. But it was never a problem. Even when a huge bouquet of roses would arrive for my birthday. All it did was remind him that he'd forgotten my birthday. But it wasn't serious. Gino loved me, and I knew it."

"What was it then?"

"I don't know. Gino . . . Alex sometimes brought some weird guys with him. Well dressed guys, but with . . . bodyguards, I guess. Not the kind of people you took photos of! Gino didn't like having them in his restaurant. He said they were Mafia. He said you could tell as soon as you saw their faces. They were more real than in the movies!"

"Did he say anything to Narni?"

"No, can you imagine? Narni was a customer. When you run a restaurant, you don't make comments. You serve the food, that's all."

"Did Gino's attitude toward him change at that point?"

She stubbed out her cigarette. It was a long time ago, but it was a period on which she hadn't yet turned the page. Even ten years later. In her head, there was probably a photo of Gino in a gold frame, with a rose placed beside it.

"Gino started getting nervous. Anxious. He'd wake up in the middle of the night. He said it was because we were working too hard. It was true, we never stopped. The restaurant was always full, and yet we weren't rolling in money. We made a living. Sometimes I got the feeling that we were making less than we had at first. Gino said the restaurant was like a treadmill. He started talking about selling. Moving somewhere else. Working less. He said we'd be just as happy."

Gino and Gélou. Adrien Fabre and Cûc. The Mafia always took away with one hand what it gave with the other. There were no free rides. You couldn't escape the racket. Especially if the racketeer had built up your clientele for you. And it didn't matter who that clientele was. That was the way it worked everywhere. To a greater or lesser degree. Even in the smallest neighborhood bars from Marseilles to Menton. It might not be a lot. One undeclared pinball machine. Or two.

To make matters worse, Narni had been in love with the owner's wife. Gélou. My cousin. My Claudia Cardinale. Ten years ago, I remembered, she'd been even more beautiful than she was as a teenager. A mature woman, in full bloom. The way I like them.

"They had a little argument one night," Gélou went on. "It's just come back to me. I don't know what it was about. Gino wouldn't tell me. Alex was eating alone, as he sometimes did. Gino sat down at his table, to have a glass of wine with him and chat. But Alex just finished his pasta and left. Without eating anything else. He barely said goodnight. But he looked at me, for a long time. Before he went out."

"When was that?"

"A month before Gino was killed . . . Fabio!" she cried. "You don't mean to say that . . . "

No, I didn't mean to say anything.

After that night, Narni didn't set foot in the restaurant again. He called Gélou, once. To tell her he had to go away on a trip but he'd be back soon. He didn't show up again until two days after Gino's death. Just in time for the funeral. He was around a lot at that time, helping Gélou with everything, advising her.

She told him she was planning to sell up and leave the area. To start all over again somewhere else. He helped her with that too. He was the one who handled the sale of the restaurant, and he managed to get a very good price. From a relative of his. Gradually, Gélou came to rely on him. More than on her family. Admittedly, once the sadness had passed, the family had minded its own business. Me included.

"You could have called me," I protested.

"Yes, maybe. If I'd been alone. But Alex was there and . . . I didn't even need to ask."

One day, almost a year later, Narni suggested a trip to Gap. He'd found a small business he was sure she'd like. And a villa, on the lower slopes of the Bayard pass, with a magnificent view of the valley. The children, he said, would be happy there. A new life.

They viewed the house, like a young couple looking for their first home. Laughing. Making plans, whispering. That night, instead of going back, they stayed in Gap for dinner. It got late. Narni suggested they spend the night there. The restaurant doubled as a hotel, and there were two rooms available. She found herself in his arms, without quite knowing how. But she didn't regret it.

"It had been such a long time . . . I . . . I couldn't live without a man. I thought I could, at first. But . . . I was thirty-eight, Fabio," she said, as if apologizing. "The people around me didn't like the idea, especially in my family. But you don't live with your family. It isn't there at night when the kids have gone to bed, and you're alone in front of the TV."

And this man was there, this man she'd known a long time, who'd waited for her. This elegant, self-confident man, who had no money worries. He'd told her he was a financial adviser for a Swiss company. Yes, there was something reassuring about Narni. A whole new future was being laid out for her. Not the one she'd dreamed of when she'd married Gino. But a damn sight better than the one she'd imagined when he died.

"Besides, he was often away on business trips. In different parts of France, and all over Europe. And that was fine too. I was free. I could come and go as I pleased. Spend more time with the kids. Just when I was starting to miss Alex, he'd come back. No, Fabio, I haven't been unhappy these last ten years."

Narni had gotten what he wanted. That was the one thing I couldn't deny. He'd loved Gélou so much, he'd been prepared to raise Gino's children. Was that why he'd killed him? Out of love? Or because Gino had decided not to cough up another centime? What did it matter? The guy was a hitman. He would have killed Gino anyway. Because Alexandre Narni was like everyone in the Mafia. What they wanted, they took, sooner or later. Power, money, women. Gélou. It only made me hate Narni even more. For daring to love her. For sullying her with all his crimes. With all the death he carried around in his head.

"What's going to happen now?" Gélou asked in a toneless voice.

She was a strong woman. But it was a lot for a woman to take in, all in one day. She had to rest before she broke down completely.

"You're going to rest."

"Not at the hotel!" she cried, horrified.

"No. You're not going back there. Narni's like a mad dog now. He must know that I know. When you don't come back, he's sure to figure I told you everything. He'd kill anyone if he had to. Even you."

She looked at me. I couldn't see her. From time to time, her face was lit momentarily by a passing car. I was pretty sure her eyes were empty now. Like the landscape after a tornado.

"I don't think so," she said softly.

"You don't think what, Gélou?"

"That he could kill me." She paused for breath. "One night, we'd just made love. He'd been away quite a long time. He'd come home very tired. Demoralized, it seemed to me. A little sad. He took me in his arms, tenderly. He could be tender, I liked that about him. 'You know,' he said, 'I'd prefer to lose everything rather than lose you.' He had tears in his eyes when he said that."

Goddammit! I said to myself. Now I've heard everything in this fucking life. Even that. The story of a tender hitman. Gélou, Gélou, why did you let go of my hand that Sunday at the movies?

"The two of us should have married."

I was talking bullshit.

She burst into tears and sheltered in my arms. On my chest, I felt her tears soaking my shirt, my skin. I knew they'd leave an indelible stain.

"I'm talking bullshit, Gélou. But I'm here. And I love you."

"I love you too," she said, sniffing. "But you weren't always there."

"Narni's a killer. A dangerous guy. Maybe family life agreed with him. And maybe he really loved you. But it doesn't change anything. He's a professional killer. He'll stop at nothing. In a business like that, you don't shut up shop so easily. Killing is his job. He has to answer to people higher than him. Guys even more dangerous than he is. Guys who don't kill with guns, the way he does, but control politicians, industrialists, the army. Guys who don't care about human life . . . Narni can't afford to leave survivors. He couldn't let Guitou live. And he can't let you live. Or me . . . "

I let my words hang in the air. I didn't expect anything from life anymore. But one day I'd imagined it the way it could be. And I'd ended up loving it. Without guilt, without remorse, without fear. Simply. Life is like truth. You take what you can get. You often get back what you've given. It was as simple as that. Rosa, the woman I'd lived with the longest, had said to me, before she left, that I had a limited vision of the world. It was true. But I was still alive, and it didn't take much to make me happy. Death wouldn't change anything.

I put my arm around Gélou's shoulders.

"What I'm saying, Gélou, is that I love you and I'm going to protect you from him. Until all this has been sorted out. But before that, I need you to kill him in your head. To destroy even the smallest scrap of affection you have for him. If you don't, I won't be able to help you."

"That makes two men I'll have lost, Fabio," she said, with an imploring look.

I still had the worst thing of all to say to her. I'd hoped I wouldn't have to.

"Gélou, imagine Guitou. He's just had his first night of love, with a beautiful girl. Then he hears strange noises in the house. Maybe a scream. The scream of someone being killed. Terrifying for anyone. No matter how old they are. Maybe Guitou and Naïma have been sleeping. Maybe they're making love again. Imagine their panic.

"So they get out of bed. And Guitou, your son, who's a man now, does something not every man would have done. But he does it, because Naïma is watching him. Because Naïma is absolutely terrified. Because he's afraid for her. He opens the door. And what does he see? That bastard Narni. The guy who's always lecturing him about whites, blacks and Arabs. The guy who sometimes beats your boy so badly, he gives him bruises that are still there more than two weeks later. The guy who sleeps with his mother. Who does with his mother what he himself has just done with Naïma.

"Imagine Guitou's eyes at that moment, Gélou. The hate in them, and the fear too. Because he knows he doesn't stand a chance. And imagine Narni's eyes. Seeing the boy in front of him. The boy who's been defying him for years, who despises him. Imagine it, Gélou. I want you to have all these horrible pictures in your head! Your son in his underwear. And Narni with his gun. On the point of shooting. Without hesitation. In the right place. With a steady hand. A single bullet, Gélou. A single fucking bullet!"

"Stop!" she sobbed.

Her fingers clutched at my shirt. She was close to hysterics. But I had to go on.

"No, you have to listen to me, Gélou. Imagine Guitou again. Falling, smashing his forehead on the stone steps. His blood gushing. Which of the two do you think thought about you at that moment? In that fraction of a second after the bullet left the gun and before it lodged in Guitou's heart? I want you to put all that in your head and keep it there. Otherwise, you'll never be able to sleep again. For the rest of your life. You have to see Guitou. And you have to see Narni as he fires that gun. I'm going to kill him, Gélou."

"No!" she screamed through her sobs. "No! Not you!"

"Someone has to do it. To obliterate all that. Not to forget. You'll never be able to forget, and neither will I. No, just to clean up the mess. Clear a space around us. In our heads. In our hearts. It's the only way we can even think of surviving."

Gélou clung to me. It was like when we were teenagers, huddled in the same bed, telling each other scary stories. But the stories had caught up with us. They were real. We could go to sleep, of course, holding each other tight, the way we used to. Snug and warm. But we knew that when we woke up, the horror would still be there.

The horror had a face. And a name.

Narni.

Without saying another word, I started the car. I'd reached the point where I couldn't wait anymore. I drove quite quickly through the little streets, which were almost deserted at this hour.

It was still like a village here, full of old houses, some of them from colonial times. There was one, in a Moorish style, that I liked a lot. The kind you see at El Biar, in the hills above Algiers. It was abandoned, like quite a few of them. The windows of these houses no longer looked out, as they once had, on vast grounds, on gardens, but on concrete apartment blocks.

We climbed some more. Gélou let me drive. She didn't care where I took her. Then the huge golden Buddha appeared on the side of the hill, bathed in moonlight, towering majestically, serenely, over the city. The temple, which was relatively new, housed a center for Buddhist studies. Cûc was waiting for us there. With Naïma and Mathias.

This was where she'd hidden them. It was Cûc's secret garden. The place she came to find shelter whenever things weren't going well. Where she came to think, to meditate. To reconnect with her roots. With the land where her heart was. Where it'd always be. Vietnam.

I didn't believe in any god. But this was a sacred place. A place of purity. There was nothing wrong once in a while, I told myself, in breathing pure air. Gélou would be fine here. With them. They'd all lost something in this affair. Cûc a husband. Mathias a friend. Naïma a lover. And Gélou everything. They'd know how to take care of her. They'd know how to take care of themselves. To heal their wounds.

A monk greeted us at the entrance. Gélou huddled in my arms. I kissed her on the forehead. She looked up at me. There was a kind of veil over her eyes, a veil that was about to be torn.

"There's one more thing I have to tell you."

And I knew it was going to be something I didn't want to hear.

# 21.

## IN WHICH YOU SPIT INTO THE VOID, OUT OF DISGUST AND WEARINESS

I drove back in the Saab. I'd switched on the radio and found a station playing tango. Edmundo Riveiro was singing *Garuffa*. It was the music that best matched my mood. My heart was like a bandoneon after what Gélou had just told me. But I didn't want to think about that. I wanted to dismiss her last words, to push them as far from me as I could. Even to forget them.

I had the impression I was channel hopping between other people's lives. Catching soap operas in the middle. Gélou and Gino. Guitou and Naïma. Serge and Redouane. Cûc and Fabre. Pavie and Saadna. I always came in at the end. When the killing started. And the dying. Always too late for life. For happiness.

That must have been how I'd gotten old. By hesitating too much, not grabbing happiness when it was staring me in the face. I'd never been good at doing that. Or at making decisions. Or taking responsibility. Or doing anything that might commit me to a future. I was always too afraid of losing. And so I always lost.

I'd seen Magali again, in Caen. In a small hotel. Three days before leaving for Djibouti. We'd made love. Slowly, taking our time. All night long. In the morning, before getting in the shower, she'd asked me, "What do you want me to be? A teacher or a model?" I'd shrugged, without answering. She'd come out, dressed, ready to leave.

"Have you thought about it?" she'd said.

"Be whatever you want," I'd replied. "I like you just the way you are."

"That's clever," she retorted, giving me a quick kiss on the lips. I'd embraced her, feeling desire for her again. "I'm going to be late for my classes."

"See you tonight."

The door had closed. She hadn't come back. I'd never seen her again, never been able to tell her that what I wanted her to be, more than anything, was my wife. Faced with a basic question, with a choice, I'd sidestepped the issue. And I hadn't learned my lesson. I didn't know what would have become of Magali and me. But I was sure that Fonfon would have been proud to know the two of us were happy. He wouldn't have been alone now. Neither would I.

I switched off the radio when Carlos Gardel launched into *Volver*. Tango, nostalgia—it was better to stop. That kind of thing could drive me crazy, and I needed a clear head. To confront Narni. There were still a few things about him I couldn't figure out. Why had he showed up yesterday, when he could have stayed in the shadows and kept searching for Naïma? Maybe he'd thought it was easier to trap me once he'd sent Gélou back to Gap? It didn't really matter anymore, I told myself. I didn't know what he was thinking, and I didn't care.

I took the coast highway. Past the harbors. Just for the pleasure of seeing the waterfront from above. Going from one harbor basin to the next. Treating myself to a view of the moored ferries all lit up. My dreams were still there. Intact. In those boats ready to cast off. Going somewhere far away. Maybe that was what I should do. Tonight or tomorrow. Leave, at last. Drop everything. Follow in Ugo's footsteps. Africa, Asia, South America. All the way to Puerto Escondido. He still had a house there. A little fisherman's house. Like mine in Les Goudes. With a boat too. He'd told Lole about it, when he came back to avenge Manu. Lole and I had often talked about it. About going there. To that other house in the middle of nowhere.

Once again, it was too late. Would killing Narni help me straighten out my life? But settling accounts wouldn't make up for all my failures. And how could I be so sure I'd kill him?

Because I had nothing to lose. But he had nothing to lose now either.

And there were two of them.

I entered the Vieux-Port tunnel, and came out beneath the Saint-Nicolas fort. In front of the old careening basin. I drove along Quai de Rive-Neuve. Marseilles was bustling at this hour. It was the time when people were thinking about what kind of food to eat tonight. West Indian. Brazilian. African. Arab. Greek. Armenian. Vietnamese. Italian. Provençal. There was a bit of everything in the Marseilles melting pot. Something for every taste.

On Rue Francis-Davso, I double parked next to my own car. I transferred Redouane's gun and a few cassettes to the Saab. Then I set off again, along Rue Molière, by the side of the Opéra, Rue Saint-Saëns, left onto Rue Glandeves. Back to the harbor. Close to the Hotel Alizé. There was a space free. It was ideal. Between the pedestrian passageway and the sidewalk. It must be an expensive space. That's why nobody had taken it. But I'd only be five minutes, no more.

I went into a phone booth, almost in front of the hotel, and called Narni. That was when I saw the Safrane, double parked in front of the New York. With Balducci at the wheel, I guessed, seeing the smoke drifting out through the window. My lucky day, I said to myself. Better to know they were here than imagine they were outside my house, waiting for me.

Narni answered immediately.

"Montale," I said. "We haven't been introduced yet. But we could do that now. How about it?"

"Where's Gélou?" He had a fine, deep, warm voice, which surprised me.

"Too late to worry about her health now, old buddy. I don't think you'll be seeing her again."

"Does she know?"

"She knows. Everyone knows. Even the cops know. We don't have much time left to settle things between ourselves."

"Where are you?"

"At my house," I lied. "I can be there in forty-five minutes. At the New York, that OK with you?"

"Fine. I'll be there."

"Alone," I said, for my own amusement.

"Alone."

I hung up, and waited.

It took him less than ten minutes to come down and get into the Safrane. I went back to the Saab. Here we go, I said to myself.

I had my plan. I just had to hope it was the right one.

Because of the congestion, which I'd banked on, I spotted the Safrane on Quai de Rive-Neuve. They'd decided to go via the Corniche. If that was that they wanted, it was fine by me. Let's go.

I drove a long way behind them. I was planning to catch up with them up by the David statue, at Rond-Point de la Plage. Which I did. As they drove toward the Pointe Rouge, I came up slowly behind them and flashed my lights at them. Then, without stopping, I went around the statue and turned onto Avenue du Prado. They couldn't do a U-turn until they got to Avenue de Bonnevoie. That would get them riled up. But it gave me time to reach the bottom of the Prado without any risk. I would wait for them there, on the shoulder of the Prado-Michelet traffic circle. Then the chase would start.

I took the pistol and the bullets out of the plastic bag. I loaded it, cocked it, and placed it on the seat. The butt toward me. Then I put on a ZZ Top cassette. I needed them. The only rock band I liked. The only genuine one. I saw the Safrane. The first notes of *Thunderbird*. I started the car. They must be wondering what I was playing at. It amused me to know they weren't in control of the situation. If they were nervous, it was to my advantage. My whole plan depended on their making a mistake. A mistake I hoped would be fatal.

Green light. Yellow light. Red light. I zoomed along

Boulevard Michelet without having to stop once. Then Carrefour de Mazragues, at top speed. After Le Redon and Luminy, the road started. The D559. The road to Cassis via the Ginette pass. A favorite with Marseilles cyclists. A road I knew by heart. From there, many paths led to the *calanques*.

The D559 was a narrow, dangerous road with lots of bends.

ZZ Top started *Long Distance Boogie*. Billy Gibbons was great! I hit the coast at 68 mph, the Safrane hard on my heels. The Saab seemed to me a little sluggish, but it responded well. I doubted that Gélou had ever put it through its paces like this.

After the first big bend, the Safrane pulled out. They were already trying to overtake me. They were in a hurry. The front of the car drew level with my rear window and Narni's arm came out. He was holding a gun. I changed down to fourth. I was doing close to 65, and I took the second bend with great difficulty. So did they.

I regained ground.

Now that I was here, I was starting to have my doubts. Balducci seemed like a crack driver. Not much chance you'll be eating Honorine's *poutargue* now, I told myself. Shit! I was hungry. You idiot! You should have eaten first before you launched into this. This was just like you. Plunging in, without even taking time to breathe. You didn't have to deal with Narni immediately. He'd have waited for you. Or he'd have come to get you.

Of course he'd have come.

A nice plate of spaghetti *matriciana* wouldn't have gone amiss. A little red wine with it. Maybe a red Tempier. From Bandol. Maybe you could find it in the other world. What are you talking about, bozo? After death, there's nothing.

That's right, after death, there's nothing anymore. Just darkness. And you don't even know it's dark. Because you're dead.

The Safrane was still behind me, still hard on my heels. But that was all it could do. For the moment. After the bend, they'd try to overtake again.

Well, there's only one solution, Montale, you've got to pull this off, OK? Then you'll be able to gorge yourself on anything you like. Hey, it's been a long time since I last ate bean soup. Yes, with thick slices of toast drizzled with olive oil. That'd be good. I accelerated a little more. Or a stew. That'd be good too. You should have told Honorine. So she could marinate the meat. Would the Tempier go well with that? Of course it'd go well. I could taste it . . .

A car was coming down in the other direction. It flashed its lights. The driver, seeing us climbing toward him at that speed, was in a panic. When he came level, he honked like a maniac. He must have been really scared.

I shook my head, to chase away the cooking smells. My stomach was going to join in, I could feel it. There'll be time to see about that, later, eh, Montale? Don't get excited. Calm down.

Calm down.

Doing 62, on the fucking Ginette pass, that was easier said than done!

We were rising above the bay of Marseilles. It was one of the most beautiful views over the city. It was even better a little higher, just before the descent to Cassis. But we weren't here for the sightseeing.

I went back into fifth. To gather my strength. I slowed down to 55. The Safrane was immediately on my heels again. The bastard was going to pull out.

A hundred yards, just another hundred yards. I changed down to third. The car seemed to leap. I went back up to 62, just after the fourth bend. In front of me, a straight line. Nine hundred yards, a thousand yards, no more than that, and the road would turn right. Not left, as it had up till now.

I accelerated, the Safrane still on my heels.

68.

It pulled out. I turned the volume up to maximum. The wailing of the electric guitars in my ears.

The Safrane came level with me.

I accelerated.

74.

The Safrane also accelerated.

I saw Narni's gun against my window.

"Now!" I screamed.

Now!

Now!

I braked. Hard.

68. 62. 55.

I thought I heard a shot. The Safrane overtook me and went straight into the concrete guardrail and overturned and took off into the air, all four wheels facing the sky.

Five hundred yards below were the rocks, and the sea. Nobody had ever made that leap and come out alive.

*Nasty dogs and funky kings*, ZZ Top were screaming.

My foot was shaking on the pedal. I slowed some more, and stopped as calmly as I could, close to the guardrail. The shaking had spread all over my body. I was thirsty, dammit. I could feel tears streaming down my face. Tears of fright. Tears of joy.

I started laughing. A loud, nervous laugh.

The lights of a car appeared behind me. Instinctively, I switched on the hazard warning lights. The car overtook me. A Renault 21. It slowed down and parked fifty yards farther on. Two guys got out. Big strapping guys in leather jackets and jeans. They started walking toward me.

Shit.

Too late to realize how stupid I'd been.

I put my hand on the butt of the pistol. I was still shaking. I'd never be capable of lifting the gun. Let alone aiming at them. As for firing . . .

They were here.

One of the guys tapped at my window. I lowered it slowly. And saw his face.

Ribero. One of Loubet's inspectors.

I breathed a sigh of relief.

"That was some dive they took, huh? You OK?"

"Shit! You scared me."

They laughed. I recognized the other one. Vernet.

I got out of the car and took a few steps toward the spot where Narni and Balducci had taken the plunge. I was unsteady on my feet.

"Don't fall," Ribero said.

Vernet came up beside me and looked down.

"It ain't gonna be easy getting a closer look at that. Can't be much left, though."

The assholes were laughing.

"How long have you been following me?" I asked, getting out a cigarette.

Ribero gave me a light. I was shaking too much to be able to light it myself.

"Since this afternoon. We were waiting for you when you left the restaurant. Loubet had called us."

When he'd gone to take a leak. The bastard!

"He likes you," Vernet said. "But when it comes to trusting you . . . "

"Wait," I said. "Did you follow me everywhere?"

"The ferry. The meeting with your cousin. The Buddha. And now here . . . We even had two guys staking out your house. Just in case."

I sat down on part of the guardrail that had escaped the carnage.

"Hey! Be careful! Don't fall now!" Ribero laughed again.

I didn't have any intention of jumping. No way. I was thinking about Narni. Guitou's father. Narni had killed his own son. But he didn't know it, didn't know Guitou was his kid. Gélou had never told him. Or anyone. Except me. Earlier.

It had happened one night in Cannes. There'd been a movie premiere, followed by a lavish meal. To her—the girl who'd grown up on the alleys of the Panier—it was magical. Robert

De Niro was sitting on her right. Narni on her left. She couldn't remember who else was there. More stars. And there she was, in the middle. Narni placed his hand on hers and asked her if she was happy. His knee was against hers. She could feel his warmth. A warmth that penetrated her body.

Later, they all ended the night in a club. In his arms, she let herself go. She danced. She hadn't danced like that in years. She'd forgotten what it was like. Dancing. Drinking. Having fun. In the crazy way she had fun when she was twenty. She lost her head. Forgot all about Gino, the children, the restaurant.

They were staying in a luxury hotel. The bed was vast. Narni undressed her and made passionate love to her. Several times. She rediscovered her youth. She'd forgotten what that was like too. But there was something else she'd forgotten, though she didn't realize it till later. That it was her fertile time of the month. Gélou belonged to a generation that didn't take the pill. And she couldn't stand the coil. Not that there was any risk. It had been a long time since she and Gino had fooled around at night after the restaurant closed.

She'd have remembered that night her whole life anyway. Kept it as a wonderful memory. Her secret. But then she realized a child was on the way. And Gino's joy overwhelmed her. Gradually, the two images of happiness became one in her mind. The images of the two men. She didn't feel any guilt. And when she gave birth, supported as never before by Gino, she presented this man who loved her, the love of her life, with a third boy. Guitou.

She was a mother again. She'd regained her balance. She devoted herself to her children, to Gino. To the restaurant. Narni still came, but he didn't excite her anymore. He belonged to the past. To her youth. Until the tragedy, when Narni reached out a hand to her in her distress and loneliness.

"Why should I have told him?" Gélou said. "Guitou belonged to Gino. To our love."

I'd taken Gélou's face in my hands. "Gélou . . . "

I didn't want her to ask the question that was on her lips.

"Do you think it would have changed everything? If he'd known Guitou was his son?"

The monk was standing there. I'd signaled to him. He'd put his arm around Gélou's shoulders and I'd left, without looking back. Like Mourad. Like Cûc. And without answering her question.

Because there was no answer.

I was spitting into the void. Where Narni and Balducci had plunged. Forever. I spat out all my disgust. All my weariness.

The shaking had almost stopped. All I wanted was a big glass of whisky. My Lagavulin. Or even a bottle. Yes, that would have gone down well.

"Do you have anything to drink?"

"Not even a beer, old buddy. But we can go grab one, if you like. As soon as we get back down to earth," he joked.

The two of them were starting to bug me.

I lit another cigarette from the butt of the previous one, without their help this time. I took a long drag and looked up at them.

"Why didn't you intervene before?"

"It was your business, Loubet said. A family affair. If you wanted to play it that way, it was fine with us. Why not? We're not going to weep over those two scumbags. So . . . "

"And . . . and what if I'd taken the plunge instead of them?"

"We'd have gotten them. The gendarmes were waiting at the other end. They wouldn't have gotten through. Unless they'd gone on foot, through the mountains. But I don't suppose mountain hiking was their favorite sport . . . We'd have collared them anyway."

"Thanks," I said.

"Don't mention it. As soon as we realized you were taking the Ginette pass, we figured it out. Maybe you didn't notice, but we kept the road clear, didn't we?"

"That too!"

"There was just that one car that slipped through the net. No idea where it came from. Maybe it was a couple of lovers who'd been fucking in the scrub. I guess they cooled down pretty quickly!"

"And where's Loubet?"

"Interrogating two kids," Ribero said. "I think you know them. Nacer and Redouane. They were picked up this afternoon. The idiots were still riding around in the BMW. They drove to La Paternelle for a meet with Boudjema Rassef. We had guys staking out his place. As soon as he met up with them, we pounced. It was quite a haul. The prayer hall was a real arsenal. They were getting ready to move the stuff. We think Ressaf was in charge of that. Shipping the arms to Algeria."

"Tomorrow," Vernet said, "there's going to be a massive raid. At dawn, obviously. It'll sweep them all up. Your little notebook was great, Loubet said."

Everything was coming to a conclusion. As it always did. With its share of losers. And the others, all the others, the lucky ones, were asleep in their beds. Whatever happened. Here, or anywhere on earth.

I stood up.

It wasn't easy. I felt really drained. They caught me just as I fainted.

# EPILOGUE

## IT'S THE SAME NIGHT, AND THE SHADOW ON THE WATER IS THE SHADOW OF A BURNED OUT MAN

We had our drink, Ribero, Vernet and I. Ribero had driven the Saab as far as the David statue at Rond-Point de la Plage. Now, with a whisky warming my stomach, I was feeling a whole lot better. It was only a Glenmorangie, but it fitted the bill nicely. They were more the peppermint cordial types.

Vernet finished his drink, stood up and pointed to his left. "Your place is that way. You going to be all right, or do you still need us to be your guardian angels?"

"I'll be all right," I said.

"Because it's not over yet. We still have a lot to do."

I shook hands with them.

"Oh, by the way, Loubet strongly recommends fishing. He says it's the best cure for what you have."

And they laughed again.

I'd just parked outside my door when I saw Honorine come out of her house. In a dressing gown. I'd never seen her in a dressing gown. At least, not since I was a kid.

"Come, come," she said in a low voice.

I followed her inside.

Fonfon was there. With his elbows on the kitchen table. Cards spread out in front of him. They were playing rummy. At two in the morning. They'd been living it up while my back was turned.

"Are you OK?" Fonfon said, giving me a hug.

"Have you eaten?" Honorine asked.

"I wouldn't say no to some stew."

"What do you mean, stew?" Fonfon cried. "Stew! As if we had nothing better to think about."

They were the way I liked them.

"I'll make you a little *bruschetta*, if you like. It won't take long."

"Don't worry, Honorine. What I need more than anything is a drink. I'll go fetch my bottle."

"No, no," she said. "You're going to wake them all up. That's why Fonfon and I have been waiting for you."

"What do you mean? Wake who up?"

"Well, in your bed, there's Gélou, Naïma and . . . oh, I can't remember her name. The Vietnamese lady."

"Cûc."

"That's it. On the couch, there's Mathias. And in a corner, on a little mattress I had, there's Naïma's brother. Mourad, is that his name?"

"That's right. And what are they doing there?"

"I don't know. They must have thought they'd be better here than someplace else, I suppose. What do you think, Fonfon?"

"Well, I think they did the right thing. You want to sleep over at my place?"

"Thanks. That's kind of you. But I don't think I'm sleepy anymore. I'm going out to sea for a while. It looks like a good night."

I kissed them both.

I crept into my house like a thief. I took a new bottle of Lagavulin and a jacket from the kitchen, and a warm blanket from the closet. I put on my old fisherman's cap and went down to my boat.

My faithful friend.

I saw my shadow in the water. The shadow of a burned out man.

I rowed out, in order not to make any noise.

I thought I could see Honorine and Fonfon embracing on the terrace.

That's when I started to cry.

God, it felt good.

## About the Author

Jean-Claude Izzo was born in Marseilles, France, in 1945. Best known for the Marseilles trilogy (*Total Chaos, Chourmo, Solea*), Izzo is also the author of *The Lost Sailors*, *A Sun for the Dying*, and a collection of essays on the Mediterranean, *Garlic, Mint, & Sweet Basil*. Widely credited with having created the modern Mediterranean noir novel, Izzo died in 2000 at the age of fifty-five.